About the Author

Jane Lark is a Kindle bestselling author and a writer of authentic, passionate and emotional Historical and Contemporary romances. She loves writing intense relationships and she is thrilled to be giving her characters life in others' imaginations.

www.janelark.co.uk

 @JaneLark

PRAISE FOR JANE LARK

'Jane Lark has an incredible talent to draw the reader in from the first page onwards'

Cosmochicklitan Book Reviews

'Any description that I give you would not only spoil the story but could not give this book a tenth of the justice that it deserves. Wonderful!'

Candy Coated Book Blog

'This book held me captive after the first two pages. If I could crawl inside and live in there with the characters I would'

A Reading Nurse Blogspot

'The book swings from truly swoon-worthy, tense and heart wrenching, highly erotic and everything else in between'

BestChickLit.com

'I love Ms Lark's style – beautifully descriptive, emotional and can I say, just plain delicious reading? This is the kind of mixer upper I've been looking for in romance lately'

Devastating Reads BlogSpot

The Tainted Love of a Captain

JANE LARK

A division of HarperCollins*Publishers*
www.harpercollins.co.uk

Harper*Impulse* an imprint of
HarperCollins*Publishers*
1 London Bridge Street
London SE1 9GF

www.harpercollins.co.uk

A Paperback Original 2017

First published in Great Britain in ebook format by
Harper*Impulse* 2017

A catalogue record for this book
is available from the British Library

ISBN: 9780008260613

Set in Minion by Palimpsest Book Production Ltd, Falkirk,
Stirlingshire

Printed in Great Britain

Acknowledgements

I'd like to take the chance, before you begin, to say a thank you to the editor who discovered *The Illicit Love of a Courtesan,* the first of the Marlow Intrigues books, and believed in my writing and this series so much that she signed up all seven of the main books in the series.

When I decided to offer HarperImpulse *The Illicit Love of a Courtesan,* as it had already been published through a small independent publisher I wasn't sure HarperImpulse would want it. My belief was that previously published books were often not wanted and so I only sent a tentative email saying 'would you be interested in seeing it?', it wasn't even a submission. I can't tell you how surprised I was to then receive an email saying, yes, with an expression of absolute excitement.

I was really surprised because I hadn't sent the book, so Charlotte couldn't have read it, but she'd said yes … I asked her then, 'wouldn't you like to read it before you say yes?' The answer was, 'I already have.' Charlotte had bought and read the story. How wonderful! She has since then always believed in, and supported, my work and I cannot say how brilliant it has been to know I have had an editor who believes so wholeheartedly in my writing and is able to see what you see as readers.

Thank you, Charlotte Ledger, for fulfilling my lifetime dream and giving me this amazing chance to get my stories out into the world and bringing my work to life. Thank you too, to Suzy, who has taken up the baton of editor and polished off the last two books.

And thank you to my family for putting up with me spending all my time with a laptop in front of me!

Plus, I ought to remember in this, my great-uncle Baba, the black sheep of my Grandma's generation, who lived in the small family cottage next to hers in Mobley, near Berkeley Castle in England, the namesake for Harry's nickname.

Chapter 1

Gareth's touch on Harry's arm drew Harry's attention away from his dog. 'Is that not the woman we saw here yesterday?'

Harry looked across his shoulder and smiled. 'I believe so.'

It was a blustery day and in the grey sky above seagulls called out as they played on the breeze, flying into it and then letting it sweep them back. The women's skirts were blowing about their legs as they held onto the brims of their bonnets.

The dog barked because the stick had been lifted and not thrown yet. Harry looked at the waves and hurled the piece of driftwood he'd picked up to play their game. Ash turned and ran after it, all enthusiasm, inspired by the energy in the weather. A few minutes later the dog returned, with the stick in her mouth and her tail wagging violently Harry patted the Dalmatian's head and took the stick from her mouth then hurled it into the sea again. The pebbles on the shore stirred with the movement of both the dog and the waves as Ash raced into the foaming water.

'She is smiling broadly and my bet would be she is smiling at you.'

Harry glanced over his shoulder once more. The woman was speaking to her female companion, who from her appearance he would guess to be a maid. He looked at his friend. 'Or you.'

'No. Definitely you.'

'How can you be sure?'

'I have neither the looks nor the reputation that make women whisper.'

Harry laughed as Ash returned. 'You have a scarlet coat with epaulettes, the uniform works wonders, Captain Morris,' he mocked his friend, then took the stick from the dog's mouth and threw it into the shallow part of the waves again. Ash followed it.

'The woman could not be more obvious. She has not taken her eyes off you.'

'Then perhaps it is some young miss who has heard of my reputation and sees a monster to point at.'

'She is not looking at you in disdain.'

Harry smiled at his friend's amusement. He did not care why the woman was looking at him. Let her look. Ash came back and Harry threw the stick a few more times as Gareth continually glanced back and recounted how the woman continued to watch while she walked back and forth, beside her maid, along the path at the head of the beach.

When he'd had enough of being observed, like a spider in a jar, Harry looked at Gareth and suggested it was time to return to their barracks in Preston. He had to get back anyway. He was on duty later.

Harry walked off the pebbly beach as Gareth sent one last smile in the unknown woman's direction.

They walked to the inn, where they'd left their horses side by side.

Ash kept close to Harry's horse as they rode back, nipping at the horse's hind legs on occasion if she had a chance.

Harry dismounted. The brick paved yard in the centre of the barracks was a huge square and the stalls about it held several hundred horses. He led Obsidian into one of the giant stable blocks, to her stall. He took off her saddle before brushing the horse down, while Ash retired to the corner of the stable and watched.

When Harry walked out of the stall the dog followed.

Ash slept under the desk by Harry's feet as Harry served his hours of duty through the night and in the morning when Harry tumbled on to the bed in his quarters, Ash climbed up and lay beside him. Harry fell asleep as he stroked the dog's ear.

A deafening explosion rang in his ears and it resonated through his chest. Then there were screams of retaliation and the thunder created by a cavalry charge. Harry awoke and sat up. His nose and mouth burned with the smell and the acrid taste of gunpowder and his mind was plagued with the sight of wounded men, blood and death. It was a relief to be awake.

He stroked Ash's neck and the dog licked his cheek. 'You, scallywag, Ash.' He rubbed her stomach as she rolled onto her back.

Ash had come from a litter his sister Mary's husband had bred for his son to choose from. Harry was offered one of George's spares. The offer had been the gift of more than a dog, though. Harry had needed something to make him smile and his sister had spotted his need and given him Ash. He'd accepted the gift for the kindness it was and chosen the runt of the litter, although Ash's playful character had grown beyond the weak puppy he'd carried away tucked inside his coat.

The dog sat up and licked his face again. 'Good day to you too, you silly animal, Ash.'

Ash's name had come from Harry's niece, Iris; Ash for the sake of the black dots on her white coat.

Having Ash to amuse and pet had helped still his mind. It had quietened the sudden, violent visions during the day. The impacts of fighting a farcical war without enough equipment, ammunition or food and medicine were cut deep into his mind and the scars opened up whenever he was idle. His nightmares were of the tents full of wounded men as often as they were of the battles. He'd seen more men lost to infection and fever than cannon fire or bullets.

He'd joined the army as an eager young man, keen to discover the thrills of the life of a soldier and leave the stifling safety of his family home behind. For years he'd lived carelessly, supported by them, with a casual disregard for anything but his own pleasure. He'd been a flippant young man, breaking all his righteous father's rules, even when he'd first become a soldier. But that was not the man who had returned from the war. War had tainted him and his family had seen it. But good God, he did not even recognise the man he'd once been now. That innocent, foolish man was a stranger to him as much as this man had been a stranger to the family he had rebelled against for no other reason than to express his individuality.

'Come along, let us go for a run.' Harry shoved the dog off the bed, then climbed out of it himself. He washed and shaved, then picked up his dark-blue trousers and pulled them on. Next he put on his shirt, tucked it in and drew his braces up over his shoulders before putting on his black neckcloth. Lastly he slid his arms into his scarlet military coat. That last garment was the thing which defined him as a lancer, a cavalry man.

His fingers ran over the epaulette, which announced him as a captain, then brushed down the sleeve, knocking off any lint. He swept off the dust from his other sleeve and then secured the brass buttons in their regimental button holes, following an upward pattern. The routine of dressing each morning and returning himself to the man who was ready and prepared to fight, had become a ritual. He clothed his soul and his thoughts, hiding them to ensure they were never exposed.

He sighed out a breath. 'Ash,' he called the dog to his heel. They left his room together and walked to the stable to prepare Obsidian. The horse and the regiment were a family that understood him and they were his home now. The Crimea had set him apart from his family. The knowledge, the wounds in his head, were things he could never share with them, or his old friends. But everyone lived with such memories here.

Yet the dog had been a good thought of his sister's. Ash was in his military family too. War may have set him apart, but his family still sought to reach out to the stranger they had found amongst them on his return. As his family could not look after him from a distance. Ash's role was to watch him and lift his spirits when they were low.

Fifteen minutes later he was riding at a trot, with Ash beside the horse, as they travelled the two miles towards Brighton's beach.

He could have ridden in another direction, but the sea always seemed to pull him towards it.

The taste of salt filled the air. He breathed it in and kept breathing slowly. It cleansed his senses of the haunting stale smells of the gunpowder and blood and the foul odours of death. He could see the sea in the distance through the avenue of houses.

He left Obsidian at the inn he regularly used for that purpose, then walked on with Ash, and a stick for Ash, ignoring the bustle of passing carriages and people in the busy street. Yes, the dog was a very good addition. Without Ash he would not have come to the beach each day. His visits to the beach had become his moments to escape – they would have felt like running away without Ash to entertain. With Ash these moments had become the sanctuary he ran to.

'Fetch!' he yelled as he walked out on to the pebbles and hurled the stick. Ash barked with loud excitement and her eyes followed the stick's flight through the air.

Harry watched it too, isolating his thoughts and himself, shutting out his awareness of the bathing carts and those managing their occupants and the others walking on the beach, letting his thoughts slip out of the past and the echoes of the nightmare he'd dreamed.

He'd been invited to play cards with a retired colonel tonight. Colonel Hillier. He presumed because those playing believed he would bring money into the game, with a Duke for a brother. The truth was that he had already spent, or rather gambled away, most of the arrears of his allowance that had been given to him by his brother on his return to England. Equally, most of his pay that had built up during his months abroad had been lost at the tables.

But not all the money had been lost since his return; there had been many nights during the regiment's progression towards the battlefields in the Crimea in which bets had been made and promissory notes written. Gambling on the outcome of a hand of cards had been the closest thing to freedom there.

The notes had all been called in and paid on his return and now he was poor until he received the next payment of his allowance from his ducal brother, or his next wage.

Laughter rang out behind him, in a woman's tone, from the walkway along the head of the beach. The familiar sound pierced through the dustsheet he'd thrown across the world to separate himself from it.

He looked back.

The woman, who kept watching him, was there again. For the fifth day. With the same maid. He looked away, out to sea. He was not interested in any young misses. His life was not a life for an English wife.

Ash returned with the stick. Harry took it from her mouth and threw it again, ignoring the woman, despite her desire to obtain his attention as she spoke in an overly loud voice. He continued playing with Ash and disregarding her, as he had done every other day, until she ceased promenading back and forth.

Once she'd gone, he left the beach and walked to a coffee shop in the town. The coffee shop was close to the Royal Pavilion, with its bizarre Indian-style architecture. The Palace made him smile. It seemed to be laughing at its grandeur. Ash came inside with Harry and sat beneath the table as Harry drank the dark, bitter coffee. It gave him a renewed boost of energy. He and Ash walked back to the inn, collected Obsidian, then returned to the barracks.

He dined in the mess room with the other officers and then it was time to ride back into Brighton for this unknown retired colonel's card party. His Lieutenant Colonel and two other officers Harry did not know particularly well, accompanied him, as they were also invited. Gareth had not been included, probably because he did not have wealthy origins.

Harry was the one who stepped up to the door of the tall terraced property and knocked.

The door was opened by a male servant, who held the door wide. Harry handed his hat over to the servant as he stepped in. Masculine laughter rang from a room off the square hall.

When Harry entered the room the laughter had come from, the other men were not in uniform, nor were they men Harry knew.

It was going to be an odd evening. He would rather have drunk and played cards with the officers who were his friends. But he had agreed to this; flattered by the invitation and out of a desire to play cards with a seriousness that would grasp the attention of his mind and silence other thoughts. His heart raced at the idea of holding the cards as he saw the money lying on the table and recalled the challenge of the game. He could also do with winning.

'Colonel Hillier.' Harry bowed to his host as the grey-haired, old, portly man acknowledged his new guests with a gesture of his hand. Chairs were pointed to at a strange semicircular table; it was half of a table, which stood before the fireplace and it had an open middle, presumably so it did not burn. Harry had never seen one like it before.

When Harry sat, the heat from the fire touched his legs. It was May and there had been the aftermath of the storm yesterday, yet it was not particularly cold, he was going to sweat in his coat. A contraption attached to the table bore a decanter; it swung on a runner, which meant it could be passed about without the need to be lifted. It was swung to those who had joined the table as a new hand of cards was dealt for each man and then passed along.

Relief filled Harry as he picked up the cards. This was a constant that had been with him since before the Crimea. He'd spent hours at card tables with his cousins during their dissolute years and the pleasure to be found in a card game had lasted throughout the war. When he'd returned, playing cards had provided a base for normality. He was once again in a place in which he could face reality.

But those he had previously played with, his cousins, were wed now and happily settled with their wives and children. Life had progressed without him. Everything had changed here. He was a soldier and nothing besides that now.

He looked at the cards he held and then at the faces of those about the table, trying to judge which men were his competition.

'Charlotte!' Colonel Hillier called.

Harry was aware of the woman walking into the room, but he did not look, his mind was on the cards and the game.

'Bring my box of cigars, would you?'

'Yes.' It was a young woman's voice that answered.

When she returned, a rose perfume scented the air. The perfume was very like the one his mother used. The scent increased in intensity as the woman came closer, circulating about the half table, holding out the open box of cigars as each man then helped himself.

When she reached Harry, he looked up. My God. The woman from the seashore. She had the most striking auburn hair, full of rioting curls, and she had remarkably large, beautiful hazel eyes that hinted at the colour of bracken in autumn. He had noticed neither thing from a distance, but then her hair had been beneath a bonnet.

'Thank you.' He took a cigar from the box.

She smiled at him as colour tinted her pale skin a deep pink while her eyes opened wider, as though she was also shocked to encounter him here.

His invitation had not been due to her, then; the thought had crossed his mind.

He looked back at his cards, but his thoughts and attention were now partly drawn to the woman.

When she finished handing out the cigars, she walked back about the men with matches to light their cigars. He watched her face when she lit a match for him. She looked only at the task, and yet when he sucked on the cigar, holding it to the match to draw the flame and light the end, he sensed her staring at him.

Did her father know that she walked with her maid along the shore each afternoon and watched him?

She left the room once her task was complete. But some of his thoughts remained with her even then. She was a very attractive woman. He had never really looked at her when he'd been on the beach. Yet his mind's focus on her was involuntary; she was a young miss and he was not interested in such women. His mind, however, begged to differ on that point this evening.

She returned to the room five times to circulate with cigars or refill the decanter. All tasks a servant might have completed, but the Colonel called for his daughter to undertake them. Perhaps this odd collection of men had been invited not solely to play cards but to obtain a suitor for his daughter and this was his version of a shop window to sell her attributes.

Harry smiled as he won his fourth hand.

He leant back in his chair as the money on the table was passed along to him and his gaze clashed with the woman's. Their gazes had met several times. She coloured and looked away.

If this card game had been played in a gentleman's club, where the women were available, she would not be colouring as she met his gaze but looking alluringly and by now he would have beckoned her over and invited her to sit on his knee as he played, effectively claiming her for the night. Perhaps he would go in search of a woman after this. The escape that could be found in a bed with a woman had been the other constant surviving from his old life.

He did not seek a woman when he left the Colonel's, richer by the grand sum of fifty pounds; the Colonel's auburn-haired daughter was still too much on his mind. If he lay with a woman it would be the Colonel's daughter in the bed in his mind and that felt sordid. Instead he returned to the barracks and climbed back into the narrow bed that he shared with Ash.

~

'You have a letter, my friend.'

Harry awoke and sat up instantly, his hand reaching for his sword, which lay on the floor beside his bed. Instinct. But the instinct was overridden when he saw Gareth. 'Must you walk in without knocking? One day I will not awake fully and your throat will be cut.' Harry turned to sit on the edge of the bed. The letter was thrown on to the covers beside him.

Gareth merely laughed as Harry picked the letter up.

He expected it to be from a member of his family. All of his brothers and sisters wrote to him on occasion, along with his mother and father. Even his cousin and friend, Henry, had kept in contact and sent him amusing anecdotes while Harry had been away. But Harry did not recognise the writing and when he turned the letter over there was no imprint of a seal in the wax.

'Do you want to come for a ride with me, for a proper gallop, without the dog?' Gareth asked as Harry opened the letter.

Harry looked up. 'Yes.' It was Sunday and neither of them had any hours of duty.

'I'll give you forty minutes precisely,' Gareth answered, before turning and walking out of Harry's room.

Harry's hand settled on Ash's head and stroked behind the dog's ear as he looked at his letter, which came from an unknown source.

Dear Captain Marlow,

I am so glad I have discovered your name. I have been longing to know it for three whole weeks and now I know it I can write to you.

I have seen you on the beach with your beautiful dog. It is charming the way you and she play your game of fetch.

The woman from the shore. The Colonel's – very forward – auburn-haired daughter. She should surely not be writing to him.

I wonder, that is I hope, that you might be willing to walk with me along the seafront one day, perhaps today. I can be there at four. If you are going to the beach today? There is no need to write back, simply meet me if you can.

Yours sincerely,

Charlotte Cotton

Cotton … A frown pulled at his brow. It was not the retired Colonel's surname. A step daughter then? Perhaps?

She was in Harry's mind again, then, as he dressed. With her large, fascinating hazel eyes and her vivid hair.

He let Ash accompany him to the stables, then left the dog in Obsidian's stall before leading the horse out into the middle of the huge stable block full of whinnying and neighing horses.

Gareth was waiting outside, sitting astride his horse. 'Are you ready?'

'I am,' Harry answered as he mounted. The weather today was bright, warm sunshine.

They smiled at one another before they turned the horses. Then left the barracks at the pace of a trot, talking as they rode. They rode out to the hills at a canter before letting the animals have their heads in a gallop. It was as good for Harry as it was for Obsidian to feel the wind whipping at him as Obsidian cut through the stillness of the world at a raging gallop.

At the top of the cliffs they stopped and looked down, watching the sea.

Harry looked back towards Brighton and thought of the woman who would be waiting there for him at four. He had no intent to go, or rather, he might go to exercise Ash, but he would not communicate with the woman ... He said aloud, 'The woman on the shore—'

'The one who has been watching you?'

'Yes.' Harry looked over at his friend as they walked their horses farther along the cliff path.

'What about her?'

'If you give me a chance I will tell you.' Harry laughed, then continued. 'I know who she is.'

'You have spoken with her? When? What did she say?'

'Last evening at Colonel Hillier's. She is his daughter. Or perhaps his step-daughter. They do not have the same surname.'

Gareth broke into laughter that came from deep in his throat.

'Why is that amusing?' Harry charged.

His friend drew in a deep breath to quell his mirth. Then smiled broadly. 'You fool, Harry. I never had you down as a naïve man.'

'Naïve ...' Harry's eyebrows lifted.

'She is his mistress. Not his daughter.' Gareth laughed again.

His mistress ... Lord. He'd had no idea. He swallowed and looked ahead. 'She did not behave like his mistress.' He thought of how regularly her colour had heightened and how she had looked away. Yet the fact the Colonel had used her to serve them fitted Gareth's definition.

'I have not seen her so I did not recognise her on the beach, but I have heard the woman is an outstanding beauty. Everyone comments on her when they have been to Hillier's.'

Something scratched along Harry's spine, like a knife on stone. It was the word, 'everyone' that had stirred the sensation. The image in his head was something he did not want to picture. 'She is beautiful.' She was. Her auburn hair and her eyes seemed even more attractive now he knew she was a touchable, attainable woman, another man's, but only because that man paid for her keep. Yet the thought of being able to touch her conjured up more images he did not want to see.

She had asked him to meet her. He wanted to do so now. Would it be wrong for him to speak with her?

He debated the question internally during their ride back to the barracks and as he brushed Obsidian down. He was undecided when he ate his luncheon and he remained undecided even after that. It was not until half past the hour of three that he made up his mind.

He would go and he would speak to her. He saddled Obsidian again and took Ash with him as he normally would. Having Ash beside the horse quietened his doubt. If he changed his mind he could just walk down to the waves.

He left Obsidian at the inn, then walked towards the sound of the sea. The noise of the water washing up on to the pebbles began to ease his soul and he could taste the salt in the air.

She was there, with her maid. They were on the path at the head of the beach, a few yards away. He crossed the street. She walked towards him and intercepted his path. 'Captain Marlow!' she called. 'Well met!' She spoke as though she had not written and he therefore presumed the maid did not know that this interchange had been orchestrated.

He bowed, slightly. 'Miss Cotton.' What was the etiquette for a man's mistress? He knew how to behave with whores and with respectable women, but a mistress was somewhere in between. 'Would you care to walk with me?' He lifted his arm, in the way he might have offered his arm to one of his sisters or cousins.

The maid held back to walk a few paces behind them as Ash

13

looked up at him with eyes that asked why he had not walked on to the pebbles. Harry clicked the fingers of his free hand and tapped his leg to tell Ash to stay at his side.

'I like your dog. What is her name?' Miss Cotton said loudly. He presumed for the benefit of the maid as much as for an answer.

'Ash. She was named by my niece.'

She looked at him as though the fact that he might have a niece was a bizarre thought. 'Oh.'

He smiled. Her colour had been high since the moment they had faced each other, but now it became even redder.

'Your dog has a very pleasant nature.'

'Yes, she does.'

'I am glad you came,' she said in a quieter voice, leaning closer to him as he'd seen her do when she spoke to her maid. 'It took me so much courage to write. But you have never looked at me here. Then you looked at me last night and I wrote in a rash moment because I have had a great desire to know the man with the lovely dog. I hope you do not think me too forward.' Her back straightened when she had finished her conspiratorial whisper and her chin lifted high. There was a sense of dignity in her posture, no matter her status.

'I was not sure that I would come.'

Her head turned and she looked at him about the rim of her bonnet, her fingers pulling on his arm a little. 'I admire you as much as your dog. I have wanted to meet you as well as Ash.'

'I am aware. I have seen you watching me.' He breathed in. 'It was flattering.' He had not thought so a day ago and yet having seen the woman up close. Yes, the interest and attention of such a beautiful woman was flattering. Her large, expressive eyes, within the shadow of her bonnet's brim, were particularly fascinating and the curls of her vibrantly coloured hair peeked from beneath the edges of the bonnet, providing a temptation to touch it.

She smiled. 'I think it is lovely how you play with the dog. There seems such regard between you as you play. So, yes, I have been watching your games and admiring you and your affection for Ash, from a distance. It is very charming to watch. Your friend has looked back at me, but you have no more than glanced. You have given me no opportunity to compliment you before.'

'I thought you were …' He had been about to insult her and say that he'd thought her respectable, which would tell her that now he thought she was not. 'I thought you someone different.'

'Who?'

'No one in particular, simply a young woman looking for a husband and I would make a poor candidate for that.'

Her colour had descended, but now it heightened again. It was strange to be with a woman who blushed so freely and frequently.

'How long have you had Ash?'

'Months only, since I returned from the Crimea. She was a gift from my family.'

'Oh. You have a wife?'

He smiled at her. 'No. She was a gift from my sister and her husband, which is why my niece named her.'

'Oh. What is your first name, Captain? I did not hear it last night.'

'Harry, Miss Cotton.'

'That is a happy sounding name. My name is Charlotte.'

'I know. You wrote it in your letter.'

'Oh, I did, didn't I?' She laughed, with an embarrassed note, her posture was not as stiff as it had been, she had relaxed a little.

Her former stiff posture had possibly been a nervous stance rather than an expression of dignity.

He patted the hand that lay on his arm, in the way he might have done to reassure any respectable woman. 'I have another name, I am Uncle Baba to my nephews and nieces. The nickname was first coined by my sister's husband. He defined me as the black sheep of the family.'

Another brief laugh escaped her mouth; this was a sound of pure amusement. 'That is an unusual name, how did you earn it?'

'Do you really wish to know?'

'Should I not have asked?'

'Suffice to say I am from a rigidly good and respectable family and my older brothers were very well behaved. I … I prefer to enjoy life.'

'How long is your regiment to be in Brighton?'

'It is hard to tell. One never knows when orders or a crisis may draw us away.'

'I hope it is for a while at least. I like watching you with Ash.'

He smiled.

'Tell me about your sister and her family?'

Harry went on to tell her about all of his family. His eldest brother, who sometimes seemed more like a second father he was so severe, inflexible and demanding – though he did not mention that John was a duke. Then he talked of his brother Rob and Rob's quiet wife and their precious daughter, Sarah. She was the only child Rob and his wife would be able to have and she was therefore precious to them all. Then he talked of his younger siblings. His sisters, Helen and Jennifer, had married while he'd been in the Crimea. They had married twins and so were now sisters and sisters-in-law. His brothers, David and Daniel, were just finishing university and beginning their lives. His sister, Georgiana, had only recently been launched upon London society and then there was Jemima, the youngest of all, at fourteen.

Charlotte, Miss Cotton, listened avidly, watching his face while he spoke, smiling and laughing as he talked of the antics of his younger siblings and nephews and nieces.

'Have you any family?' he asked at the end of his long description about his. He'd never asked a whore such a question. He'd never known anything about the women he paid to share a bed. But nor had he told such women about his family. Conversation was not normally a part of the exchange. But nor had he walked anywhere with a whore's hand on his arm in this way, and he had never felt a need to reassure a woman of that background before as he'd sought to reassure Charlotte earlier.

'Yes.' She did not smile when she answered and her voice sounded flat.

Whenever he spoke of his family words babbled like the ripples on a flooding brook. He may have been an ill-behaved son, who was a constant nuisance to his father and at times an annoying brother, and he may have felt a stranger amongst them a few weeks ago but, even so, there would always be love between them. Ash was testament to that.

'I have an older brother and a sister who is ten years younger than me.' She did not go on. Thoughts of her family did not flow into her words.

'Do you see them very often?'

'No. I have not seen them for years.'

His eyebrows lifted. He was unsure what to say. The reply had been spoken so bluntly. He took a breath. 'I did not see my family for two years during the war. But they wrote to me frequently and regaled me with tales of the things they did. My cousin too. Henry writes some very amusing letters about his bookish wife Susan and his daughter.'

She smiled. She seemed to like listening to him more than speaking and so he continued talking about his family; after all, he had so many brothers, sisters and cousins it was an endless subject.

They walked along the seafront for almost an hour as he talked continuously, while she listened.

But it was Charlotte who ended the conversation. 'I am sorry, Harry, I must stop you, I have to go. Will you be here again tomorrow?'

'I am on duty in the day tomorrow, but I will be here at five to exercise Ash.' He had obligated himself then, when his hours here with Ash had become important to him. He did not particularly want to exchange them to entertain a woman with conversation. 'But if you come here, then you may stand beside me, if you wish, as I throw the stick for Ash. But I cannot deny her the pleasure of the game for two days.'

She laughed. 'If I am able to escape the house at that hour I would be happy to stand with you.'

Her fingers slipped off his arm and he bowed slightly. To a whore … But she was not that, not in the same way as the women he'd known. She confused him. 'I shall meet you again tomorrow afternoon, then.'

'I hope so, but I cannot promise.' She smiled, in a way that expressed her liking for him, but with none of the open desire to attract his attention a normal whore would have deployed. Then she turned away.

His gaze followed her as she joined her maid. She glanced back at him. He smiled at her. The smile he received in return he would describe as flirtatious, but it was still not like the looks he received from the women in a gentleman's club.

He looked down at Ash and stroked the dog's head. 'Come on, girl, let's play for a while before we go back.'

He walked down to the shore.

Miss Cotton hovered in his thoughts for the rest of the day and when he retired to his bed she was still there. He was unsure of what to think, of whether he should allow himself to think anything. He had enjoyed her company and his fascination with her eyes had become a fascination for her character, her silences and blushes.

Chapter 2

When Harry collected his letters, there were three. One from his sister, which largely contained stories about the cleverness of her children and asked after Ash on behalf of Iris. The next came from his younger brother, Daniel, saying he was thinking of a military career and asking for Harry's view.

God, how to respond on such a point to his little brother when his mind cried out daily with the haunting visions of men cut through by swords or lances or blown to pieces by cannon and shots from a rifle? He'd seen their bodies fall into the mud. Then there were the men he had visited lying in filthy sheets in make-shift hospitals, where the air had been foetid with the smell of their putrid flesh rotting on their bones. He could not encourage his brother to become a soldier.

The third letter was another invitation to Colonel Hillier's. The men he'd played with probably wished to win their money back. He smiled, then took the letter to the mess room, where he could write back and accept. He did not accept for the benefit of a game, though, but for another opportunity to see Charlotte.

They had met twice more on the beach while he'd played with Ash. But he was still interested in seeing her at the Colonel's house. He was trying to decipher how things stood with her. A woman who was paid for her bed sport and yet named as belonging exclusively to one man.

His lieutenant colonel was also invited and so they rode into Brighton together.

When they walked into the hall, as a servant shut the front door, Colonel Hillier came into the hall to greet them. It was unlike the previous occasion when Harry had visited the house.

He welcomed Harry's lieutenant colonel first, then looked at Harry and held out a hand. 'You have eyes remarkably like those of a woman I once knew, Captain Marlow.' He shook Harry's hand then turned away.

It was an odd statement and one that discomposed Harry to the point he made the decision not to accept any more invitations. The man had a mistress and yet perhaps he had a leaning either way and favoured men and women. Harry was not that way inclined. He looked at Charlotte differently, though, when she was called into the room to offer them a cigar from the wooden box.

She did not smile at him in the same open way she had done at the seashore. But as she walked about the men who were gathered at the unusual half-circle table her gaze favoured Harry, her eyes expressing the connection they had formed in the last few days as they'd conversed, a budding sort of friendship.

Harry's eyes were continually drawn to her too; whenever she came into the room she pulled his attention away from the card game.

He had a very strong desire to bed her. Even the thought somewhat released the tension in his body and his mind, quietening the guilt that always hovered in his soul. If merely thinking about lying with her could make him feel better, then how much better would he feel if he did it?

He stared back at his cards. Why should he not accept the opportunity? She was not a virtuous woman and she had approached him, after all. Did it matter, then, that she was paid by another man?

Perhaps it would be stealing, in a way. Yet surely Hillier paid for her hours and not her body. She was not his slave. He did not own her.

Harry refilled his glass, losing focus on his cards and consequently as he refreshed the brandy in his glass again and again he lost hand after hand.

He left Hillier's sixty pounds down but with a desperate desire for the hours until he was to meet Charlotte again to hurry past. His decision on the woman was made. She was desirable, she had made herself available and he wished to partake.

~

Charlie stood on the uneven pebbles waiting for Harry. He approached from the street that contained the inn where he kept his horse. Ash walked at a swift pace beside him, keeping up with the long strides of his master.

Harry always looked so handsome and very grand in his manner. He walked with a determined stride and his dark-blue trousers, with their outer yellow stripe, seemed to make him taller and his vivid scarlet coat made his slender, muscular figure more defined.

He was the prettiest man she'd ever seen; it was that which had made her watch him and his dog. He was fascinatingly attractive, almost too handsome to be real. Yet now she had spoken to him she knew he was real and as beautiful as he'd looked from a distance.

Before he had come to Mark's she'd been longing to ask the other officers who played cards who the man who entertained his dog on the beach was? But she had never dared.

It was the dog that she had seen first and then she had watched Ash run up the beach and her attention had been drawn from Ash to her master. The closeness he seemed to have with Ash had made her want to stop and watch them and then she had noticed that Harry was even prettier than his dog.

Then he had come to Mark's. Captain Harry Marlow. It was a wonderful name, too. It made her smile. Harry.

'Hello!' he called from a few feet away.

The pace of her heart beat lifted in a fluttering sensation.

Since they had been talking each day, her heart felt as though it had grown the wings of a butterfly. 'Hello.'

'How are you?' he asked as he joined her.

Charlie glanced back along the path at the maid who'd walked with her. She had left Tilly a few feet away to mind her own business and Tilly had not come nearer to listen, which was what Charlie feared. But if anything had been said to Mark about her liaisons with Harry, which it probably had, he had not complained to her about it.

She looked at Harry, again, turning her back on Tilly. 'I am well. How was your game last evening?'

'Must you ask?' He threw the stick out into the sea. 'Do you not know?'

'No.'

'Then do not ask.'

She laughed as Ash returned with the stick.

Harry looked at her after he'd thrown the stick again. 'I have a question to ask you, though.'

'Then you must ask it.' She was very forward with Harry. She kept surprising herself. But it was the atmosphere he exuded. He always spoke so liberally it made her more confident to reply. But she had been forward with him from the beginning because she had been desperate to know this man with his dog. So desperate she had dared to write. But she had told herself that a woman of her status need not worry over what was right or wrong or fear the judgement of others. She had transcended those things. It was the one benefit of her status – she might do as she wished and she had wished to meet Ash and speak to Harry. That was not a crime.

Her chin lifted and her back straightened in denial of the

22

accusation of forwardness that continued charging at her in her head.

Harry turned and faced her fully as Ash ran into the shallow, frothing ripples, chasing the stick as the tide pulled it out on a retreating wave. 'If I hired a room in an inn, would you come there with me?'

'Now?' To … Oh … She had not thought about where this might lead. She had thought of nothing other than that she admired him and she had wanted to know him. But. 'My maid is with me.' Her heart had jolted suddenly into a sharp pace.

'Tomorrow. Would you meet me there?'

Her heart was pounding as hard as her father had used to pound a hammer on a straight bar of iron to twist and curve it to make a horse's shoe. She had not imagined, and yet she had in daydreams sometimes thought about what it would be like to kiss Harry.

But to make this a sin…

Ash shook the sea water off her coat, spraying them both. Then Harry took the stick from Ash's mouth, lifted it and held it out of Ash's reach. The dog barked and leapt around, waiting for it to be thrown again, then it was and Ash went racing after it.

Harry looked at her. 'Will you?'

'Yes.' She spoke without thought. She spoke from longing. Yes, she would like to be with a man like Harry. If she must share a bed with a man, then why could it not be with a man like Harry? She was being forced into sin anyway.

When Ash returned next, Charlie took the stick and threw it out again, though it did not go as far as it would have if Harry had thrown it. She spoke about the dog, commenting on Ash's ability to swim in the waves, to hide her awkwardness and move the conversation away from more personal, embarrassing things.

She had agreed to share a bed with him. She would not be able to sleep this night. She must think of a reason not to bring

Tilly tomorrow. Tilly might have laughed with her over the pretty dog and the attractive officer Charlie had pointed at in the distance, but she had not approved of Charlie speaking with Harry. She would certainly not approve of her going to an inn with him and if she told Mark that … She did not want Mark to know. He would spoil this. She was sure he would.

When Harry told her it was time for him to return to the barracks, he also said, 'Shall I meet you in the street outside the inn tomorrow?'

Her heart thundered in her chest as though a bolt of lightning had struck her. 'Could we not meet at the corner, there?' She pointed to the street he usually appeared from. 'I would feel uncomfortable standing outside an inn alone.'

'Of course, forgive me. I did not think. Yes. Let us meet on the corner.' He bowed slightly and when he straightened his very pale-blue eyes looked directly into hers, as though looking for an answer to something.

He had beautiful eyes. They were his most notable feature. His hair was dark and his eyelashes and eyebrows dark and against those his blue eyes were a striking contrast.

He took hold of her hand, lifted it and pressed a kiss on the back of her kid glove.

Warmth rose in her skin, no one had kissed the back of her hand before. She pulled her hand free, bobbed a curtsey, which was silly, smiled and then turned away.

He would think her a fool now.

She glanced back. He was walking away with Ash at his side.

She held the hand that he'd kissed. She could still feel the heat of his grip as he'd held it. Her heart beat out the rhythm of a hammer strike once more. Tomorrow…

When she had written to ask him to meet her, she had not thought things through; she ought to have realised where it might lead. Yet perhaps she had known, really. She had wanted to know the handsome man and his dog with a desire that had become an obsession and she had dreamed of him. Now she pictured him in her imagination instead of seeing Mark when they did that.

Hush mind! She did not want to think of that. She would not think about it outside of the room in which it must be done.

But with Harry…

Do not think! She ordered herself. She would do it to preserve their friendship. She would do it because she enjoyed his conversation and she liked looking at him and playing with his dog.

When she returned to Mark's house she found a reason to remain in her room until dinner and she hoped she did not have to go to Mark's room later.

He did not ask for her.

~

Once Harry had completed his hours of duty, he let Ash run in the barracks' yard, then took the dog to the stable. He left him there when he walked Obsidian out of the stall.

He had dreamed of Charlotte last night. But then he had not lain with a woman for a couple of weeks and the need to do so was flooding his blood. The sense of escape achieved was as addictive as it was to gamble or drink.

He patted Obsidian's neck, then set his foot into the stirrup and lifted up, swinging his leg across the animal's rump to take his seat in the saddle.

'Where are you off to without Ash?'

Harry looked across the yard at Gareth, who strode towards him. A strange sensation tightened the muscle in his stomach. Fear. He did not want his plans for the afternoon disrupted, and yet – there was guilt too. An emotion he knew well. But it was a guilt he could not really explain. Perhaps it was because he wished to keep this secret and keeping secrets meant that there was a sense of doing wrong. 'For a ride.' Was all he said in answer. They

25

all had hours when they wished to be alone, Gareth would not think it odd.

His friend nodded, then turned away.

Harry rose up from the saddle, gripping Obsidian with his thighs, urging the horse into a trot and then he rode out of the stable yard. Leaving the barracks and the army behind.

The inn's groom took Obsidian as he had every other day, only today there was no Ash and Harry did not immediately leave the inn but walked inside to ensure there was a room available. He had not checked yesterday. There was.

He walked along the street, his heart pulsing faster than it normally would. She was not waiting for him on the corner. Yet it was better that he awaited her rather than her being left to loiter. It would have been awkward for her. As she had made him aware yesterday, she was not a street prostitute.

She appeared after about five minutes, walking quickly towards him. She lifted her hand and waved when she saw him. He lifted his hand and acknowledged her. His heart began to pulse harder, it had never raced at the thought of bedding a woman before. Or perhaps it had happened the first time, but that had been a long time ago.

'Hello,' she spoke first and smiled in a shy way.

Another undefinable emotion twisted around in his chest, aching not clasping. 'Hello. Shall we?' He lifted his arm, as he would have to a woman he'd asked to dance at a ball. She wrapped her fingers about it, gently holding his coat sleeve.

They walked the short distance to the inn in silence. He had no idea what to say.

When he opened the door of the inn for her, her hand let go of his arm and she walked in ahead of him. He did not stop to speak to the clerk, but directed her up to the room through the press of his palm against the curve of her lower back above where the skirt of her dress flared out.

He pushed open the door of the room. She walked in, then

stopped about eight feet away from him. He locked the door, then faced her. 'So ...' Where did he begin with this woman? With every other woman he'd lain with there had been no hesitation. They had agreed a payment or the price was already set by the club or the brothel and they had come to a room and begun.

'I feel so awkward,' she said, then laughed in a self-conscious way. But her laughter broke the ice that had settled over the moment.

A sound of humour escaped his throat too. He laughed at himself. 'I do too. Isn't that silly?'

'Yes.'

'I should have ordered food, or something to drink, chocolate for you ...' Why? They were here for one thing. This was being truly ridiculous.

She shook her head slightly. 'I am neither hungry nor thirsty.'

God. He was both, but not for food or water. 'Let us begin by removing our hats and gloves, shall we?'

He took his hat off and set it on a chest near the door, then stripped his gloves off and left them there too. When he looked back at Charlotte she was untying the bow of her bonnet. Her pale hands shook.

He had not even seen her hands naked before.

What a strange thought.

She slid her bonnet off.

He walked across and took her bonnet and gloves from her. Then carried them over to the chest to set them down beside his hat. She was watching him when he turned back. He smiled. 'Will you take the pins out of your hair? It is a very pretty colour. I would like to see it down.'

She began pulling the pins out at once, her hand still trembling. He walked over there and helped, looking only at her hair, searching out the silver and pearl heads of the pins.

Her hair was such a vibrant copper colour and a mass of tight curls that tumbled on to her shoulders as the pins came free. He collected the pins in the palm of one hand. Then walked over and put them beside their other items.

Bedding a whore had never been like this. Charlotte engendered a need to be solicitous.

Yet he still wanted to be in the bed with her.

He turned and walked back, his hands lifting. He wanted to touch her hair. He held the curls and rubbed the strands between his fingers. The colour glistened in the sunlight from the window, changing as amber did when the sun shone through it. His gaze turned to her face and then his fingers clasped, closing about her hair, at her shoulders, as he leant to kiss her.

Her mouth opened as his did and her tongue reached forward to play with his while her hands came to the back of his head.

He pulled away and looked down at the buttons on the front of her dress, then began undoing them.

She started working the brass buttons on his coat free. Her hands were still trembling but they worked with the haste that he felt in his blood as he hurried too.

This was more like the encounters he was used to.

When she had undone his coat her fingers slipped beneath it and ran over his cotton shirt. The sensation was abrasive on his skin in a way that was arousing. It was the first time a woman had touched him like that while his clothes were on.

He undid her buttons to below her waist, then pushed her dress off her shoulders. 'Help me take it off.'

She smiled in that shy way she had on occasion as she pulled her arms free from the sleeves, then he helped her get the dress over her petticoats.

'Turn,' he requested.

She did so, and then he undid the tapes holding her petticoats in place and once she was free of those and they were set aside he began unlacing her corset. She breathed heavily as he worked, sounding anxious as well as awkward. Yet she had kissed him just

28

as any whore would kiss and unbuttoned his coat with a haste any whore might have.

When her corset was put aside he took off his coat and his shirt. She stripped off her stockings.

'Take off your underwear and jump into the bed,' he said as he sat down on the end of the bed to remove his boots.

A nervous sound escaped her throat that seemed to pretend laughter as she slid down her drawers and pulled her chemise off quickly, before lifting the sheet and blanket and slipping beneath them. Her body was pink with what he guessed was embarrassment. So odd for a whore.

She smiled at him with that essence of shyness as she held the covers up to her neck, no matter that it was a warm day.

He smiled too and continued smiling as he pulled off his boots, hoping to ease any anxiety she had. Then he stripped off his trousers, underwear and stockings all in one, so that he was naked too, before turning to find his sheath out of his coat. He slid it on, then smiled even more broadly as he climbed beneath the covers with her. The feeling in his chest was warm and full. It was no longer tight or painful. It was ready to know freedom and pleasure – with this woman.

He had never cared about it being with any particular woman before. But there was a sense of excitement that the woman would be Charlotte.

Her hand lifted to the back of his head and braced his skull through his hair as his hand reached to the place between her legs. He stroked her there as they kissed. He had never been selfish with women; he'd always ensured they had pleasure too. The experience was better for them both if that was the case.

~

Harry had dressed himself in something, but he had not immediately turned her on to her back and invaded her, neither with his body nor his fingers. He was just touching her, stroking.

His mouth lifted from hers then his head lowered and he kissed the edge of her breast.

'What did you put on?'

He looked up. 'A sheath.'

'Oh. Why?'

His smile said she was being foolish and that she ought to understand. 'To protect you from the risk of a child and us both from disease.'

She wanted to ask what disease, but he had thought her naïve for asking about the sheath and now was not the moment as his fingers continued to gently stroke the place between her legs.

Warm, nice, feelings skimmed through her nerves and across her skin.

He started sucking her nipple. That was done very gently too.

She shut her eyes, shutting out the room and the world as her fingers combed through his hair. Life had been cruel to her. But Harry … She had seen Captain Marlow and wanted to know him and this was her choice. For the first time in years she was doing something that was her choice, with no sense of persuasion or force.

His fingers slipped inside her and stroked, just as he'd stroked on the outside of her body. She let the feel of that, and only that, fill up her mind. Her fingers pressed into the skin and muscles on his back.

The emotions and feelings that rose from the points he touched spun like a whirlpool in a river. She had never felt such things when Mark touched her. When Mark touched her she felt cold and empty. But all those things were left in the room, in his home and pushed out of her thoughts.

She rocked up against Harry's hand, enjoying every sensation, longing to feel them more strongly as his tongue pressed against her breast while he sucked her nipple and his fingers stroked in and out.

Harry's lips lifted off her breast, pulling it as he sucked her nipple one last time, then his hands dented the mattress on either side of her.

She opened her eyes as he moved over her and her hands traced the contours under his skin, over his chest and arms, then settled on his shoulders as his gaze met hers.

When he pressed into her, it was done slowly, and still gently. 'You are very pretty,' he said as he began to move.

'And you are very handsome.'

He smiled at her as he continued working. It was still nice, even with him inside her. He had sweetened it with gentleness. Enchanting sensations swirled through her lower body, gradually rising in intensity, grasping her attention. She did not think of other things as she did with Mark. It was impossible to think of other things with Harry.

Her fingers combed back Harry's short hair, then trailed over his skin again, following the bulges of the muscles on his arms and his chest, as she rocked up against him, while he pressed into her with a slow enthralling pace.

With Mark it was always hurried and forceful, and often painful, but this ... there was no pain, and no force – it just was. And it felt ... beautiful. She had never thought she would say that about joining with a man, but he was even more beautiful without clothes and this was wonderful.

The feelings in her body spun higher, as though Harry's movement whipped them up like a strap flicking at a spinning top. These feelings had risen from her stomach to her chest and were in the back of her throat and then they broke like a wave on the shore, frothing and washing out into her arms, her mind and her legs. She cried out with the pleasure of it.

Harry's pace did not change, but his head lowered and he kissed her neck, her collarbone and her shoulder. She sighed and inside – writhed. The sensations danced through her continuously, racing over each other like waves tumbling on top of one another as she was thrown about in their white foam.

After a while, although she had no idea of how long because she had lost all sense of time, he clasped the back of her thighs and rolled on to his back, pulling her on top of him. Then his hands lifted and pressed either side of her head, his fingers curling into her hair as she knelt over him and he pushed up into her. His pace then was quicker and more powerful. Though even then he did not rush but moved in a way that seemed to focus on his pleasure. But the movement brought her pleasure too.

He turned again, tipping her on to her side.

It was like a sensual dance. Their arms and legs were all tangled up as they moved about the bed, in various positions that brought up different feelings inside her.

Harry knew how to do this in a way Mark did not and all the time her fingers ran over his skin, touching and appreciating as she looked at his beautiful eyes and face and her body grasped at every sensation and let wave after wave of pleasure wash over her.

Then finally Harry rolled her on to her back once more and pushed hard into her over and over, his pace quick and sharp, and then she felt his release throb inside her. Only it did not spill inside her, it spilled into the thing that he wore.

He withdrew from her body and lay on his back.

She rolled to her side and her arm reached across to hold on to him. The emotions still swayed inside her. 'I have never enjoyed it before.'

He laughed. She could feel and hear the rumble of it in his chest.

'How many men have you lain with, then?'

'Only Mark.'

'Colonel Hillier is the only one?'

'Yes.'

'Then how many years have you been with him?'

'Seven.'

He breathed out a long breath, as though her answer had disturbed him. Then his hand rested on her head and his fingers began playing with her hair.

~

Charlotte sat up suddenly, her hand pressing on his stomach. The motion woke him.

Lord, he'd fallen asleep. 'What hour is it?' He sat up too, throwing back the covers.

'I have no idea. I fell asleep.'

They had slept together, then. He walked over to fetch his pocket watch from his coat. 'Six.'

'Oh dear.' When he looked back she was already hurriedly pulling on her underwear.

There was a jug of water and a washing bowl on a stand in the corner, he washed out the sheath and then began to dress.

She turned with her corset in her hand. He had only succeeded in putting on his underwear. 'Will you help me?'

'Yes. Turn around.'

She held her corset against her stomach as he threaded the laces at the back. It was far easier undoing the thing than it was doing it up. He had never done that before. When he'd left women before he had left them in a room in a bed or at the door, placing money on the bed or into their hand.

This was a very strange affair.

When he was done, she glanced across her shoulder. 'Thank you.' Then she stepped away and picked up her petticoats.

He attended to himself. Put on his stockings, then his trousers, then pulled on his shirt and tucked that into his trousers as she buttoned up the front of her dress. He was tugging on his boots as she came across the room to fetch her hair pins.

He slid his arms into his scarlet coat and then secured the

buttons watching her, fascinated, as she deftly twisted her hair and then stuck pins into it to keep it up. Her hair was a magnificent colour. So bright. If it was dressed formally, as his mother's and sisters' hair was at times, she would stand out in any ballroom.

She picked up her bonnet, then realised he'd finished dressing and was watching her. She smiled with that hint of awkwardness and the shy nature that had been there before they'd used the bed. When she put on her bonnet and tied the ribbons her hands trembled as they'd done when she'd come up to the room. 'I think I will be in trouble.'

He did not know what to say to that. 'I'm sorry.'

'It is not your fault we fell asleep.'

No. It was not. But it had been a very odd thing to do.

'I must hurry.' She walked past him and opened the door before he could reach it. Then she hurried on down the stairs ahead of him.

He breathed steadily, keeping the pace of his breaths calm, even though his heart pumped harder in an uncommon way as they walked through the inn and then out into the street. He walked as far as the corner with her, though she did not give him the chance to offer his arm because her steps were so quick.

At the corner she looked at him. 'Thank you. I enjoyed it. Will we do it again?'

Lord … Will we do it again? The words echoed through him. 'Yes.' The answer came from his tongue without thought, but now it was spoken the thought followed, and yes … He wanted that. 'I am on duty until the evening tomorrow, but the day after I will be free.'

'Shall I meet you here at the same hour?'

'Yes.'

'Goodbye, then.' She bobbed a ridiculous little curtsey at him.

'Goodbye, Charlotte.'

She turned and walked away, hurrying once more. He watched

her until she was out of sight. Then he returned to the inn to collect Obsidian.

Everything felt strange, different. Which was absurd. Sleeping with a woman changed nothing. Yet certainly he was calmer than he remembered being in a long while and his mind continually reflected on images and sensations from the time he'd spent with her, it did not recall images of war.

It had been different from any other encounter he'd had with a woman, though.

She had been … He did not even know how to describe it. Refreshing, certainly. But it was not that; it was the way she had performed, or rather not performed at all. When they had been in the bed she'd done nothing like a whore. There had been no sound, or movement, that had felt forced, acted or exaggerated. It had simply been what it was – the only honest encounter he'd ever had with a woman. And he had not even paid her, when he would have paid triple for the service she'd given him. He felt so relaxed.

Guilt pierced through his ribs with a sharp pain that resembled the sudden lance of the tip of a sword. He had not paid her. Ought he to have given her something? Yet she had not asked, nor acted as though she expected payment. But unlike the other women he had been with, she was in the constant care of one man. Kept. For Hillier's attentions. For seven years … For seven years she had only lain with one, old, man.

The thought stirred strange emotions Harry did not care to define.

When he rode into the stable yard at the barracks, Gareth was there.

'Hello.' Gareth called out. 'I have been looking out for you. Are you in the mood for a drink?'

'Yes.' Harry suddenly had a desperate need for a drink.

He dismounted, then walked into the huge block of stables with Gareth beside him.

'You were a long time. You had me worried,' Gareth stated as Harry undid the saddle's girth strap.

Yes. He could not believe he had fallen asleep. With every other woman, when the deed had been done they had thrown him out through the door, their money earned, no matter how pleasurably.

'I mastered a few demons,' Harry answered. He had. Harry gave his friend a twisted smile as he took the bridle off Obsidian. He could tell Gareth, but he would not. He had a desire to continue keeping his liaisons with Charlotte a secret.

Gareth fetched a curry comb, so did Harry, and together they brushed Obsidian down as Ash watched from the corner of the stall.

Ash was at Harry's heel when they walked back into the barracks. Harry stroked the dog's ear. He ate in the mess room and drank with Gareth, using the liquor tonight not to blur the images of war but to blur his memories of Charlotte.

The liquor failed in its task. When he retired to his bed, thoughts and memories still flooded his mind. He saw money being set into women's hands, by him, and recalled the tremble in Charlotte's hands. He felt the movement of her body and heard her breaths. Then he saw her holding open the cigar box for him to take one and then he saw Colonel Hillier welcoming him into his home.

You have eyes remarkably like those of a woman I once knew …

He had probably done something foolish today.

Yet nothing in his thoughts or emotions cared if there were consequences.

Chapter 3

He did not take Obsidian to the usual inn on the day he had agreed to meet Charlotte and nor did he hire a room at that inn. It had probably been foolish to meet her at the usual inn he used, the inn most of the officers used. He ought to keep their association more discreet – she was under the protection of another man.

Instead, once he'd met her, he walked farther along the sea front with her and then led her into a quiet, narrow street. They walked along that, talking and laughing, then turned right, into an even narrower street. In that street he took her into an inn, where he'd hired a room.

The room was smaller than at the last inn. But on this occasion he had thought to order fresh lemonade for her and some small, sweet currant buns topped with icing.

She turned and smiled at him as she took off her bonnet and then her gloves. 'The refreshments are a very nice gesture; it was kind of you to think of that. What is the drink?'

'Lemonade.'

'I have never had it.'

That was a ridiculous notion. Who in the world had never tried lemonade? He crossed the room and poured some for her. Then held out the glass.

She took the glass from him and sipped from it. 'It tastes sour and sweet all at once.' Her expression spoke of the difference between sour and sweet too.

His lips pulled up into a smile and then he laughed before picking up an iced bun. There had been no blushes or hesitation in her movements or her conversation today.

He took a bite of the bun, then held it out to her. 'Here, eat this, it will reduce the sourness.'

She bit into the bun as he held it, then he let go and let her hold it.

'Mmm. That is nice.'

He picked up another and ate it, then poured himself lemonade and drank the glass down. The lemonade brought back memories of his childhood home and that sense of love that came with thoughts of his family, which then brought back the vivid images of battles and their aftermath. God he hated the shame and guilt that attacked him with the bombardment of cannon shells.

He set the empty glass down, then unbuttoned his coat, raising his eyebrows at her in a gesture to tell her that he was looking forward to what would come next. That would taste sweet too.

With a cheeky smile she started undoing the buttons of her dress, hurrying to get her clothes off as last time she had hurried to get them on before they had separated.

She stepped out of her dress as he pulled off his shirt, his braces hanging loose at his sides.

She untied the tapes of her petticoats as he took off his boots. Then she sat beside him and rolled down her stockings as he took his off too. She stood, then, and turned her back to him, so he could pull the lacing free from her corset and after he'd completed the task she stripped off her chemise while he stood to take off his trousers and underwear.

When she'd taken off her drawers, he looked at her. It was a hot day, there was no need to rush for the warmth of the bed.

But there had been no need for her to do so last time, yet she had done.

She looked at him and did not move, seemingly trapped in his gaze. She had a perfectly proportioned body, small breasts, a curve to her hips and long limbs.

She took a pin out of her hair. Some of the copper spirals fell down and touched the top of one pert breast. She pulled another pin out. More hair fell. He walked forward and began taking out pins too, until all her hair had fallen.

He held her hand and tipped the pins from her palm to join those in his, then set them aside with their clothes.

When he returned to her, he looked at her hair, touching it as he'd done the other day. It was such an unusual colour. He had lain with women with red hair before but not with such a rich colour as this. He wound it around his fingers and drew her closer, tilting her head back so that he brought her lips to his.

She opened her mouth instantly and their tongues began to dance. But their interaction still felt nothing like it had with other women.

Truth and honesty. That was what made her different from the women he'd bedded before her. She seemed to hide nothing of her nature or emotions.

He let her hair go and instead squeezed her breast as they continued kissing.

In answer, her fingers stroked along his erection, before closing around it.

He continued kissing her and let her touch him. It was the usual way for a whore to reach out and arouse him quickly. But this was not that.

After a few moments he ended the kiss and stepped away from her. He was still unsheathed. She climbed on the bed as he found his sheath and put it on, then he joined her.

She lay on top of the covers, not beneath them. It was too hot and she was clearly less shy today. He knelt between her open legs and slid his fingers inside her, watching his fingers work as she reclined. Her arms lifted and lay above her head, and her eyes shut. Even her eyelashes and eyebrows were a beautiful copper colour.

The expression on her face was one of focus, her mind was concentrating on the movement of his fingers, and her breaths were shallow and slow.

With her eyes shut and her arms relaxed and resting above her head she soared to her height and sighed as Eros's bliss swept over her. Just that. Just a quiet sigh of pleasure. No writhing or crying out to make him think he was the best lover ever known. Just a short sigh of breath and sound.

He leant forward, resting the weight of his body on his hands beside her shoulders, then he looked down, angled himself and pressed into her.

When he looked back up at her face her eyes opened and the mixture of green and light brown looked at him as he moved within her. Her expression asked the strangest questions, as though she found him as much of an enigma as he found her.

Her front teeth pressed into her bottom lip as he continued working

He bent his head and kissed her again. She tasted of the lemonade and the icing on the bun.

The relief – the all-encompassing sensations of intercourse overtook him, and he let them, bathed in them, and let his spirit heal some more. Her fingertips pressed into his arms as she clung to him while he worked. Sounds of his relief carried on his breath with the sound of her pleasure.

His end came without him even attempting to change position and make this last. It did not need to last; it was the perfect escape just as it was.

When he'd finished he rolled on to his back and smiled at the ceiling, then bizarrely laughter gathered in his throat.

She leant up on her elbow and her fingers stroked over his cheek. 'You make me happy.'

His hand lifted and brushed her hair to set it behind her ear. 'You make me happy too.'

'I am going to have some more lemonade. Would you like some?'

'You are daring to risk the sourness.'

'For the sweetness that catches on another part of my tongue, yes.'

He smiled. 'Yes. I will have more lemonade.'

She got up and brought the full glasses back to the bed. He sat up and took his. She put her glass down on the chest beside the bed, then turned and brought over what was left of the plate of sugary buns.

It was the oddest picnic; sitting on top of the bed, naked, drinking lemonade and eating the buns as a warm breeze swept through the window and stirred the hairs on his skin. He'd not think about home again when he tasted lemonade, he'd remember this.

Once the sugar of the lemonade and buns had replenished his strength, he set the empty plate aside. Then with a smile, he turned and took the empty glass from her hand.

He indulged himself again, enjoying her body as she enjoyed his. He'd always believed that he gave the women he'd bedded as much pleasure as he'd received. He doubted it now. With Charlotte … The unguarded expressions on her face and in her eyes and the sounds she made said she genuinely enjoyed what he did and she was earnest in her attempt to please him in response.

When he walked her back, he did not stop at the corner where they'd met earlier, he walked on past it towards Colonel Hillier's house and damn – he thought about her with that old man. He did not want the thought in his head. He pushed it aside.

He stopped walking a street away from Hillier's. She curtsied to him, in an awkward gesture. As she'd done the other day. He smiled, rejecting a desire to kiss her, then before they separated he arranged to meet with her again the next day.

In his own bed at the barracks, in the dark, he thought of her, of being in bed with her. A sharp breath escaped his throat as he awoke from a dream aroused with hot, damp skin. He had not dreamt of war. In his dream Charlotte had been unbuttoning his trousers with a promise in her eyes.

A keenness to finish his duty and see her gripped at the muscles in his stomach.

When he met her, he took her to a different inn. He'd decided it was better not to form a pattern. But he arranged for there to be refreshment in the room once more and they lay together twice again. Both things were novelties that he'd enjoyed the day before.

He could not then see her for four days; his rota of duties did not allow it and so the urge to kiss her as they said goodbye was even stronger because he knew it would be days before he could do so again. It was also harder to not think about her with Hillier – about what might happen in Hillier's house at night.

But she had not spoken of it and he did not wish to acknowledge it. *Nor even think about it!* He yelled the words into his thoughts to silence them.

Chapter 4

There was a travelling trunk in the middle of the hall. Charlie clasped the bannister and stopped on the stairs as she looked at Mr Rook, the butler. 'Who?'

'Colonel Hillier is travelling to London, Miss.'

It was not an arrival then, but Mark about to leave. He'd said nothing to her yesterday. Yet that was not abnormal. She was his servant as much as anyone else in the house; he had no obligation to tell her anything.

She walked down the last few steps as he walked into the hall. The front door opened and men came in to lift the trunk out to the carriage.

'How long are you likely to be away?'

He looked over. 'Hello, Charlotte. I am not sure, a few days perhaps.'

A few days. She would have the house to herself for a few days.

He came to her and held her hands, then leant forward and kissed her lips. She pressed her lips back against his because if she did not he complained. Yet Mark's kisses made her wish to wipe her mouth afterwards. Harry did not make her feel like that. She liked his kisses.

The hall was busy as the final preparations for Mark's journey were undertaken. She remained there and watched, leaning back against the newel post. Then when the door finally closed behind Mark, she looked at the grandfather clock. It was twenty minutes after she had walked downstairs, a little after eleven. Harry had said he could not meet her because he had to work through the night. But if he had been working through the night then in the day he was free.

Her feet carried her across the hall and into Mark's office, where she found out some paper, a quill and ink. She was not very good at reading and writing, but she knew enough to write what she wished to tell Harry.

She took everything back to her room and sat at her dressing table, then picked up the small ink bottle to open it. Her arm accidently caught the top of her perfume decanter and knocked it over. She hastily pulled the paper out of the way and righted the decanter, then mopped up the spilt perfume with a handker-chief from the drawer. But a few drops had fallen on the paper and so it smelt of the essence of roses when she began to write.

The tip of the quill scratched out the words, then she let the ink dry, folded the letter and sealed it with wax so no one but Harry would open it. She put on her bonnet, but did not call for Tilly to accompany her on the walk. She had not taken Tilly with her on the days she'd met Harry at the inns and to take her again now would stir questions she did not care to answer.

She went to the inn she had gone to the last time she'd written to Harry and gave the letter to a boy who was clearing out the stables, with a coin to encourage him to take it immediately. Then she gave a groom, who tried to stop the boy, money to let the boy go on her errand.

The day was cloudy and the sea loud as it rolled up on to the pebbles while she walked back to the house. There had been a storm last night and it had stirred up the energy in the sea, making the waves higher and seemingly angrier as they charged up towards the seafront. Yet there were still a number of bathing carriages out in the water, where some of the wealthy had chosen to swim.

Her strides kicked at her petticoats in her haste as she hurried back to Mark's. It was going to be an intolerable day if Harry did not come. She would be wandering about the house awaiting him and she would be so disappointed. He had to come.

~

'There is a letter for you.'

Every muscle in Harry's body jolted as the envelope landed lightly on his stomach a second after he'd heard Gareth speak. Ash barked at Gareth, leaping off the bed, startled too.

Harry lay back down and let his muscles relax now he knew it was not a deadly threat but his friend.

Gareth stroked Ash's head.

'Must you keep walking into my room when I am asleep.' Harry's forearm fell on to his forehead and he shut his eyes again.

'The letter smells of perfume and was delivered by a stable boy, who said he was told to ensure you received it urgently. I am merely fulfilling the direction and I think it is fair to guess, as the letter did not come in the post or with the dispatches, it is nothing to do with your family, which the smell of it would indicate too.'

Harry picked up the envelope and smelt it, without opening his eyes. Roses. Charlotte. He opened his eyes. 'What hour is it?'

'Just past eleven.'

His duty had finished at six. He'd eaten and then come here to sleep. He'd barely slept. But he lifted the sheet and then turned to sit sideways on his bed and opened the letter. Then he looked up at Gareth. 'Thank you for this, you may go now.'

'Dismissed for a woman. You are not going to tell me who, then?'

'I am not going to tell you who, no.'

45

Gareth took Harry's hat off the peg on the wall and flung it at him, then turned and walked out of the door.

Harry laughed, picked up his hat and put it on the bed beside him, then looked at the letter as Ash rested her head on his knee. The black tip of her nose sniffed the paper as Harry read.

Dear Harry,

I have news. Mark, Colonel Hillier, is away. He is in London for a few days and so I hoped, thought, that you might like to come to the house.

Officers call here all the time, it would not be at all exceptional for you to call here as a friend. We can spend longer together here and you must bring Ash. We could take her for a walk along the shore after luncheon. If you will come for luncheon?

Tell me you will come. You must come. It is such an opportunity.

Yours sincerely

Charlie

'Charlie …' he said aloud, his eyebrows lifting. 'Charlotte … Charlie …' The shortened, less-formal name suited her. 'Luncheon …' He looked at Ash and stroked her neck, laughing quietly. Then shook his head slightly. He'd be a lunatic to go. Like everything about this affair with her it rang of oddness and imbalance. The etiquette of a relationship with another man's mistress was something he did not understand.

Was it really appropriate for him to call on her at Hillier's? Yet perhaps Hillier knew, perhaps he was allowing this. She had left his house on her own for several afternoons.

He sighed. He hated thinking about her and Hillier. He would go, for good or bad, whether it was right or wrong. He wanted to see her again, he'd not seen her for four days. The abstinence had opened a cavern in his chest that he knew would be repaired by a few moments of her company.

It had probably reached and passed midday when he knocked on Colonel Hillier's door, with Ash sitting close to the heel of his boot.

'No, do not worry. I will answer it. You can go back to the kitchen.' He heard the words, spoken by Charlotte, through the door. Then the door was opened. 'Hello,' she said in a breathless whisper.

'Hello.' He saluted her, in a teasing gesture. 'I am here as ordered, Miss Cotton.'

She reached out and gripped the cloth of the sleeve of his scarlet coat. 'Come in.' Once he had been pulled inside, she whispered. 'I am so glad you came.' Ash paced about the hall sniffing everything as Harry took off his hat.

'I have luncheon all laid out for myself in the parlour. I was going to eat alone but as you are here you must join me, Captain Marlow, with your dog!' She spoke in an overly loud voice, he presumed for the ears of the servant who had been sent back to the kitchen. 'You will, won't you?' This last sentence was said much more quietly, just for his ears.

'I will, thank you. That is very kind of you to invite me to stay as the Colonel is not here!' He smiled after he'd spoken for the ears of the servant too, then bowed slightly, in a gesture of habit, in the way he might have done had one of his sisters-in-law asked him to stay to eat.

Charlotte, or Charlie, turned and walked ahead of him, leading him to a room at the back of the house. It was relatively small and very feminine, very yellow. She held the door as he walked in with Ash at his heel, then shut it firmly, as though she shut out the world. 'This is my room,' her voice had become conspiratorial. 'No one is allowed in here unless I invite them.'

There was an immediate difference in her. Her posture became less rigid and her movements more flowing and there was a hint of mischief in her eyes and her smile too. She was more relaxed here.

He glanced about the room. 'This is a very pleasant space.'

'It is, isn't it. It is my hiding place.'

There was not much in the way of furniture, but there was a comfortable sofa and a chair.

'Look. I am prepared.'

The food was on a table in one corner of the room.

She crossed the room, passing him. 'Would you like something to eat?'

'Yes, now you speak of it, my stomach is growling at me.'

She began filling a plate for him with sandwiches and small pies, then she held it out. 'There.'

He stepped forward and took the plate from her hand. 'Thank you.' This was truly bizarre, when he'd thought this relationship could be no more peculiar.

'Well, sit then, Harry, do, you are making me feel awkward.'

He smiled and did her bidding. Then put down the plate and took off his gloves. He dropped them on the arm of the chair before he began to eat. Ash lay on the floor before him, watching Charlotte, Charlie, filling a plate for herself. 'You signed your letter 'Charlie' ...' Would she prefer him to use the name?

She sent him a smile across her shoulder.

He would guess she did prefer it.

'It is a nickname I have had since I was a child. I thought if anyone broke the seal they would think my letter from a man.'

He laughed. 'They would not have. The perfume gave the intent of your letter away immediately and if that had not, your words would have done.'

She smiled as she came to sit next to him. 'But no one intercepted it ...'

'No, no one opened it. Yet what would Colonel Hillier think of me being here, Charlotte? Charlie.'

'I have no idea what Mark will think.' Her chin lifted as she answered, in a way that denied any judgement. It reminded him of days when he had been challenged over his morals and behaviour by his father. He had always answered with an equally harsh dismissal; he had never cared for anyone else's opinion.

But now he was older and wiser and her words made him less certain of his decision to come. He did not want any trouble with a Colonel, retired or not. 'Is this sensible, then?'

Her chin lifted even higher. 'If he complains, then I shall tell him that I am allowed to do what I wish, just as he does.'

The look on her face touched him, literally, as if her fingers had pushed into his chest. Her expression said do not deny me and do not judge me. How could he condemn her? He'd not led a wholesome life. And Hillier could not own her, as Harry had thought the other day; she was not a slave.

He smiled. 'And send military men perfumed letters of seduction and tempt them into your parlour for luncheon. Am I to be snared in a web of deceit, then, Charlie?' He joked to shatter the hard look of defence and defiance that had cast across her expression.

The words succeeded and the stiffness in her posture disappeared again as a laugh broke from her throat. 'Yes, exactly that. I hope to snare you and I shall have you all wrapped up in my sewing threads.'

She stood then. 'You do not have a drink.' She poured him a glass of lemonade. 'Since you introduced me to it, I have had a kitchen maid make lemonade every day.'

His smile widened when she handed him the glass. Once he held it, he lifted the glass in a toast. 'To leading our lives as we wish.'

She raised her glass in the same gesture. 'To freedom.' Then drank when he did.

The sourness tingled on his tongue, then the sweetness flooded his throat.

He laughed a lot as they ate, because she did, and her laugh had an infectious quality.

After they'd eaten they walked Ash along the seashore as he'd always done alone. It had become normal now for her to be there. Even Ash seemed to think it right that she was there. The dog walked at her side not Harry's.

He was tired still, and the world felt surreal with that strange sensation that was a symptom of being only half awake; it gave his hours with Charlie a dream-like quality. He was lucky, probably, that they met no one from the barracks, otherwise the men might have guessed the origin of his scented letter, yet she'd seemed convinced by her desire to do as she wished, as though it really did not matter if Hillier knew.

He accompanied her home after their walk, but he did not go back inside when she invited him. 'No, I need to rest, I am on duty again tonight.'

'But will you call on me again tomorrow?'

'If you wish.'

'Of course I wish.'

He smiled and bowed his head. 'Then I will call here. At what hour?'

'For luncheon again …' she proposed.

'Very well, for luncheon.'

For the first time, she did not curtsey to him when they parted; instead she simply turned and opened the door.

When she went inside, he walked away and something clasped in his chest with a hard sudden grasp. He leant and patted Ash's head. 'Women are the strangest creatures.' Yet he'd thought he had mastered that knowledge years ago. Charlie was proving him wrong.

He had a sudden desire to break into a run, though. There was a lightness inside him, a strange emotion that expressed a sense of escapism – and the feeling had not come on the back of a physical encounter; they had not gone near a bed. This feeling was due solely to Charlie's conversation, her laughter and her smiles.

The next day he arrived at midday. With a smile on his face as he and Ash waited on the doorstep for the door to be opened. His heart had a full feeling, as though he'd just eaten a very rich meal. He had completed his duty and now he had two days to do as he wished.

Charlotte, Charlie, opened the door.

'Hello. Come in.' She took hold of his coat sleeve and pulled him over the threshold once more. Then her other hand lifted his hat off his head, before he could do it himself. She put it aside on the hall table. 'We have the whole house to ourselves, I told all the servants to go out.'

'You will have me strung up,' he said as he stripped off his gloves.

She only smiled. Then took his gloves from his hand and dropped them on top of his hat. 'I have luncheon ready in my parlour.'

'And lemonade?'

'And lemonade,' she confirmed with a nod, holding his hand and then pulling him towards her parlour.

'This is your lair I am being lured into again. Am I to be the luncheon today?'

'No, you will be dessert.'

Uncertainty lifted his eyebrows, although his smile still broke, yet that twisted a little. He was still unsure whether or not it was wise to call on her here.

They ate their luncheon in her little parlour and drank the lemonade, just as they had done yesterday, talking and laughing together. Then she stood suddenly and took his empty plate from his lap. 'Shall we go up to bed?'

He glanced at Ash, with a desire to laugh at himself whipping at his chest as his eyebrows lifted again. He was in a strange play. The set for it was perfect; in a feminine parlour. And the scene;

the demise of a lustful, sinful soldier. He was still tired from the hours he'd worked through the night, though. For two days he'd had only a couple of hours' sleep and it made his thoughts disjointed.

He looked up at her as she stood before him, trying to search for some common sense in this. 'And what will be said by the servants?'

'They are all out.'

'I know, but if anyone returns?'

'I have locked the door between the downstairs and the upstairs and only I have the key,' her pitch was proud and self-satisfied and her chin tilted upwards, just as it had done yesterday when he'd questioned her judgement.

Damn. The laugh escaped his throat. He could not help himself. The woman was so confusing and enchanting. The Charlotte he had met here, Charlie, was an entirely different person to the trembling woman who'd joined him in a bed in the inn for the first time.

He reached out and held of her hand, without standing or making his decision to accept. Her fingers closed about his as her large eyes looked earnestly at him, asking him why he had not moved yet.

He might be tired but he had learned to ensure his decisions were not slanted by fatigue. 'Are you certain this is a good idea?' Perhaps they both needed to come to their senses and stop this now. But his desire to do that was weak, his mind urged him to continue it as much as she did. He wanted to go upstairs with her.

'Yes. I am. It is the best idea,' her answer was spoken in her voice that said she intended to live her life as she wished. Her stance reminded him of his youthful self again and his constant refusal to conform to his father's and older brother's moralistic view of life. Ah. Damn the world and its judgement.

He stood up.

Damn an army that would make its soldiers march into a battle with a pitiful ration of bullets, let alone food. Damn the infections and diseases that killed the men who had survived the battles and died in filthy beds. Nothing in this world was fair or right.

Who had the power to be a judge over them for choosing to share a bed? No one. They were free to do as they wished.

The emotion that rushed through his body had him lifting a hand to embrace her neck. He wanted this as much as she did. The servants' or Hillier's interference be damned. He brought her mouth to his for a long moment.

When they walked upstairs, he led her by the hand as Ash followed them, looking at him with doubt.

If this was a wrong thing to do, then Harry was now cursed, but he would go to hell smiling.

'Where?' he asked on the landing.

'There.' She pointed to a door in the corner of the landing.

God, he had to ask. 'Is it the room you share with Hillier?'

'No.' She shook her head. 'It is my room, as the parlour is my room.'

He breathed out the disturbed sensations that began spinning in his blood on a frothing wave. He did not think he could have lain in the bed with her if Hillier had been there before him. Which was a stupid thought because when he'd slept with other women potentially hundreds of men had been in those beds before him.

He clasped the door handle, turned it and pushed the door open. She took over and led him into the room. It was another small room, like her parlour, and the bed was plain and narrow. Beyond that she had a dressing table, wardrobe and a set of drawers, and that was all. There were none of the fancy things like the jewellery boxes and ornaments he knew were in his sisters' rooms.

She stood before him smiling proudly and they still held hands as Ash walked around the room sniffing at everything. Ash had known where the letter had come from just as Harry had.

Harry's free hand lifted and stroked Charlie's neck, then he kissed her.

She kissed him back as her hand pulled loose from his, then reached to release the buttons of his coat.

It was hurried and urgent when they came together; there were still pins in her hair and the dog lay on the floor beside the bed.

It was the first time they had done this in the way he might have done it with a whore, yet it still felt entirely different. The setting and the hours they'd spent together changed everything. And Charlie ... Charlie was simply different – she felt different from every other woman in the world.

When he'd finished, he rolled on to his back, content, and his mind was peaceful as it had not been peaceful for more than a year. He closed his eyes and let that peacefulness enfold him.

Chapter 5

Charlie sat down on the edge of the bed. Harry did not wake, even when the mattress dipped as she sat. He'd slept all afternoon.

She had risen and taken Ash out for a walk about the garden, before any of Mark's servants returned, and since then she had been busy sealing her new friendship with Ash in the parlour, playing games. She'd taught the dog tricks for the benefit of some treats from their left-over luncheon; to bark when ordered and lift her paw for a shake and to roll over.

But now the others had returned and it was time for dinner and she had decided that she ought to come and wake him.

His arms rested on top of the sheets and he breathed steadily, his chest rising and falling. Her fingers stroked down his cheek.

Suddenly his eyes opened wide and he grasped her arm as he sat up. The grip hurt.

There was a moment like that and then his eyes looked at her face when he fully woke and he recognised her. Letting go of her he tumbled back on to the bed with a sigh, his arms lifting and his hands then pressing on to the top of his head.

She rubbed her aching wrist.

'Sorry,' he said. 'It is better not to wake me.'

'But it is getting late, I thought you must be hungry.'

'Lord. Yes. I am hungry. What time is it?'

'Nearly seven.'

'Really.' He sat up again. 'The servants—'

'Have returned. But they have said nothing about your hat in the hall. Mark invites other women here, though, sometimes. That is why I have my own rooms, so I can stay out of his way when he wishes. So perhaps the servants do not care and why should I not have a man here, when he is entertained by other women?'

He smiled, but not widely, and his hand lifted, then the back of his fingers ran over her cheek. 'Do you think we have taken a risk we should not have? Will you be in trouble? I suppose I should not have fallen asleep.'

'You should have done, you were tired, and this is my house when Mark is away. I have the run of it and the say of it in Mark's absence.'

A quiet sound that expressed amusement escaped his throat. 'There is so much conviction in your voice that I shall let myself be convinced by you.' He sat up and she stood, moving out of his way so he could get up. 'You are right, I am hungry, but we will go out and eat at an inn. I am not inclined to ask the Colonel's kitchen to cook for us.'

While they ate, in the inn he'd taken her to on the second day they had shared a bed, with Ash at their feet, she persuaded him to come back with her and remain for the night. This was what she wanted, to be with Captain Harry Marlow. She had delighted in his company at the seashore and she enjoyed being in a bed with him and yesterday and today she had appreciated his companionship. This was what she wanted.

When they returned to the house, she fetched one of Mark's cigars, lit it herself as she did sometimes for Mark, and handed it to Harry. They shared it as she sat on Harry's lap while they also shared a few glasses of Mark's whiskey.

She asked Harry about the places he'd travelled to with the

army and the things he'd seen of the world. He told her some horrible stories about the war and spoke of the men he'd sought to comfort as they'd suffered with their wounds and men he had seen fall upon, or carried from, battlefields. He also spoke of men who were his friends; men who had done miraculous things. Harry was a good man. Everything he said to her screamed of it. Then he told her about his horse, Obsidian. She could tell from his voice that he was fond of the horse and as kind to her as he was to Ash and as he had been to his men.

When he'd finished speaking, she said, 'Would you introduce me to Obsidian one day. I'd like to meet her.' Then she held his hand and stood up. 'But let's put Ash out into the garden now, for a moment, and then retire to bed.'

This was very different to the way she had lived for the last seven years with Mark. She had talked and laughed with Harry and now they walked upstairs for a second time holding hands, only this time it was her leading him. In her room she looked immediately at the brass buttons on his coat and began undoing them as Ash found a place on the rag rug beside her bed.

Harry let her take his coat off, smiling indulgently at her. Then she pushed his braces off his shoulders so she could pull his shirt up and over his head.

When he stripped his shirt off his arms, she began undoing her dress. He did not try to help, but instead sat on the bed and watched her as he pulled off his boots.

He seemed slightly intoxicated, but so was she and the taste of the cigar still filled her mouth. She felt naughty, as she had as a child when she'd sat on top of a hayrick chewing on a liquorice root, when she had run away and hidden when she was supposed to be in Sunday school.

She was hiding again, with Harry – she wanted to hide away with Harry forever.

When she remembered the days she had lain on hayricks, she always longed to go back in time, then she would never climb into Mark's carriage and she would hide on a hayrick forever. She hadn't known what would happen then. But now she knew the future and she wanted to stay in this moment and stop time.

When she turned her back to him, so he could unlace her corset, Harry was sitting on her bed, in only his trousers, stockingless, with his braces hanging by his hips. His fingers tugged the lacing free, jolting her body. The assurance with which he performed the task pulled strings inside her as well as pulling the lacing loose.

When her corset fell off she turned and held Harry's head, the heels of her palms pressing against his cheeks as she bent and kissed him.

His hands grasped her chemise at the hem and lifted it, then he drew it over her head and off her arms. When she straightened, his gaze dropped to her navel and his hands settled at her hips over her drawers. He pulled them down, leaned forward and kissed her stomach, then the place between her legs.

'Oh.'

Her hands rested on his head and her fingers combed through his hair as his fingers spread and pressed into the skin and the flesh of her bottom, holding her against him as his tongue explored. He moved her hips as he wished, while the movement of his tongue stirred up the pleasurable sensations she'd discovered with him. Then his fingers slid into her and the rush of emotion rolled over her. She clung to his shoulders.

He looked up at her, his eyes hazy with liquor, yet saying he was proud of his success.

She took control, pushed him back on to the bed, straddled him and undid his trousers, so she could get at him, then freed him from his underwear and put him inside her. It was her turn to control the movement, moving up, backward and forward. Seeking to catch him out with unexpected movements as his hands slid over her thighs, gently, with the flow of her motion. But he did not try to take control from her.

She moved more determinedly, her palms resting on his chest, her fingers splayed. She wanted to feel successful too, to feel as smug as he had looked when he'd brought on the rushing waves of the little death in her. She wished to make the waves crash over him, as though there had been the wildest storm.

His pale-blue eyes looked directly into hers and his lips parted slightly as he breathed more heavily, in a quick rhythm of breaths, even though it was not him who was moving.

'You are an incredibly beautiful woman, Charlie, in spirit as well as appearance.'

Her hands ran down to his stomach then up to his shoulders and on to his arms. 'You are beautiful too.' She wanted to say she loved him, the whiskey had put the words on to her tongue. But military men like Mark and Harry did not recognise or trade in the emotion of love. She had learned that long ago. Everything with a soldier was just fact, they did not welcome compassion or care. But this … This they welcomed, and this Harry was skilled at – and he was youthful and beautiful and she had drunk whiskey and her emotions were free and she was in a mood to be naughty. She laughed.

His hands came up and pressed either side of her head, then pulled her down to kiss him as she continued moving, working hard, more forcefully. She struck her body against his so that sensations exploded through her until the moment the wave came and when it came she could feel that a second later it broke over him too.

She was sweaty and breathing hard. She lay on top of him, letting her body rest on his. His hand stroked over her hair as he breathed heavily too, his chest lifting beneath her.

I love you. Her tongue longed to say the words.

After a moment, Harry's hand gripped her arm and encouraged her to move off him.

She lay on the bed beside him.

His forearm covered his eyes. 'I did not put on the sheath.'

She did not care. 'It does not matter.'

'It might. I have never forgotten before.'

What did she say? He seemed upset. No. Not upset, angry. But with himself. Her fingers touched his arm. 'I do not mind, Harry.'

He turned then, rolling on to his side and wrapped his arms around her, holding her. It was the first time he'd simply held her. 'I am sorry. I should have remembered.'

'You have nothing to be sorry for.'

He did not answer, only held her more firmly. She wanted to know what he was thinking, but she did not ask. She was not sure how to ask, or that he would answer.

After he'd taken off his trousers and underwear they got into the bed.

He lay on his back with her head on his shoulder and his arm around her as the sheet lay over their hips, so the breeze from the window he'd opened brushed over her skin. He held her all night, as she drifted in and out of sleep.

~

Harry woke in a strange bed, in a strange room and his body was pinned down by … Charlie. He laughed quietly.

Something tickled his foot. He lifted his head. Ash. The dog probably needed to go out; from the amount of daylight in Charlie's room it looked quite late to be rising. But the late hour did not matter, he was not on duty today so he did not care that they'd slept late.

The thought stirred a sound of humour low in his throat. She had cared for nothing yesterday. She'd let him spend time here and sleep here as though Hillier did not exist. He wished the man did not exist.

He slid Charlie's hand off his stomach, then carefully disengaged his arm from about her shoulders before climbing over her and off the bed. It did not disturb her. He picked up his underwear and trousers and put them on.

Her beautiful hair was splayed out over the pillow. He smiled as he pulled on his stockings and boots. Then he beckoned Ash with his hand. He and the dog left the room and went downstairs side by side, then walked on through the room in which he'd played cards and over to the French doors. He opened a door and let Ash out, then turned to the box of cigars that Charlie had brought back into the room late last night. He took one out, lit it and then walked over to the open door.

He smoked the cigar, half-clothed, his braces hanging down at his hips and his top half bare as he watched the dog discovering all the scents and secrets the garden held. There was that surreal feeling. Perhaps he had picked up an infection in the battlefield and he'd never come home at all and this, Charlie, the Colonel, all of it … Perhaps it was all a hallucination. Or heaven.

But if it was real?

If it was real then last night he had forgotten to wear a sheath. She might be with child. It had taken his brother only twice to achieve that with his wife. Or … he might be infected. She'd said that Hillier brought other women here. If Hillier or the other women carried a disease … But God, he could not think of that – of Charlie like that.

He tossed the end of the cigar into a flower border in the garden, then called Ash back to him and walked inside. He shut the door, then returned to her room and to her bed. And God, let every self-righteous person in this world point their fingers at him and call him a villain, or debauched, he did not care. Let the rest of the world care, not him, nor Charlie. He woke her up and appreciated everything about her body again and he did not use a sheath. Fool, or not a fool, let him be damned, but it had felt so good and it was too late to avoid infection now. But to try to prevent a child he did withdraw before his moment of victory.

They spent the day together, never entirely dressing, and continually returning to her bed. Although they ate at times, ringing down to the kitchens and telling the Colonel's servants that they were coming down so that the servants would stay out of their way. It was an idealistic life, the sort of life he'd never thought he wished to indulge in and yet it had a draw. It stirred emotion in his chest in the same way that a spoon spun the tea in a cup when sugar was dissolved.

They spent the night, a second night, in her bed together and while they slept he held her. It felt better than he could have ever imagined to hold a naked woman – Charlie, not any woman.

But then the sun rose and it was time for him to get out of her bed and stop pretending that he was another man in another life.

He dressed as she watched him. With Ash sitting near him. The dog's head turned from Charlie to Harry as they talked.

When he was dressed he bent down and looked at himself in the mirror on the dressing table. His fingers combed back his hair. He looked tidy enough but he'd have to shave at the barracks. He straightened and looked back at Charlie. 'Well then, it is time I headed off.'

She smiled and threw aside the sheet, getting up. 'I'll walk down with you.'

He nodded. Why was there a queasy feeling in his stomach?

There was a cloth garment on a chair near her bed. She picked that up, pulled it on to her arms and then over her head. The garment was the nightdress she must normally wear. It sheathed her body with one swift waterfall of movement.

Humour gathered at the back of his throat. This woman had so many characters and yet none of them seemed quite like a whore's. They walked downstairs together, with her clothed in only her nightdress.

As they reached the hall, his palm cradled her head and he leant and kissed her. Her fingers stroked through his hair as his free hand ran across her back. He did not want to leave her.

When he broke the kiss, her fingers fell on to his cheek. There were emotions expressed in her eyes. This was so much more than any connection he'd ever had with a whore. The emotions he saw in her eyes were those he'd seen in the eyes of his brothers, his sisters and his cousins when they'd found a wife or a husband.

He turned away.

He was a soldier. He did not have space for those emotions in his life and she belonged to another man.

He belonged to another life.

'Will you come back when your duty hours are over?'

'If I can.'

She nodded, her eyes speaking of happiness.

He smiled, then turned and opened the door and left her, his heart thumping in a heavy rhythm. He looked back once and caught her gaze just before she shut the door.

Ash walked close to his heel as they headed back to the inn, where Obsidian had awaited them for hours.

He breathed hard, trying to take control of the answering emotions and desires inside him. It would be foolish – entirely foolish, to think of her like that.

But still, in the hours he was on duty, he pushed aside the military papers he was working on and pulled over a blank sheet of paper, then wrote to his brother.

Dear John,

I have never begged for my allowance early before, as you are aware, and I find it both humiliating and uncomfortable to do so, and yet, I have discovered a reason that justifies putting myself in this place. I am not asking for the money for myself, but because I wish to support a woman. I have spent my last quarter's allowance and I want to secure this woman now. I do not want to wait. It would…

It would mean that she would have to share a bed with Hillier again if he could not support her and he did not want that to happen. He wanted Charlie to be his. But for her to be his he would need to pay for somewhere for her to live and for her food and her clothing and … he needed his next quarter's allowance.

…mean she suffered unduly. Please would you send my money early, then I promise I shall manage it accordingly from here on. I will not ask again.

Your brother,

Harry.

He sealed the letter, addressed it to his ducal brother, and then included it in the pouch of dispatches going to London.

Later in the afternoon, once his duty was complete, he returned to Charlie, but he did not tell her he'd made the request. Instead of telling her, he suggested they took Ash out for a walk along the beach. They did so and took turns to throw the stick for Ash for nearly two hours, before finding an inn where they could eat dinner.

Let this dream or hallucination, or whatever this madness was, continue. He did not want anything to break what this had become.

They spent the late hours of the evening at the house sitting on the sofa in her little parlour, playing chess, conversing and smoking one of Hillier's cigars, handing it back and forth, and drinking more of his whiskey.

When Charlie was in this careless, spirited mood it reminded him of the off-duty hours he spent with his men and the hours he'd spent with his cousins in his youth. He was entirely comfortable in her presence. They laughed and talked continuously. It was not simply their relationship in a bed that made him wish to keep her for himself, it was this too.

He did not deny another opportunity to share her bed, though, that did play a large part in his desire to keep her. They joined again and then he slept beside her with his arm wrapped around her.

In the morning they ate bread, cheese and eggs in the kitchen for their breakfast and washed it down with coffee, before returning to the bed as he was not on duty again until the evening. Then they took Ash out and ate in an inn.

Afterward he walked her back to Hillier's, then said goodbye on the steps in front of Hillier's door.

As he walked back to collect Obsidian, Harry's innards writhed. How long would it take John to reply? To act. All he had to do was send a note to Harry's bank. And how long before Hillier came back?

He sighed.

Perhaps tomorrow he should speak with Charlie and ask her, tell her, what he hoped for? But then, if he did not receive the money from John, he would be raising Charlie's expectations for something that might not be possible.

Not possible yet. Regardless of what John said now, when the next allowance was paid then he would rent a house and have her move to it, clothe and keep her.

But God, he could not stand the thought that he might not be able to do it immediately. His mind would be unable to bear it if Hillier returned and she was still in that house.

Chapter 6

Someone knocked on the office door with a firm military-style rap. 'Come in,' Harry called.

'Captain Marlow. Sir.'

Harry looked up at the saluting Major, who faced him in the small room illuminated by a single gas light. 'Yes, Major.'

'There is a woman here to see you, sir.'

A woman … 'Who?' He looked at the clock. It was only a few minutes after three o'clock in the morning.

'A Miss Cotton, sir.'

Charlie.

He stood up. 'Where is she?'

'In the officers' mess, sir. She is very distressed and injured.'

Injured … What on earth? He was walking already. 'Thank you, Major, you are dismissed.' Harry walked past him.

The sound of the heels of his boots echoed along the wood-panelled hallways as he made his way to the mess room.

She was sitting alone in the large room that was cluttered with tables and chairs. Someone had lit a single light and the gas flame made its muffled, almost crackling, sound, but other than that the room, which was often busy and noisy, was shadowy and quiet. He shut the door. Charlie sniffed away tears.

What had made her cry? What had brought her here in the middle of the night?

'Charlie …' She was still dressed in her bonnet and cloak and her hands were clasped together in her lap.

She had been looking at her hands. She looked up, but did not rise. 'Harry.'

'What has happened?' Within the shadow formed by the brim of her bonnet he could see one of her eyes looked … bruised, but it was not a dark bruise, it was a fresh crimson bruise. He walked across the room. 'Charlie.' Panic sliced him in half. 'How were you injured?'

When he reached her he squatted down on his haunches and clasped her hands as they lay in her lap. They were trembling like leaves on a tree in a breeze.

'E's thrown me out. Mark 'as.' Her words expressed a coarse accent that was not her usual tone. 'I 'ave nothin', Harry. I 'ave nowhere to live. I 'ave no clothes. I 'ave no money. Nothin'. I 'ave nowhere to go. No one to go to.'

But she'd come to him.

His grip firmed on her hands. 'You have me. I will take care of you. Now tell me what happened, how were you hurt? Did Colonel Hillier hit you?' The thought of it pierced him in the stomach as if a sword tip had pressed into his flesh.

'No. Yes, 'e slapped me, that was all.'

Slapped her. For God's sake.

'He did not intend it. I fell against the doorframe. But 'e had told me I must leave. 'E said I had to go because I let you stay, and 'e did not like it. 'E made me leave with nothin'. 'E said I couldn't go to my room. I couldn't fetch anythin'.'

'But you came to me,' he repeated. 'You did the right thing. You have something. You have me.' He squeezed her shaking fingers and refused to admit how much the sight of her distress and her injured eye disturbed him. The bright-red stain below her copper eyebrow was spreading like a spilt glass of red wine.

'Oh, Harry, 'ave I been silly? I am so afraid.'

'Come along.' He stood and pulled her on to her feet. 'You will sleep in my bed while I complete my duty. I cannot leave my post. But once I am done then we will resolve this. Do not worry.'

He held her hand tightly as he walked her through the barracks, aware that this was entirely wrong, but where else was she to go? He could not leave his post.

When they reached his room, he took off her cloak and bonnet for her. Then he made her sit, unlaced her short boots and took them off, before making her lie down. She trembled, even as she lay on the bed.

'Ash.' The dog had been sitting and watching them ever since Harry had brought Charlie into the room, disturbing Ash's sleep. He tapped the bed in front of where Charlie lay. Ash jumped up and lay beside her. 'There, Ash will keep you company until I return.'

She did not look at him. She was suffering with shock; he could see the signs in her eyes, he had seen many men with staring eyes like that in the hospital tents during the war. It expressed how wounded she must feel on the inside, just as the bruise said how wounded she had truly been.

He leant and kissed her cheek. It tasted of salt from the remains of her tears. 'Try and sleep.'

He left her. But God, his heart remained in his room when he walked back to the office to complete his duty, and his hands trembled with shock too.

One hand lifted and ran over his hair.

Her eye … If she had been slapped, she had been slapped very hard.

Damn. His instinct was to go to Hillier's, kick the damned door down, drag the man out and show him what it felt like to be hit. But that could not be done, Harry would be locked up for it and then who would take care of Charlie?

He sighed out a breath as he reached the office.

In the Crimea, night hours had been for planning, maps had

been spread out and leant over and strategies drawn up. Here …
Night hours were long tests of endurance. Nothing very much
happened, and he could not walk about the men all night to
check they were at their posts. There were records to be kept, but
his mind would not focus on them. His mind was on the woman
who lay in his bed.

He got up and walked outside to speak with the men on guard.
At least that would distract his mind for a few minutes. He was
teased when he got out there, in a light-hearted way. He was their
officer, but even so … Many questions were asked about the
mysterious, tearful woman.

Gareth appeared at the door to the office just before six, just
before Harry's duty came to a close and Gareth was to take over.
'I have been hearing tales about the night.' He walked over and
stood before the desk that Harry sat behind. 'A woman …'

Harry shook his head. 'Do not ask me. I have heard it all
tonight.'

His friend smiled. 'So the desire to ride out alone, frequently,
I take it was not to ride a horse.'

'Gareth.' Harry warned in a voice that was a reprimand.

Gareth smiled, unrepentant. 'I believe she is currently in your
room.'

'She is, but she will be gone within the hour.'

'Good, because I do not want this falling on my head in my
hours of duty. She cannot remain here on my watch.'

Harry made a face at him as he stood up. He knew he was in
trouble. He did not need to be reminded of it. 'I told you, I will
resolve it now.' And delay facing the storm that would thunder
through the barracks when the Lieutenant Colonel woke.

'Good luck,' Gareth stated as Harry left.

Harry sighed out hard as he walked towards his room. Half
of him had been in this room through every hour of his duty
since she'd arrived, waiting for the moment he could go back.
After he'd spoken to the men he'd planned his strategy of attack,

or perhaps defence. He was going to take her to an inn for now.

He knocked on the door. There was no response. Concern twisted through his stomach as he opened the door.

She was asleep, still fully clothed. Lord the emotion in his stomach rolled up to his chest. Her hair was awry, twisted bits had escaped pins, making her hair scruffy, but it was her eye that tainted her beauty, not that. The vivid red bruising had flooded her whole eye socket and spread across her cheek. It was an internal wound, not simply a bruise, and it had been bleeding throughout the night.

He squatted down and his hand rested on Ash's head as the dog looked up at him with sad, questioning eyes, asking him why this woman who had come into both their lives was lying on Harry's bed. Harry's hand lifted and instead settled on Charlie's head.

Her eyes opened, though she did not move. She was still in shock, her eyes spoke of doubt and fear. 'Harry …'

'How are you feeling?'

'Bilious.'

'I need you to come with me. I'm sorry, but I cannot let you stay here.'

'Is it the morning?'

'Yes.'

'Where can I go?' She started, leaning up on her elbow.

'To an inn.'

She sat up fully, turning to sit at the edge of the bed. 'I have no money. I cannot.'

'I will pay.'

~

'You should not have to.' This was not what she had wanted.

The pain inside her was a tight ball of agony. What had she done? She had been so stupid. But she had wanted something

70

for herself. A moment. For seven years she had lived as Mark wished and done everything as he wished. She had deserved something for herself and she had not intended for it become what it had, and yet she had not regretted that it had reached that point. She had enjoyed every hour she'd spent with Harry and especially the hours they'd spent in her parlour and her room. He had made those places special to her.

Tears rolled on to her cheeks.

'Come along, Charlie. I need to take you out of here. You should not be in my room.'

He clasped her hands and pulled her to her feet as she choked on tears. Then his arms were about her and he held her tightly for a moment. But then he let her go. 'Let us put on your boots and then we must go. Ash, you can come too.'

She sat again as he slid her boots on to her feet and laced them. Then he put her bonnet on for her and tied the bow, and when she stood once more he set her cloak about her shoulders and tied that for her too.

As they walked out she glanced all about the wooden-panelling which lined the corridors, she had not even noticed it the night before. But confusion, fear and terror of what would happen next had flooded her then. The fear still had a tight grip about her throat; it had not let go.

She had walked to the barracks in a daze; her head spinning and it still hurt. She could barely remember the walk from Brighton in the dark any more than she remembered these corridors.

But she remembered Mark returning late, in the middle of the night, in a rage. He'd called for her, shouting up from the hall and then ordered her into his drawing room. She had not wanted to go down, but she had gone to fulfil her duty. Then he'd yelled and slapped her and she'd fallen and hit her head and he had told her to leave. Just to leave. He had not even let her return to her room. Once the maid had brought down her bonnet and cloak, Mark had clasped her arm, led her to the door and thrown her out.

And now Harry held her arm as he walked her through the halls – but his grip was gentle.

When they walked out of the barracks' gate, the uniformed men saluted Harry. He saluted them in return. She bit her lip to stop herself from crying again, she was so uncertain of everything. She could not look ahead. There was no knowledge of where she would be in an hour, what she would eat, when she could change her clothes – she had no clothes beyond those she was wearing.

'We will walk to the town,' Harry stated once they'd passed the men. 'I am sorry, but I could not take the time to fetch Obsidian, men are not allowed to bring women to the barracks and the rule includes officers. I broke it by letting you stay while I served out my duty, so it is best we left at once.'

'Will you be in trouble?' Shivers kept raking through her body, even though she was wearing her bonnet and her cloak and it was a summer morning. Her arms folded across her chest. He was walking quickly. Her legs slashed at her petticoats as she tried to keep up.

He sighed. 'I will be. But it was my choice to take you to my room. Just as it was yours to take me to your bedchamber.'

'Will you be in severe trouble?'

'Yes, quite likely. But I will manage it. Have you not been in severe trouble? I think it fair I suffer too and it is not your concern, so you are not to fret over it.'

She glanced at his profile. 'Are you angry with me?'

'No, Charlie, I am angry at Hillier, and tired.'

'I am tired too.'

'I'm sure.'

'Have you the money to pay for a room in the inn for me?'

'Let that also be my concern. You will have a room and a bed and food to eat. I will ensure it. Although I may struggle with the quality of clothing, and such, that Hillier provided, you will not be left to beg.'

Yet this felt like begging, but she had nowhere else to go. Her arms fell and swung at her sides with the pace of their steps. At least she knew there would be a room, a roof and a bed. Now at least there was no need to be afraid of the next hour, and until the next night.

Harry walked with the rhythm of a march, while Ash kept pace at his heel. Her heart raced with the pace of his strides as she tried to hurry and keep up on his other side.

He took her to the inn they had first lain in together and her fingers curled into fists at her sides as her chin tilted up defensively while Harry requested a room for an indefinite stay. The man looked at her with a gaze that judged her badly. She knew that look, she had learned it at the age of fourteen.

Harry was asked for money as a down-payment. He took a purse out of his coat pocket and put some money in the man's hand.

She bit the inside of her cheek to stop the tears. She had been forced by circumstance and love for her family into accepting a life under Mark's protection; she did not want to force Harry into protecting her.

His hand held her arm as they walked upstairs and the gentle contact sent relief flooding into her blood; it seemed to express concern and caring for her despite their situation.

When they reached the room, he let her go. 'I have to leave you now, I'm afraid. I have asked them to send you breakfast up and Ash will stay to keep you company. But I must return to the barracks to receive whatever judgement my commanding officer wishes to bestow. It is better I return than wait for him to send for me.'

'I am sorry,' apologies were the only words her tongue wished to say. She had not wanted it to be like this. They had shared something she'd thought special and now it was all ruined, soiled and stained. It was not special any more, it was a need.

'It is not your fault. You must do as you wish while I'm gone. I have paid enough money for you to live here for a few days without incurring debt, so do not be afraid to order food, drink or a bath, and here.' He withdrew his purse from his pocket and gave it to her. 'This will give you something, at least, although not much, with which to find some clothes other than those you are dressed in.'

She swallowed against the lump of tears gathering in her throat. 'You will come back?'

'Yes. Of course. I just … I cannot be sure when. It is dependent on how lenient my Lieutenant Colonel feels.' He smiled, but the smile was not in his eyes, it had no depth.

She had done something terrible.

His hands lifted and he stepped forward, then he braced either side of her head. 'Do not be afraid, promise me? Relax here. I will talk my way out of this.'

Tears made his face a blur.

His lips pressed on to hers, then another kiss touched her cheek. Then he pulled away. 'I have to go. But you must smile for me before I leave, so I may remember that while I am away.'

She opened her lips in a smile, but it was probably more of a grimace.

His fingers tapped beneath her chin. 'I have to go.'

Once he'd gone, she sat in a chair and cried as Ash sat beside her with her head in Charlie's lap.

'What will happen now, Ash?'

~

It was as though the first charge of Armageddon struck Harry as he stood before the Lieutenant Colonel.

'I might demote you for this. I might have you court-martialled.'

Damn. He would be shamed forever if he faced the judgement of a military court. 'Forgive me, sir. I saw no other option at the time. Miss Cotton was in shock and injured.'

'And your mistress.' The words were snapped at Harry in an accusation.

The denial rose to the tip of Harry's tongue, but … It was the truth now, she was his, and he had been living as though that was the truth for the last few days. He bowed his head and acknowledged it.

'And you have taken her from the care of a Colonel.'

A retired Colonel, he wanted to say. He did not. It hardly mattered. He knew the army. The Colonel's rank would still have sway among Harry's higher-ranking officers. His fate was now being busily rewritten. To what?

He breathed in, in a controlled way. He had survived a war; he would survive the outcomes of this, whatever they were.

'You are dismissed. I will let you know what I decide later.'

Harry stiffened his stature and saluted. 'Lieutenant Colonel.' Then he turned with a step and walked out. Damn. Damn it.

But Lord, he did not regret what he'd done with Charlie. She had been everything to him these last few days.

When he walked past the slot for his letters, he stopped. There were two for him. He took them out and walked on towards his room. He would pack some of his things, then ride back to the inn.

In his room he opened one of the letters that was written by a hand he knew. It was from John – his older, ducal half-brother, who held the purse strings. He unfolded the paper with an eager-ness that one of his nephews might feel.

No. The word jumped out and bit at him. His fingers creased the paper as his grip on it tightened. 'No … Damn you.'

How dare you even think that I would approve such a thing … How many times have I told you, warned you, that you cannot behave so? It will break our mother's heart if she heard of you keeping a woman. No. I will not fund it. I will stop the damned allowance, if that is how you are choosing to spend it. I had thought this behaviour outgrown. I was wrong, then. I am stopping your allowance. Enough is enough.

Lord. Anger rushed into Harry's limbs with a surge of longing for a sword fight and the rage roared in his ears, yelling out inside him. He needed the bloody money, it was not want, nor desire, it was desperation now. Damn. He was not a youth to be moralised at. He'd thought he had outgrown the condemnation of his brother too. It sent a bitter taste flooding into his mouth.

He discarded the letter, throwing it on to the bed, then opened the next one.

Hillier. Bloody hell.

The letter was an outpouring of accusations, of theft and then demand. Harry was accused of stealing, both for stealing Charlie away and for taking the Colonel's food and drink. God. He had spent three days in the man's house. But he had been invited – 'By his mistress.' It was a type of madness that had come over Harry where Charlie was concerned.

Yet he still did not regret.

You owe me, Captain Marlow. Apparently the price of his theft – of Charlie – was five hundred pounds. Harry thought her priceless and he still did not regret. Let Hillier, as well as his brother, go to hell.

But five hundred, that could not be found, even if he wished to pay it, and if it was not paid as it would not be, what then?

Nausea stirred in Harry's stomach as he packed his things. His life had changed and neither time nor fate could be turned back. He'd learned that well enough in a baptism of a barrage of firing-arms in the Crimea. Guilt swept up into his mind and thrust its fists at his chest, but that, he had learned, must be lived with. Now there was simply another part to it.

He picked up his sword belt, wrapped it about his waist and secured the buckle. Then he put his pistol in his bag and pulled the drawstring tight before lifting the bag on to his shoulder. He felt as though Ash should be beside him, but Ash was with Charlie.

At the inn, he left Obsidian to the care of the stables, then walked into the reception room and asked for food, coffee and a bathing tub to be sent to his room.

His body ached to join Charlie in the room he'd hired. He had no idea what the outcome of this would be, yet he knew that he was glad to have her here. The thought of her with Hillier would have cut deeper than any sense of guilt he'd known since the war.

He knocked on the door.

'Come in!'

He opened the door and stepped into a new way of life. 'Hello.' Ash bounded over to him, barking.

Charlie was sitting up on the bed, her hair a mess. The bright bruise about her eye had become even larger during his absence; it had crept quite far out on to her cheek. The internal wound was still bleeding. He would have to watch her and make sure it was nothing more serious.

'What happened?' She slid across to the edge of the bed and got up.

'Nothing for you to fret over. I have brought my things. I will be staying here with you when I am not on duty.' He put the bag down on the floor by a chair and took off his sword, then rested it across the chair.

When the meal of stew and bread was brought up, she ate too, and they sat and talked. Her hands trembled as she ate. She was still very distressed. It made him realise how much of herself Charlie kept hidden. He had always seen the things she'd revealed, the honest and natural way she behaved, both out of a bed and in it. Yet she had said very little about herself or how she felt. Those were things, he now realised, she'd deliberately kept secret, though he did not believe she had ever lied.

'What happened last night?' he asked. 'How were you hurt, really?'

'I told you; Mark slapped me and I fell. He did not hit me.'

He had hit her, just with an open hand and not a closed one, the action was the same. But Harry did not say that; it made no difference. He would never let Hillier near her again. 'Because of us?'

'Yes.'

'How did he discover it?' Not that they had been discreet.

'The housekeeper wrote to him. He returned late and he shouted at me and smacked me and then threw me out through the front door. I had nowhere to go and so I just walked. Then I realised I was walking towards the barracks and I carried on because I knew you were there.'

'And, as I told you, that was the right thing to do.' She had not sounded as though she thought that true.

'You are not in too much trouble?' Perhaps she was uncertain because she felt guilty over the problems it had stirred up.

'No.' He did not want the worry to be hers. He'd become used to the burden of guilt; he could carry another weight.

'When are you on duty again? When must you go?'

'Tonight. We have the rest of the day to spend together.'

'But you must be tired, you have not slept.'

'I have ordered a bath, I will bathe and then sleep, and you may bathe and sleep with me. You said you were tired too earlier; I doubt you slept much last night or when I was gone.'

She shook her head.

As she sat in the tin bath before him Harry combed her hair. He had washed her hair for her too, their legs tangled and contorted about one another.

'Tomorrow, I will take you shopping and we will buy you one more dress, at least, and underwear and such things that you need.' His brother and his ill opinion be damned, Harry would pay the bill with an I-owe-you agreement, if he must, and he would use John's name and have them send the bloody bills to his brother too. He would not see Charlie suffer unduly for what they had done together. Their affair had been a joint endeavour; he should bear as much of the brunt of the results as her.

'Thank you.'

'You do not need to thank me.'

It was a strange thing to lie in a bed with her when she was his; his to keep, protect and care for. This woman, who he held in his arms, he also held in the palm of his hand. She ate by his gift now and she slept in sheets in a dry room by his gift. The knowledge was an odd feeling in his gut. He did not try to touch her in any way, but simply held her. She was still a little in shock – and the knowledge that he was now paying her … by a sort of method … did not sit comfortably with him at all.

Strange. His morals had always previously encouraged him to pay a woman.

He shut his eyes and expected to see a hospital tent, or the battlefield and hear the sound of cannons or screaming and moaning men. Instead he could still see the vivid red bruise around Charlie's eye.

He swallowed against the lump of emotion in his throat, then let the tiredness claim him.

~

A knock, a sudden, hard strike, hit the door of the room that Harry had taken for them. Harry was asleep but Charlie had been lying awake beside him for a little while. She sat up.

The door was hit again.

Charlie climbed off the bed. 'I am coming, wait,' she said it quietly as she walked towards the door. Harry had worked all night and he'd been sorting things out for her benefit for most of the morning; she did not want to wake him unnecessarily. It was probably only someone come to take away the bath tub they had used. She did not attempt to dress fully, but she picked up Harry's coat and put it on over her chemise. She was not indecent, she had her chemise and drawers on.

She opened the door a little and peered around it. 'Hello.'

'Miss Cotton.' The door was pushed open wider. It was Mark's manservant, his valet, Mr Perrin.

The moment threw Charlie back years, to the stupid young girl who had taken this man's hand and climbed up into the Colonel's carriage, and later Perrin had collected her from her mother's house and brought her here to Brighton. She swallowed against the fear in her throat. All the emotions that she'd known then and thought she'd conquered were inside her again.

'You are to come back,' he said. The words were an order. She was being recalled.

But. 'No.' Her chin tilted up in defiance. She was with Harry now. 'No.' This was where she wanted to be. She was not young and as pliant as dough to be manipulated any more. She did not want to be Mark's any more.

'You will come home with me, Miss Cotton.' Perrin's hand lifted as he stepped forward.

'No. She will not.'

Mr Perrin looked beyond her.

Charlie turned.

Harry walked towards them. He'd woken, risen and he must have moved with stealth and speed because he'd collected his sword without her even hearing. He unsheathed the sword as he moved, with a whisper of steel. In the next second the tip was directed at Mr Perrin's chest, at the level of his heart, at a flat, sideways angle as Harry held out his elbow in a posture that said he was prepared to lunge.

Harry's stance spoke of a knowledge of exactly how to kill a man and all the muscles beneath the skin of his upper body were taut and ready to do it.

'She will not, and if you do not go I will push this sword into your chest with a force that will make the steel pass through your clothing, flesh and between your ribs, to skewer your sour heart.'

This was the first time she'd faced Harry the soldier. This was the man who rode his black horse towards the fight on a battlefield, knowing that he would kill or be killed. Fear whispered through her with the same quiet sound as when he'd withdrawn his sword. He scared her like this and he was only clothed in his underwear.

She touched his chest. 'Harry.'

He looked at her. It was as though he did not see her immediately. He looked through her at first. But then he focused and his hand that held the sword fell. Then he looked back at Mr Perrin. 'Go.'

Mr Perrin did not move. 'If you want her, you have to pay for her. The price is five hundred pounds as you have been told. Colonel Hillier said if you do not have the money you cannot have her.'

'He threw her out,' Harry's words were dismissive.

'He has changed his mind.' Mr Perrin looked at her. 'You are to come with me, Miss Cotton.'

'No. My mind has changed too,' Charlie stepped closer to Harry and wrapped her arm about his waist. 'I want to be with Harry. I have a right to choose. Colonel Hillier cannot force me to go back.' She was not that girl who had felt trapped into leaving her family to put food back on their plates. She had come to Harry and he was taking care of her.

Harry's chest moved with his breaths, but his body was still rigid and ready to strike. He was holding on to his temper tightly.

Mr Perrin looked at her. But she was not afraid now because she knew Harry would slash him with the sword if he made a move to take her. 'If you stay, Miss, he owes Colonel Hillier five hundred pounds. Or someone does.' She did not move. He turned away then.

Harry stepped forward and closed the door, then turned the key in the lock to secure it. He turned and looked at her, his hand that carried the sword hanging at his side. 'I'm sorry.'

Five hundred pounds ... Did Mark really expect Harry to pay him. 'Did you know about the money?'

'There was a letter at the barracks.'

She swallowed. She dared not ask if he would pay it. He should not have to pay it. She did not want him to pay for her.

'Charlie.' He'd seen her becoming lost and had called her back to him. His free hand lifted.

She went to him again and his hand embraced the back of her head and drew her forehead to his shoulder. 'Do not worry. He did not own you. He cannot force you to go back or make me pay him anything.'

She shook her head. No. Mark did not own her. But it had felt as though he had.

Harry's hand ran over her hair as the tears returned. It was not sadness that kept making her cry. It was only that everything was so muddled.

'You do not need to worry,' Harry repeated. 'I will keep you safe.'

Once they'd dressed, they took Ash out for a walk, but then Harry had to return to the barracks for duty.

'You are to keep this door locked. Do not open it for anyone but me in the morning. Ash will stay with you and keep you company,' he said as he put his sword on and buckled the belt.

She was sitting on the bed with her hands in her lap. She did not want to be alone. But he had to go. Her head nodded her acceptance.

'Charlie.' He crossed the room, then leant and cupped one side of her face as he kissed the other. 'Do not be afraid, simply be careful. If you lie down and sleep I will be here when you wake.'

She nodded again, then stood so she could hold him. *I love you.*

His arms came about her as hers wrapped about his neck and she breathed in his smell.

There had been nothing that felt sexual between them since she'd gone to the barracks, but there had been these gestures that seemed affectionate. She hoped he had deeper feelings for her too. *Love.* It would make her feel less guilty for forcing herself on him.

He kissed her hair, then let her go. 'I have to get to the barracks.' She nodded and bit her lip as he left.

Chapter 7

His hours of duty had been another night of strategy planning. Five hundred … He did not have it, and even if he did, why should he pay for her? She had come to him by choice. Paying for her would feel sordid.

No, he did not want to pay. But he did want her.

There had been a quiet emotion whispering through him all day. It told him to do more. It urged him to make this into something he could be pleased with. Something that would feel satisfying, not make him feel hollowed out with more guilt.

'Marriage.'

He breathed out.

That was what had been on his mind. Marriage.

Should he?

The desire to do it was building like a snow storm in a flurry of flakes that had begun to blind him. He could not focus on any of the work he was supposed to be doing.

He sat back in the chair, staring at the papers before him. Then he stood. He would walk out among the men on guard.

Marriage…

He had always said he would never marry. What good was a

wife to an army man, who was continually on the move and often uncertain he would live to see the sunrise of another day.

But in this situation, with Charlie, there was no other choice that he found acceptable.

When he left the barracks at the end of his duty, his belief that the idea was right was still multiplying. He had two days now, with no duty. He had the time to consider his life and what he wanted to do with it and resolve this.

He ordered salted ham and eggs sent to the room before he walked up.

When he tried the handle the room was locked, as he'd requested of her. He tapped the door gently. 'Charlie.'

The door opened in a moment. She had not been asleep. Yet … she had not entirely obeyed his order to keep the door locked, she was in her chemise and drawers and it reminded him that someone would have had to help her with her lacing; she must have called for a maid last night to help her undress. Had she been scared?

'Harry.' Her arms wrapped about his midriff, clinging on to him, so that he had to bustle her backwards to walk into the room. It was the way his youngest sister had always clung to him on his homecomings, like a monkey.

The memory of his smallest sister made him think of something else too. If there was marriage there could be children, yet he had already ceased wearing his sheath. There could already be a child, no matter that he'd withdrawn. He had not worn the sheath since the day he'd forgotten it.

'I have ordered breakfast.'

She had still not let him go.

When she took off his hat, he leant and caught her lips with a kiss, then pulled away and smiled at her. Her eye was no worse and the scarlet in places had turned darker. She was no longer bleeding behind her eye, it was starting to heal.

She let him go and set his hat aside. Then as he took off his gloves, she returned and her fingers began unbuckling his sword belt. He was not in the mood for playing around with her, though. Not when her eye looked so sore and he felt so damned guilty.

He took over the task of taking off his sword belt and turned his back on her, facing the chair as he slipped it off, then set the sword down. 'Did you sleep?'

'Yes. But you must be very tired.'

He looked back at her. 'I am used to managing with only a small amount of sleep, it is a part of being a soldier.'

There was a knock on the door. Charlie's head spun as she looked in the direction of the sound.

'It will be breakfast,' Harry said reassuringly, but he ensured that he was the one who opened the door. It was breakfast.

They ate at the small table, facing one another, with her in her underwear. Through the thin cotton he could see her breasts shaking as she moved and lifting as she breathed in. Something twisted in his stomach that would not be resistant to taking her back to bed for exercise, not sleep. Yet there was the weight of guilt and the burden of empathy pushing the thought down.

After the meal he stood up to undress and retire, to sleep. Another knock struck the door. A harder knock that held an intent. It was not the inn's servers coming to fetch the empty tray.

Harry lifted a hand, telling Charlie to stay where she was, well away from the door, as he went over to it. He picked up his sword and unsheathed it, then walked to the door without a word as the knock struck again. He opened it. Then re-sheathed his sword as the major saluted.

'Captain Marlow. Sir.'

Harry saluted in return, in recognition of his junior officer. 'What is it?'

'I have been asked to bring you back to the barracks, sir. There are orders.'

There are orders … What bloody orders? He had been looking forward to his hours off duty.

He looked back at Charlie, who was hiding out of sight, in her underwear. He smiled, then wrapped his sword belt about his hips, slid the leather through the buckle and pulled it tight, securing it before turning and picking up his hat and gloves. He lifted a hand in her direction, in a slight gesture to say goodbye, deliberately not speaking as he did not want his man to know she was in the room. He walked out of it then.

The lock clicked home in the door behind him once he'd walked two paces. The Major probably knew she was in there. He must have heard it too, but at least she had listened to Harry's advice.

This was another charge of Armageddon. 'You have a new posting, Captain Marlow,' his Lieutenant Colonel stated as Harry stood before him, in the official stance a soldier had to express before a superior officer – especially when the superior officer had been giving him a dressing down. He had known he was in trouble, but a new post. Where?

'Sir.' He could not stop the note of surprise slipping into his voice. 'I did not think the regiment—'

'Not the regiment, Captain Marlow, just you. You are being transferred to another regiment. A cavalry regiment that is leaving for India in six weeks. You will have four weeks' leave and then you must report to your new regiment in Plymouth.' He held out the letter, with all the information written on it, the dates and details so quickly planned to dispose of Harry.

This was Colonel Hillier's doing. He had wished Charlie out of his house and on the streets, not in the keeping of another man. Now the man, who had embarrassed him by taking his mistress in and staying with her in his house, was to be disposed of. It would leave Charlie without a protector. That was the intent.

It would not, though. Harry's decision had already been virtually made and now the decision cemented in his chest. He would marry her. She would have to go with him. That was all. They would both go to India. Lord. Less than a week ago they had been idling in her bed and playing carelessly in her small parlour and now his future had been entirely rewritten.

But so what? The emotions within him did not reject it.

He bowed.

'You may pack your things now and go and report to your new commander on the date there.'

Thrown out of his regiment and the barracks, his home, as quickly as that. With no chance to say a proper goodbye to his men, or his friends. It was as Charlie must have felt the other night as she was pushed through the door into the street. Only he had a family and numerous homes he could always go to and now a posting in India. Another option would be to refuse it and retire from the army, but the army was all he knew. He would not want to have to find a new career or live on his share of his grandfather's inheritance, kept by John. When he was working, accepting that money was one thing, but to live off it entirely, when it was gifted by John … No, he would not go cap in hand and beg his brother to reinstate his allowance. He was a soldier and he would stay a soldier.

Harry saluted, then turned on his heel with one step and walked out.

He had moved half his things to the inn already. He packed the other half as the men came to him to say goodbye – word and rumour had travelled. Gareth was the last to come, but Harry would guess that he had been at the heart of the rumour spreading. He would have made sure the men knew they were about to lose Harry. They had passed through so much together in the Crimea. The men in his regiment were like brothers. The relationship between soldiers who had survived a war was different to any other. But the attachment was something controlled, though. There had been a constant fear of loss that could distract and cause deaths and so connections were held away from the heart as guilt was forced back too.

When Harry finished packing, Gareth gripped his arm.

They were close, they'd turned to each other to deal with the pressures of command. Gareth had been to Harry what his cousins had been when he was younger. They had behaved badly together and fought hard together, loved women (in the sexual vein of the word) and lost men together. But even with Gareth, all those shared emotions had been held away from his heart. Stone. That was what a military man needed in his chest, not flesh that could be wounded.

And Charlie? How did she fit within that life, where a man only ever gave half of himself because the grim reaper stood behind him? How much of himself could he give to Charlie? Not all, never all, he needed a firm heart. But his body already felt as though he had given a greater part of him than he'd ever shared before.

Harry embraced Gareth then they left the room and walked through the halls together. This was a strange goodbye. A goodbye he'd never imagined saying, as he'd never pictured himself as a married man.

Gareth stood with him as Harry saddled Obsidian, jesting and mocking Harry for letting a woman sway his life. Harry smiled and laughed, even though inside he was windswept by shock. Just as Charlie had been yesterday.

He shook hands with Gareth before he mounted the horse.

Gareth lifted his hand in a final parting gesture. 'We must communicate in writing. I wish to hear how this domesticated life you are planning works out.'

Harry smiled. 'I shall be awaiting that tale too.'

His friend laughed.

'Captain Marlow! Captain! Sir!' Harry looked as one of the men hurried across the yard. He held up a letter.

More bad news, no doubt.

'This just arrived in the packet for you, sir. I'm glad I caught you.'

Harry leant down in the saddle to accept the letter. 'Thank you.' The writing was his father's.

He pushed the letter inside his coat, between the buttons on his chest. Whatever his father had to say could wait. He saluted the man, saluted Gareth and rode Obsidian out of the barracks, with the remainder of his belongings in a roll strapped behind the saddle.

And so his new life began.

He read his father's letter as he walked up to the room from the inn's stable, the second half of his belongings over his shoulder.

The belongings of the rest of his family filled huge rooms and houses.

The memory of home and his family made him smile, that was where he'd go now, for the weeks before he was to report at Plymouth.

Harry! What the hell do you think you are doing? The letter began, which did not bode well for the remains of it. John had ratted on him then.

It was an entire letter of reprimand and complaint. The sort of diatribe he had received in his youth from his moralistic father. Yet again the sort of complaints he had expected to have outgrown. When would they allow him to make his own decisions regardless of their views? At what age? Eighty?

How dare you consider this … You have been told again and again …

Yes, he had been warned against sleeping with women who chose to be paid. He had always retorted, 'was that not better than seducing an innocent woman,' or 'misleading some barmaid or a serving girl into thinking there might be more'. But now, as he read those words, his refusal to listen stung him with an accusation from his own mind as he saw Charlie and heard her words. She had been seven years with one man and yet she'd never enjoyed it nor ever been happy, from what he could tell. So why had she done it, then? Why did other women? For money, not pleasure, certainly, and he had traded with them for the use of their flesh, telling himself it gave them as much pleasure as it had given him. His father's words cut with a poisoned tip of a lack of integrity when he read them today and saw them through the lens of his association with Charlie.

If your mother hears...

They had always been the primary words of his father's complaint. He had been terrified of Harry's mother knowing that he associated with such woman, as though she would be tainted merely by the knowledge of Harry's unsavoury behaviour.

Well, his father would be swallowing his words soon when Harry rode up the drive with Charlie wearing his ring on her finger. They had denied him the money to keep her, but hopefully they would not deny her.

The letter was addressed from Harry's brother's estate in Kent, his parents, and probably all of his extended family, were there for the summer. They gathered at John's estate once a year, or sometimes twice, sometimes for Christmas too.

That would be where he would go then, via London. He needed a marriage licence, and then he would go to John's and introduce his wife to his family before he went to India.

His new life and his new strategy were prepared.

~

Charlie was dressed and waiting for Harry. She had been looking through the window, trying to see when he came back, but the first she knew of his return was the sound of his footsteps on the stairs.

Once she'd heard the soldiers leave with him, she'd immediately rung for a maid to help her dress. Her hands had shaken as she'd tried to stand still while the woman had laced her corset, and her palms had been cool despite the warm weather and yet damp with sweat. She'd been scared someone else would come or that Harry would never return. He had obviously been in a lot more trouble than he'd led her to believe. She had caused that trouble.

But what would be the outcome.

After she'd dressed, she'd taken Ash down to walk beside the sea. She'd known Harry would be a while. The sound and the energy of the waves had calmed her mind a little, but all the time she'd been wary of the possibility of one of the Colonel's servants watching her. She had continually looked across her shoulder. She had been mindful of Harry too and what might be happening at the barracks. What if he had been put into the cells there? That thought had made her return to the inn in the hope that he would be there.

He had not been here then. But now he was.

She opened the door before he knocked, she was so certain the footsteps were his. The sight of him in his uniform, so strong and bold, grasped about her heart just as it had this morning when she'd opened the door to him.

He smiled at her, his lips twisting to one side slightly, in a way that apologised as he lifted another canvas bag from his shoulder and let it fall on the floor.

She wrapped her arms around his neck and hung on. 'What happened?' He had no need to apologise. Any request for forgiveness should come from her lips, not his. She had begun this by pressing her friendship upon him. Then she had urged him to come to Mark's and stay there.

'I have a new posting,' he said.

She let him go. 'To where?'

He smiled as he took off his hat and gloves. 'India.'

Oh. Lord. A sound of shock and pain escaped her lips. A sound she would have preferred him not to hear, but he ignored it anyway and looked down to unfasten the buckle of his sword belt.

'Do not worry, it means you will have me to yourself for four weeks.' He looked back up as he took the belt from his hips. 'Or perhaps not all to yourself. We will go to my family. They are all together in one place. It will inevitably mean you must share

92

your time with my nephews and nieces, but if we are to be in India for years, as I imagine, then I would like to see my family before we go.'

We…

His hand slid into his trouser pocket. Then lifted. His fingers held something.

'Charlie, you are going to have be saddled with me I'm afraid. I cannot leave you here. I can neither protect you nor afford to set you up here while I am away – and regardless I want you with me. So, there is only one answer for it. You must marry me!' It was a ring in his fingers. A gold band. 'This will have to do, as both your engagement and wedding ring, I'm afraid. I bought it from a pawn shop in the Lanes.' He laughed. 'I hope you will forgive it, but I do not have much ready cash at the current time.'

She swallowed against the tears building in her throat. Then she blinked them from her eyes. How silly. But they were happy tears.

'Thank you.' She had thought he would leave her behind when he'd said he had to leave, but to marry her … 'Thank you,' she said again as she looked at the ring, unable to believe this. A month ago she had been living at Mark's and Harry had been a beautiful stranger on the beach.

A rough sound of amusement broke from his throat. 'I had never expected myself to say those words, but if I had ever imagined it, thank you, was not the answer I would have anticipated.'

She looked up. 'Sorry.'

'Thank you and sorry.' His lips quirked in a challenging smile.

I love you. The words whispered through her head, but she would not speak them. This marriage offer had come about because he felt there was no other solution. It was not a thing of the heart. She did not care what had made him say it, though. She could see that he meant it and the offer saved her from the streets and whatever may have come then. 'Thank you.' Those words slipped from her mouth again.

He laughed at her. 'Let me put this on for you.'

She held out her hand. It was shaking again. He held it steady while he slid the ring on as far as her knuckle. When he released her hand she slid it up her finger the rest of the way. It fitted.

He looked up from the ring and into her eyes. 'We are to be married then, Charlie. We will go to London and get a licence and marry there. Then we'll go to my brother's estate. I'll not subject you to the stares of my family as you stand at the altar, as you do not know them. Though, the church that is a part of my brother's property is very pretty and you may say you'd have preferred it.'

She still did not know what to say, yet him speaking of his family reminded her of hers. She had not seen them for seven years, but she wrote at times and they would want to know that her circumstances had changed and where she was. 'May I write to my family and tell them?'

'Of course. I need to rest,' he said as he began unbuttoning his coat. 'We'll not set off until tomorrow. You have plenty of time.' He stripped off his coat. 'There is a quill, ink and paper in the things I brought with me yesterday, and I can give you the direction. It is on a letter from my father in my coat pocket. You may write while I sleep.'

As though he sensed her unease, his hand lifted and he held the back of her neck and pressed a kiss on her lips, before letting her go and smiling. Then he sat on the bed, took off his boots and stockings, then his braces and his shirt.

She watched, her arms at her sides. The sense of awkwardness in the air was as heavy as that which had been in the room the first time they'd come to this inn.

He stood and stripped off his trousers, then lay down on top of the bed, not beneath the covers, wearing only his underwear, tied low and loose on his hips. 'Will you open the window?'

'Will the noise from the street not disturb you?'

'No, Charlie, I have slept in a tent while cannons have been roaring their defence. I can sleep through the noise from a street.' She nodded as for the second time the truth of the life Harry had led as a soldier crept into her mind.

She was to go to India now and live that life with him.

He was asleep in moments as the summer breeze brought slightly cooler air into the room.

She looked at the ring, splaying her fingers so she could admire it better. A ring. She … Wicked Charlie Cotton. Was engaged. To Harry. The beautiful Captain Marlow.

A part of her would never believe this could have happened and that part was so happy. Yet another part of her was weighted by guilt with the sense that she had forced him into this. He would not have chosen her, or this, had she not written to him, or if Mark had not turned her out on to the street and she had gone to Harry. Harry was simply an honourable, good man. Who did good things.

She had gained the attention and protection of a good man. But how would that progress? Would he always be good to her, kind, thoughtful, even caring – and yet his heart empty?

Her heart was full. But not only with love, with so much pain. She was afraid as well as happy and her stomach turned over, churning with uncertainty. She had known for years what was expected of her and she had never been happy with it, yet at least she'd understood it. She did not understand anything any more. She had no idea what her role would be – no she did, she would be a wife.

He breathed quietly in his sleep, unmoving.

Despite him saying he could sleep through noise she tried to be quiet as she looked for the materials to write with; he had woken easily enough when Mr Perrin had knocked.

She found the things and laid them out on the table.

She could see her brother, her mother and her little sister in her mind, only her sister was no longer little, she was twelve. She would probably not even recognise Ginny if they passed each other in the street, it was so long since she had seen her.

For moments she stared at the blank paper, not knowing what to write. The feather tip of the quill brushed her cheek. She wondered what her brother and mother would think of her news. Surely they would be glad for her – and yet they lived on Mark's land, in Mark's property, and he had been giving them money for years. She knew why he had asked Harry for money. He wanted Harry to pay back everything Mark had spent on her and given to her brother, and more. Mark would stop paying her brother now.

But she had stayed with Mark for seven years, was that not long enough to live unhappily? And her brother was a man now and working in the forge; he could provide for her mother and Ginny and his wife and child.

Would Harry be unhappy with her, though?

She glanced back at him, hoping that in seven years he would not feel unhappy with her after spending those years forced into a marriage with her. He had not touched her in the way a man did in bed since she'd gone to him at the barracks … and yet he had asked her to marry him.

Marry him! The words shouted through her soul and she dipped the tip of the quill in the ink.

Dear Mama, Rodney and Ginny,

You will never guess my news, I know. Even though you may have heard some of it, you cannot know it all. Colonel Hillier is done with me.

That was a lie, and yet she knew that Rodney would be angry with her if she told the truth because Mark would no longer give him money.

I have been thrown out and yet I have made a friend of another man. A friend who has been loyal and respectful and kind, Mama, he is very kind. You will like him I know. He is an officer too. A Captain. Captain Marlow. And he has asked to marry me!! I told you, you would never guess it.

I am to be his wife, and we are going to India on a ship, half way across the world, and so I wanted to write and tell you that I am safe and happy, with Harry. We are going to visit his family. Their address is at the end of the letter, if you wish to write to me there. I shall be there for four weeks, or a little less, and then we sail.

I shall write to you when we reach India too and tell you where you may write to me there. I shall be Mrs Marlow remember, though, if you write to me at Harry's brother's.

I hope you are all well. I hope the harvest is good and all your friends in the village are well too.

For seven years she had not seen the friends she had grown up with and she had never dared write to them. She had been frowned on and spat at before she had left.

Harry still lay quiet on the bed.

He'd said the letter with his brother's address on it was in his coat pocket. If she wrote the address in the letter then she could seal it and take it to the post master to send it, and give Ash a walk at the same time.

She went over and quietly picked up his scarlet and gold coat, with Ash watching her, then felt in all of the pockets until she found the roughly folded letter.

She opened it, then took it over to the table and copied the address from the top right-hand corner.

Ash's eyes questioned what she did, and yet the dog did not make a sound. Ash must know the smells on the letter she would be remembering a home that Harry knew.

The smell of the small cottage she had grown up in was

something Charlie would always recall, the heavy scent of peat burning on the fire with the wood and the sweet smell of bread baking.

She folded her letter and used Harry's wax and the blank end of his seal. There was an image at one end. He had a mark that would tell people he had sent the letter.

When her letter was addressed, she looked back at the one Harry had received. Her gaze fell to the signature. *Lord Edward Marlow*, was signed beneath a large cross. He had said the letter was from his father. A lord … Had he told her that? Perhaps, in the beginning and she had forgotten. Since the beginning he had only ever spoken of his family by their Christian names. He had not mentioned titles.

She could not resist looking up to the top of the letter. She was not a clever reader, she was slow and this was written in an unknown hand. Yet she could spot enough words to recognise the intent of the letter.

His father wanted Harry to leave her. He thought she was not good enough for Harry.

If your mother hears…

You cannot keep this woman.

You have to leave this woman alone. It is not right.

Harry rolled to his side and a low sound came from his throat as though he was dreaming.

Her heart raced as she refolded the letter, trying to make it look untouched. Harry had read this, though, and then bought a ring and asked her to marry him. Why? And why did he wish to take her to meet this family who did not want her there.

Her stomach churned with the nausea created by the uncertainty inside her.

No. She would be happy. She would be. Harry had chosen to marry her despite his father's complaints. Surely that must mean he did not feel trapped. He would not have gone against his family if he felt forced.

Her hands were shaking once again when she picked up her letter. But she wanted to walk outside now even more than before, she needed air and time to think. Time to try to understand her new future.

India. She could not imagine it, though.

'Ash,' she whispered, to call the dog to her heel. Ash glanced at Harry but then looked at Charlie. The dog had been given a new mistress these last few days but Ash had accepted her. Charlie would pray that Harry's family accepted her too. Yet she had been told long ago, by the vicar in her village, that God did not hear the prayers of a sinner. The memory made her lift her chin as she walked out of the door and down the stairs. She had denied such rebukes then; she would not listen to them now.

She walked briskly, occasionally looking across her shoulder for Mark's servants but if any of them were watching her they did not show themselves. Mark had probably thought his threat had been heard. He was used to people who conceded and Harry was now disposed of – sent to the other side of the world so he could no longer keep her. Only Harry had defied that; he would not concede and nor would she, not any more.

Pride became a new emotion in her stomach that defied her fear of the future and of Harry's family and of Harry's reasons for asking her to marry him. She would be proud to be his wife. She would be the wife of an officer and she would be able to hold her head high and look down on those who had looked down on her.

A part of her longed to return home and show them all. The part of her that was still angry even after all these years.

She paid for the postage of her letter with money she had taken from Harry's purse, then walked down to the sea.

The pebbles turned noisily under her feet as Ash found a new stick to play with and then bounded about Charlie. She threw the stick as Harry had done on all those days when she'd watched him from the path and not come near.

She returned to the inn two hours later and when she shut the door of their room she did so with a little too much force so the wood bumped against the frame. Harry woke and he sat up abruptly, his hand reaching out as though he sought for a weapon.

She ignored the movement and untied the bow of the ribbons on her bonnet. 'Sorry I woke you. Do you feel rested?'

He smiled then let a sound of amusement escape from his mouth. 'Yes, until the last moment when I thought your entrance a cart of explosives.'

'Sorry,' she said again

'No need to be sorry that my mind is scarred by war. That has naught to do with you.' He turned and sat on the edge of the bed. He was breathing harder than normal as though the dream had truly shaken him.

'May I fetch you anything?'

'A tankard of ale would be welcome.'

'I'll walk down and bring a jug for you.'

She stiffened her shoulders and her posture as she walked back down to the taproom. She was stronger today. Recovered from her shock. She was ready to defend herself if she must as she had done before. She would not listen to his family if they judged her badly nor listen to her fears. She and Harry could be happy. They were alike that was why they suited. He was scarred and she was scarred and so they did not judge one another as others might judge them.

When she returned to the room, holding a jug and two tankards, she smiled at him knowing she looked like a tavern wench with the items in her hands. 'Ale for the Captain.' She lifted the jug.

He smiled.

She set the tankards down on the table and filled them. He got up, walked over and accepted the tankard she held out. He drank all the ale in it immediately then set the tankard on the table beside the jug as he wiped his mouth with the back of his hand. She had only sipped her drink but he took it out of her hand and set that down too.

Then he kissed her. His mouth pressing down on to hers, and his tongue reaching into her mouth as his hands clasped her hair in the way he often did.

She would be happy. They would be happy. He could not feel forced not when he was defying his family and not when he could kiss her like this.

Her arms rose and rested on his shoulders. Then he picked her up and carried her to the bed and did not even undress her but merely lifted her skirts and petticoats and through the gaps in their clothing made use of the bed in the way a bed ought to be used – for pleasure.

Chapter 8

The carriage continued through the maze of London's streets, rocking from side to side on the cobble, like a boat at sea, and creaking as though it would fall apart. The old ruin of a bounder he'd hired had seen far better days and yet with his cash low he had hired the carriage on a promissory note to be paid either when he received his next wage or when his brother relented and paid him his next allowance.

In the meantime he and Charlie were going to be acting the poor relations. That was one of the good things about this new posting; he now had four weeks in which he might live off his family until he received his next wage.

'Where are we going?' Charlie asked. Her words drew Harry's attention away from the view out of the window.

'We are going to John's town house. I doubt anyone will be there, so we will have it to ourselves for a wedding breakfast tomorrow.'

'And today …' Her voice carried a teasing pitch, hinting at him to take her to a bed.

For the last two days they had been acting as they had acted during their days in her parlour and her bedchamber at Hillier's. As though they were careless. 'We will enjoy the run of his home.

But first, after I have dropped you off, I must go to speak with my brother's solicitor and find out what I need to do to arrange our wedding. Then I hope I will have time to take you shopping. We will use my sister-in-law's modiste. The woman will know exactly what you need.'

He looked out of the window, again, his hand holding hers with their fingers laced together on his thigh as the carriage turned through the very familiar streets. Something squeezed at his heart. This was a home-coming he had never imagined.

'We are here,' he said when the carriage turned and he saw his brother's giant Palladian mansion behind its wrought iron railing and gates.

Charlie leant across him to look. 'Where?'

'There.'

'There is only one huge house and nothing …' She pulled back looking her question at him.

'Yes. The huge house.'

'Oh my goodness, Harry!'

He smiled, thrilled that she was impressed. Sometimes it was fun to be the brother and grandson of a duke and a nephew of several too.

She sat back looking absolutely horrified. 'You did not say …'

'Why should I say so. Although I think I did mention once he was duke. Where did you expect a duke to live, in a hovel?'

'I do not even remember you saying that.'

'Well regardless we are here and this is where we will spend the night. Though, as I said I do not think any of my family are here.'

The carriage turned into the small area before the house and stopped in front of the door.

Harry let go of Charlie's hand and rose to open the carriage door then jumped down with Ash following. He knocked down the step and held out his hand to take Charlie's. He imagined the panic inside the house generated by an unexpected caller.

A porter opened the door as Harry turned to lead Charlie up the steps.

'Captain Marlow, we are not expecting you.'

'I know you are not, but I'm sure you can have a room made ready quickly. One for the two of us.' He leant towards Charlie. 'It will not be as magnificent as you are imagining on the inside, everything will be covered in sheets to keep off the dust.'

'It is like a house put to sleep,' she said as they walked in, her head and her eyes turning everywhere.

The porter watched her, asking silent questions Harry did not answer. It was none of the man's business. 'You will have a room prepared …' he prodded.

The man looked back at him. 'Yes, sir.'

'One with a sitting room so we have no need to interfere with the rest of the house. We are only staying for one night.'

The man bowed. 'We will have a room ready in two hours, sir.'

Two hours. Perhaps it was better that Charlie stayed with him then.

'And I need one of the grooms to take care of my horse?' John always left a couple of his horses in the stables here, there would be a groom available.

'Yes, sir.'

Charlie stood on the black and white chequered marble floor, her gaze spinning about the columns, the marble fireplaces and walls and the stairs that wrapped about the walls at either side of the room. His hand lifted and his fingers pressed beneath her chin closing her mouth. She looked at him and smiled, her large eyes wide.

'I need to go outside and see to Obsidian. Wait here.'

She nodded then her head tilted right back so she could look at the painting on the ceiling.

A groom came to untie Obsidian from the back of their hired carriage and Harry had him take Ash to the stables too before returning to the hall.

Charlie was still staring at the ceiling, her arms hanging at her sides. She looked as though the room had overwhelmed her, swallowing up her confidence. He clasped her hand. Perhaps it would be good for her to see his brother's wealth in small doses. It was right to take her out of this place and with him. 'Come. As there is not a room ready we will go to see my brother's solicitor together.'

She nodded at him in the way she had of looking suddenly lost. There were still two sides to her. There was the confident Charlie who cried out to the world that she was careless and happy, despite anything that might try to deter it. Then there was this uncertain side of her that sometimes crept through. For some reason he had a feeling she had kept this side of herself a secret from Hillier. He could not even say why he believed it, and yet he did. He had realised in Brighton that she was keeping parts of herself hidden even from him.

She was defiant again when they sat down in Phillip's office. John's solicitor, Phillip, managed all of John's formal business and was also John's brother-in-law. So Harry knew as he took a seat, by tomorrow and probably before the deed was even done, John, and therefore his father, would know Harry's intent. But Phillip Spencer was the sort of man who knew everything. He was the same age as John, they had been school friends too, and since he had worked for John he had become the font of all knowledge.

'I did not know you were coming to London, Harry. I did not realise you had more leave. What can I do for you?' Phillip shook Harry's hand before returning to his seat. He did not even speak to Charlie, but he'd glanced at her, in a way that implied he was wondering who on earth she was.

'I need a marriage licence today and a church tomorrow,' Harry answered diving straight in.

'And you think I might provide them …' Phillip's eyebrows lifted. His gaze shifted to Charlie for a moment then he looked back at Harry.

'No but I am sure you know how to obtain them. How do I go about getting a licence?'

Charlie was sitting with her back straight as though she was at attention, and her chin was up high in that defiant posture that said she cared for no one's opinion but her own. He assumed she feared she was being judged. Unfortunately, she was probably right. But they would likely have to deal with a lot of that in the next few days. No. He would deal with it. He would damned well threaten every member of his family if they did this.

'Forgive me, but this is madness, Harry,' Phillip said more quietly as if he did not wish Charlie to hear when she was sitting in the bloody room.

'I am posted to India, I wish to take Charlie with me and this is the way to do it. There is not time for delay.'

Phillip sighed.

Perhaps Phillip did not like this but he would have to bloody well do it. Harry's brother employed him.

'Will you be our witness too?' Phillip's behaviour said that it was a bad idea but who else did Harry have to do it.

'John is not going to be happy with you.'

'John can go to hell for all I care. I do not give a damn what he thinks.' Harry's ire and impatience brimmed over. 'I can go and ask a priest, I just thought it would be easier to come to you. You know everything.'

Phillip sighed again. Phillip hated to do anything John would disagree with and yet Harry was John's brother, surely that loyalty would transfer. 'Go to the offices at Lambeth Palace you can obtain one there.'

'And where can I use it.'

There was another sigh. 'There is a small church I know of and an elderly vicar with a good nature. I will arrange the wedding for you, if you obtain the licence. What hour do you wish to be married?'

Harry glanced at Charlie. She looked at him blankly. He looked back at Phillip. 'Ten. Then I can be at John's in the afternoon.'

'You are taking her there …' Phillip's tone expressed a mix of astonishment and outrage.

Were they the emotions he would face at John's? He reached over and clasped Charlie's hand. Well damn them all if it was. But he saw his sister Mary's face and he did not believe that all of his family would judge Charlie so badly after all Mary's husband had not been a saint. He had eloped with Mary and been forgiven.

Harry sat forward. 'Would you write down the address of this church for us?'

Phillip pulled over a sheet of paper. Then reached for a quill. Everything in his body language expressed his distaste of the idea.

Perhaps Harry should keep Charlie in town and forget about going to see his family. But now he had spoken with Phillip if he did not go to John's within a day John and his father would come looking for him. There was no doubt of that. They had done it before or at least his father had.

Phillip blotted the address and then slid the paper across the desk.

Harry stood and took it. 'Will you be staying with John and Kate this summer?'

'I do not think so. I am busy here.'

Harry gave Phillip a nod. 'Thank you. I will see you in the morning. At this church, at ten.'

Phillip nodded his agreement.

'He hates me,' Charlie whispered as she grasped Harry's arm once they'd walked out of the room.

He squeezed her fingers against his side. 'He does not hate you. He is angry with me. Did I not tell you, I am considered a trial to my family? Uncle Baba. The worthless black sheep, in my father's flock, with a fleece that cannot be dyed and altered to match his values as he wishes.'

She leant closer to him as they walked along the hall of the offices. 'You are not bad, you are the kindest man I have ever met.'

He opened the door and held it for her to go out, emotion tightening about his throat as though it would strangle him. Was he a good man? He had always thought he was, and his family had only ever teased – yet now, in the last weeks, he had come to wonder. He was not sure that he had always made honourable choices. And during the war … It was the bitter recollection of hurried choices that had always been the thing his mind could never stand.

But he was confident with this choice and he did not care if Phillip or any of his family disagreed.

She waited in the carriage when he went into the Palace at Lambeth to ask how a man obtained a licence to marry without banns being called. It took half an hour to obtain the right man who could give him such a licence. But that man then sent him out to the carriage to obtain the birth date of his intended wife.

He opened the carriage door and leant in. 'Charlie …' She was sitting in the far corner, looking out at the Thames. Her head turned and she looked at him. Her eyes were shimmering, as though there were tears. Damn. Phillip had upset her more than he'd realised. Harry would have to write to him tonight. But now … 'What date were you born? I need to know for the licence.'

'April the sixteenth, eighteen-thirty-four.'

'Thank you. I shan't be too much longer.' He turned away, denying the shout in his head. He'd done the calculation instantly. Twenty-two. He'd thought her older than that. Twenty-two and she had been with Hillier for seven years, she'd said.

Since she'd been fifteen.

Fifteen! The age she had gone to Hillier screamed at him repeatedly as he walked back inside the palace.

Damn. Guilt had made him feel nauseous for months since the war and in the last few days he had learned to doubt his beliefs about women since he'd met Charlie and that too had thrust fists of guilt at his stomach. But now his conscience shouted and growled at him as his father and John had always done over his behaviour with women who'd chosen to be paid for sex. John had always claimed the women had stories Harry could not know. Stories that had forced them to reach a point at which sex with a stranger was worth the money they received in exchange.

God. It sickened him to think of the stories he had not heard spoken in the minds of the women he'd shared beds with.

But most of all, it was Charlie's unspoken story haunting him. He wanted it told – he wanted to know it now – and yet a part of him did not want to request it because he was unsure he could bear to hear it. He had to know, though. He cared about her and he wished to understand.

Fifteen…

When he returned to the carriage, the document they needed was within his coat, against his chest.

Tomorrow she would be his wife and today … he would hear her story. But not now, let them shop for pretty things and he would put them all on his brother's bill. And when John or his father cursed him for marrying the former mistress of another man he would accuse them both of being hypocrites. He was giving Charlie a happy ending, a life she deserved. She had never seemed really happy in the beginning; now there were moments when the pressure on them was eased and glimmers shone through of what things could be for them if cruel fate left them alone.

When they returned to John's, the porter told Harry a room had been made ready for them. He led Charlie upstairs by the hand as she hung on to his grip, looking everywhere, though nothing but the plasterwork and ceiling paintings were on show. All the portraits were covered with dustsheets.

The suite of rooms they had been allocated was usually the suite his parents stayed in. It felt odd when he walked in; he had frequently come into these rooms to visit his parents over the years. They were the largest rooms, apart from John's.

Dinner was served at a table in the sitting room. Then Harry requested a cigar and whiskey – to share with Charlie – though he did not tell the servant that.

Charlie's eyes were still darting everywhere as they talked. The sitting room in the suite was more than four times the size of her little parlour and probably twice the size of Hillier's sitting room.

'Did you grow up here?' she asked as he lit the cigar. He laughed because she whispered the question, as though she did not want it to be overheard by the furniture.

She had been asking him question after question about his family over dinner. She now knew exactly how many men he was related to in the House of Lords and her pretty eyes had been getting wider with each second.

'No. I have visited often as a child and as a man, but this was never my home. My father owns a house that is much smaller than this, on land that is only a few dozen acres. That is where I grew up.'

She nodded, though her eyes continued to express her bewilderment.

'Would you like some?' He held out the cigar. Her hand already embraced a glass of whiskey.

She nodded and reached out to take it from him.

She was sitting forward in her chair; he was sitting back in his. He reached over and passed the cigar to her.

'Harry …' her voice was uncertain.

'Yes.'

'You have not asked me where I grew up?'

No. He had not known where to begin with the conversation. Fifteen … But where better to begin her story than at the start. 'Where did you grow up?'

'Not in a place like this.' She sucked on the cigar, then blew out the smoke.

But that had been obvious, she would not have needed to be a man's mistress if she had. 'So where, then?' he prodded.

'In a very small cottage. My father was a blacksmith. He worked in one side of the house and we slept in the other. It was one long room. We slept behind a curtain—'

'We …'

'My brother and I, my little sister slept in the room with my mother.'

'Your mother … You have never mentioned your father until today—'

'He died when I was eight, just after my sister was born.'

'And then …'

She sucked on the cigar again. There was a look in her eyes now, that careless defiance she had at times. 'We were hungry and I wore rags and we lived on charity. Mrs Hillier and the vicar's wife brought us bread and broth to eat.'

Mrs Hillier … Good God. He sat forward in the chair. He had not realised there was a Mrs Hillier and that Charlie knew her. But what age had she said she was? Eight …

'They gave us clothes too and my mother took washing in and I helped her do that, and Rodney worked on the farms.'

'Rodney …'

'My brother.' This was all said so bluntly. As though she was speaking of someone else's family. There was no real emotion in her voice and yet she was an emotional woman, he had seen that side of her.

She held the cigar out for him to take back.

He took it and asked the question that had been in his mind all afternoon. 'And you left home when you were fifteen? Is that right?'

Her eyebrows lifted as if she was surprised that he knew.

'You told me the date you were born today, Charlie, and you have told me how long you were with Hillier; seven years. You were fifteen.'

She blushed, then sipped her whiskey, glancing down at the glass to avoid his gaze. Then she looked back up.

He raised his eyebrows at her, asking again without words. He wanted to know. He wanted to understand.

'Yes.' She did not progress.

'How, Charlie? Tell me. Please.'

She looked back at her glass. 'I was not fifteen. I was fourteen when it began.'

A bilious sensation spun through his gut; when what began?

'I was not where I was meant to be. I was always up to mischief. That was what my mother used to say. She told me it was my own fault. But I liked Sundays. I liked to be on my own or with my friend, not in Sunday school or church. I was on my own ...'

Lord, where was this going? His palms became clammy with fear. He sucked on the cigar once more, then held it out to her, his hand was shaking; the hand of a man who had held a sword and a pistol square and strong in battle.

She looked up at him as she took the cigar. There was still that disengaged look in her eyes. She was reciting this story to him as he might speak of a battle. The memory was shut away and not allowed to be joined and mixed with emotion – because if it became mixed with emotion that emotion would drown him. What of her?

She looked directly into his eyes. 'He invited me to go for a ride in his carriage and he offered me cake and jam and a cup of sweet tea.'

'Good God, Charlie.'

'You think I did wrong too ...?' She sucked on the cigar then blew out the smoke.

'No. I think he did wrong. You were a child.'

She shrugged. 'He gave me money afterwards, to give to my mother and my brother.'

'How old was your brother, then?'

'Nineteen.'

Too young to stand up to a man who had the force of the British army behind him. My God. Harry wanted to return to

Brighton and push his sword deep into Hillier's cold heart. 'What did his wife say?'

An odd smile twisted her lips, a bitter smile. 'She saw me leave the house in Mark's carriage, when Mr Perrin took me home.' He could finally glimpse an element of emotion through her armour. 'She hated me. She started the rumours and then everyone knew what had happened. I was an outcast, spat at, and some of the people threw stones. Children who had been my friends threw stones.'

'Charlie …'

She shrugged again.

'What did you do?'

'Stayed out of everyone's way. But then people would no longer give their washing to my mother and so we had less and less money and Mrs Hillier and the vicar's wife no longer brought us food or clothing. My little sister used to cry all the time because she was so hungry.'

'Charlie …' He had not thought he'd be shocked. He had slept with whores all his life. He had spent years in the army.

She smiled and handed the cigar back to him. Then her chin lifted. 'So I went back to him. He agreed to give my family money if I stayed with him. So I stayed with him so that my little sister would no longer wail with hunger and my mother would not cry. He sent me to Brighton and he would come and visit me at first, but then Mrs Hillier died and he moved to Brighton.'

'Charlie …'

'What do you feel?'

What did he feel? 'I have no idea.'

She sipped the whiskey and then her head tipped to the side. 'Does it disgust you?' He had a feeling she was slightly intoxicated; she had drunk four glasses of wine with her dinner as well as the whiskey.

'No.' He disgusted himself. What were the stories of the women he had lain with in brothels … Rape. It had begun for her as rape at the age of fourteen and then she had been forced to turn to the man who had raped her to protect her from the havoc he had caused. Hillier had destroyed her life and she had stayed with him for seven years. Harry could not even imagine how she had done it.

Damn it. She had learned to reconstruct her heart out of stone too, she must have done.

'Do you still wish to marry me?'

'Charlie, do not be ridiculous. I am hardly the man to judge you. You have lain with one man before me, for all the wrong reasons, but one man besides. I have lain with two hundred or more women. Or have I not told you that? Well, if I have not, you know it now. I have always used women who work in brothels and no one else until you. Do you still wish to marry me? I think it far more likely that you have cause to turn me away. Will you?'

She shook her head. But then the truth was she had no choice as she'd had no choice with Hillier.

'You are allowed to say that you do not want to marry me if it is not what you wish for. My family would support you if I cast you off. John is a saint. He would not see any woman injured by me.'

She blushed, but then she drained her whiskey glass and set it on the table between them, stood, and came over to him. He sat back in the chair again as she made a seat of his lap and then held the cigar for him to take back. 'I want to marry you,' she said as she gripped his neck and then she pressed her lips on to his.

It went no further than that. The cigar was still alight and he had a glass of whiskey in his other hand. She made herself at home on his lap, though.

He had never thought he would find a woman who could make him want a wife. Yet he had. She fit him, and fit his life – regardless of the situation that had made him make this choice, and he was going to give her her happy ending. He stubbed out the cigar and drank the last of his whiskey. Then he wrapped his arm about her shoulders and slipped the other beneath her legs and stood up.

'I am taking you to bed. Tomorrow is our wedding day and I will not allow you to be tired or have a headache from drinking too much.'

She laughed as she gripped his shoulders.

When she sought to begin a sexual exchange in the room, though, he stopped her. 'Not tonight, I feel as though it would be bad luck. Tomorrow.' But it was not only that, his parents had slept in the bed and Hillier and her, when she had been fourteen, was still in his mind.

Damn.

Chapter 9

Charlie woke, screaming. The sound erupted from her throat and jolted her awake.

Her throat…

She'd screamed in her dream and she must have screamed aloud.

She sat up.

Harry had woken and was sitting up too. He looked shaken, his muscles were taut, as though he'd braced himself for defence. Her screaming must have woken him and her nightmare had probably stirred one of his. They made a pair … 'Sorry. I did not mean to wake you.'

He smiled at her, then lifted an eyebrow. 'Did you have a dream?'

'Yes.' She had been at home and a child again, the child who had climbed up into the carriage with Mark. Why had she made that choice?

'A bad dream?' he clarified.

She nodded. Tears gathered in her eyes and blurred the room.

'Do not worry.' His arms came around her as the memories behind the conversation they'd had last night spun about her, drowning her in images and feelings from the past. She had relived them in her dream. They were memories she'd pushed aside. She did not want to recall them. She did not want them in her head.

His hand stroked over her hair. 'It is because you let the memories out of their box last night and talked of it. The dreams will go away again; it is the same with war. I never speak.' His voice had lifted with a lilt of humour. He'd said the last words to make her laugh.

She did laugh, although the sound broke, it was not laughter that she felt in her soul.

After she'd told him about Mark, he'd told her more about his rich, noble brother, uncles and cousins. His past was very different to hers. He had grown up in luxury and love. He'd had everything he could have wanted. She'd had nothing beyond her family and a simple happiness, even though there had been hunger at times – until she had been fourteen. She was a long way beneath his status in life. Yet he did not appear to care nor judge her at all. He'd said he still wanted to marry her.

His fingers touched beneath her chin and lifted her head so he looked into her eyes. The pale blue of his said he was speaking honestly to her. There was an openness in his eyes that had never been in Mark's. 'May we agree on one thing before we marry? You must feel free to talk to me about anything. If you have a bad dream or feel like crying you must not hold anything in. I know how it feels to hold those emotions in; you need not any more. If you wish to talk, ignore my guidance to hold it back, you may talk. You must talk.'

Strangely, because he gave her the permission to cry, the tears dried. Instead it made her not want to cry, but to hold it in. She had stopped weeping over such things for years until she'd met Harry and she wanted to be with him, so why was she crying? This was the best thing that had happened to her.

His fingers braced her chin as he looked even harder into her eyes, as though he sought something. But then his gaze changed and his eyes just looked at her face. 'I promise to make you happy.'

'And I promise to make you happy too,' she answered.

'Charlie, that is one thing I know you will do.' He kissed her, pressing his lips against hers for a moment, but only that, then he pulled away. 'Shall we dress and prepare for our wedding, then?'

She smiled. 'Yes.' Yes. She was going to be married today. He knew everything about her and he was going to marry her anyway. There was that sense of pride swelling in her chest. She was going to be so proud to be his wife. He had said he'd make her happy. She knew he would. Simply walking beside him and knowing she was his and he was hers, made her happy.

He helped her dress as he dressed too and she put on one of the gowns he'd bought for her yesterday, a pale-green muslin with a dark-green leaf print. He had said yesterday that the colour set off her eyes and her hair. She put on her new straw bonnet too, with a cream ribbon.

'You look magnificent,' he said as he strapped on his sword belt.

'You do too, but then you always do.'

He smiled.

When they walked downstairs her arm was wrapped about his.

'When we come back, before we go to John's, we will eat and I will give you a tour of the house while they prepare our luncheon.'

She could not believe the size of the place and yet he'd said this had never been his home and she took heart in that. Without those words this would have terrified her. He'd paid no attention to their difference in status, yet if she had to live this life, she would feel embarrassed every hour of every day at her own lack. She did not fit in this grandiose place. She had fitted with Harry, though, in his small barrack room and her parlour, and in the inns.

As they reached the last flight of stairs descending from the first floor she looked down and saw the porter there. He was opening the door wide. 'Good morning, Lord Framlington.'

Charlie's gaze shot to look at Harry. She could not remember which member of his family Lord Framlington was. Her heart jumped into a sharp, fast rhythm as a man stepped through the door.

She thought of Harry's father's letter, the wording swiped at her with the force of the slap Mark had landed, which had knocked her off balance. Harry had said last night that his family would look after her if she did not marry him. She had not believed that. He might love them but she had seen the words his father had written about her.

Her fingers clasped his arm. 'Will we be in trouble?' she whispered.

He looked at her and laughed. 'From Drew … No. He is my rogue of a brother-in-law, remember? I told you.'

His sister Mary's husband. Yes, she recalled the name now. She would have to begin reciting the names of his family once a day so she remembered them all.

'Hello!' Harry shouted as they kept walking down the steps.

'Uncle Baba! Good Lord! You are a surprise!' The man looked at her, but said nothing, then looked back at Harry. 'What are you doing here?'

'Getting married,' Harry said, smiling as he continued walking down, while the man stood just inside the door, which the porter shut behind him.

The man frowned. 'I take it you are joking.' He walked across the room. There was a look of … it was more than surprise; it was shock in his eyes.

'No. I am absolutely serious.' They stepped from the bottom stair together and Harry lifted his elbow, as though to present her. 'Meet my soon-to-be wife, Miss Charlotte Cotton.'

'Well, good grief.' The man was still frowning, but he lifted a hand and stepped forward, implying a wish to take her hand. 'Miss Cotton. How have you captured him? What did you do?'

Harry laughed. 'You will scare her off, Drew, and I would have thought you must have heard all about it by now.'

Charlie accepted the stranger's hand. He bowed, then let her hand go.

He looked at Harry again. 'All about what?'

'I spoke to Phillip yesterday and asked him to help me arrange the marriage. I am sure he would have written to John.'

'I was not staying at John's, I came from home on business. I have heard nothing.'

Harry clasped her hand, as though to reassure her, as he carried on talking. 'I think we will be disapproved of, but I do not care. I am posted to India in six weeks and so there must be some haste about the matter.'

The man's eyebrows lifted once more. 'Well, Mary and I know all about a hasty marriage and your family's disapproval.'

'Then you will be on our side and a voice with me against their judgement. Tell me that will be so, because I am counting on it.'

'Of course,' the man smiled.

'Why are you here? Is your business in town urgent? Do you think you can spare us an hour to be a witness?'

'I will put off my business indefinitely for the spectacle of seeing Mary's little terror of a brother wed. Where are you getting married?'

Harry withdrew the piece of paper with the address on it from his pocket and handed it over.

His brother-in-law looked up and smiled again. 'It is where I married Mary. You can use my carriage if you wish, it is outside, ready. I presume you hired that wreck of a bounder out there? You can let it go and travel to John's with me.'

'Thank you.' Harry took back the paper. Then they were all walking across the hall, she one side of Harry and his brother-in-law the other.

Her heart thumped out a hard pace of nervous fear. She was

to step into Harry's life then, and she had been afraid of doing that when it was a silent, empty building. What would this place and his world be like when it was full of people?

She did not speak in the carriage, but sat and stared out of the window as Harry held her hand firmly and talked with Lord Framlington. They travelled into a less-affluent area of London.

She had never been to London before and so she had no idea where they were.

A small church stood on one side of the street, surrounded by a wall and tombstones. It seemed wedged into the space.

She saw the church in the village where she'd grown up, with its churchyard, which looked out across the fields.

Harry climbed out of the carriage, held out his hand and helped her down. 'Do not be nervous,' he said in a quiet voice so his brother-in-law would not hear.

When Lord Framlington climbed out, he looked about the street. 'Lord. This brings back memories. Sadly they would probably not be good memories for Mary. Which is perhaps why we have never come back for a sentimental view of the place.'

'Good morning.' The man from the office yesterday approached them, walking out from the churchyard. Phillip – that had been what Harry had called him. Another man and a woman with auburn hair walked beside Phillip.

Harry looked across at them. 'Phillip. Rupert. Meredith.'

Charlie had not expected all these people. She only wanted Harry here.

'I invited Lord and Lady Morton as they were in town. I thought there should be more witnesses, but I'm sorry ...' The man called Phillip smiled at Lord Framlington, then at Harry. 'I see you have already made arrangements.'

Harry smiled too. 'No. Drew's arrival was coincidence.' Harry glanced over his shoulder at Charlie. 'Charlie, this is my father's cousin Rupert Stanforth and his wife Meredith. Rupert is the Earl of Morton.'

The Earl ... and so it began. She was standing with a Lord and an Earl and they had not even been wed, but Harry did not appear to think it odd for her to be beside him. He still held her hand.

The Earl bowed stiffly. Charlie curtsied as deeply as she was able, though it was unpractised and wobbly. The woman bobbed a slight curtsey back at her.

This was all so bizarre – her life was contorting in a hall of bowed mirrors. She was meeting an earl and Harry had spoken of dukes last night. She was not sure she could do this. Yet none of them would be in India. In India it would be only her and Harry in somewhere like one of the rooms in the inns.

'The bride and groom?' They all looked towards the church.

The vicar was walking towards them, wearing a long, black gown.

'That is us.' Harry lifted their joined hands.

'Come along then, come in.' The vicar beckoned. 'Have you the licence?'

Harry let go of Charlie's hand and delved into his coat pocket. She felt as though she was standing on the beach in Brighton while the waves roared, washing the pebbles around and the seagulls cried out above her. In the houses behind her on the seashore, normal life continued; families together while she stood alone.

Harry looked back. She tried to tell him with her eyes – she could not do this. She wanted to run. She would not fit among his family when these people discovered the truth...

He looked about the others. 'Go in. We will be there in a moment.'

When they were only feet away she clasped Harry's hand. 'I do not know them, I—'

'They are my family and we need witnesses.'

'They will judge me, they—'

'They will not.' He shook his head and held her hand with

both of his. 'Drew is the one that calls me a black sheep and he was the worst of rogues himself, yet my sister saw into his heart and fell in love with him. He will think nothing bad of you. And Rupert has a stiff upper lip but he married Meredith over some scandal, so he is in no place to condemn us either. Do not worry about what they think. I would not have invited them. Perhaps they are the misfits of my family, but even so they are a part of my family.'

Her teeth pressed gently into her lower lip as she fought the fear that sought to overwhelm her.

He pulled her hand. 'Come along, they are waiting for us and I want to marry you.'

The beat of her heart thudded through her body as she conceded and let him draw her towards the church. If she had ever dreamed about being married she would never have imagined this. But with Harry … She just wanted to be with Harry.

I love you. The words whispered through her head again as he pulled her on into the shadowy porch of the church. She had not walked into a church since she'd been fourteen.

The vicar now wore a white robe over his black dress and the others stood in a group at the bottom of the aisle.

Harry stopped, and turned to her. 'Let me have your ring back?'

Oh. 'Yes.' She took off her gloves.

'I'll take them.' He took her gloves, then took off his hat and set it down on a pew. Her gloves were left in his hat as she took off the ring and handed that to him.

He smiled, then raised his elbow, implying she should hold his arm. Her fingers clasped the scarlet woollen cloth. Then they walked through the small group of people he had called misfits and on up the aisle.

Perhaps these people were the best congregation for their wedding – she was a misfit too – and Harry had said he was a misfit in his family? *It is the same with war. I never speak.* Harry seemed to understand her. No one else had ever understood her choices.

Harry slid the ring back on to her finger, then held her hands and looked into her eyes through the rest of the service. Not once did he look at either the vicar or his family and he spoke only to her. This marriage was for them. In weeks it would just be the two of them in India. He knew that too. It was only about them, no matter who watched.

India … She was going to India.

Her fingers clung to his. He was a solid, good man. She felt safe when he was with her.

'Charlie …' He prompted in a whisper.

She glanced at the vicar, she was meant to have replied. What was she supposed to have said? 'I do …' he whispered at her.

Oh. She looked at Harry. 'I do.'

He squeezed her fingers. 'I do,' she said again quietly to him.

'I know,' he whispered back, with humour in his eyes.

This was their moment.

'I now pronounce you man and wife!' The vicar called out about the echoing church.

Harry leant forward and she looked up so he could reach beneath the brim of her bonnet and kiss her. He still held both her hands.

'I did not expect to say this today or perhaps ever; congratulations on your marriage, Harry.'

Harry let go of one of her hands and turned to face his brother-in-law. 'The unexpected can sometimes floor us with a single blow.'

The man laughed. 'So now, is there a wedding breakfast?' He spoke more quietly, 'and if so, are we inviting Rupert?'

Harry smiled and whispered back. 'Why not, because you think him dull?'

'He is dull.'

'Yet, it is my wedding and I am inclined to include him. Be nice to him, Drew.'

Drew. She captured the name and tried to hold it in her mind.

'Rupert. Meredith. Phillip,' Harry stated, looking past Drew. 'We are going back to John's for luncheon, would you care to join us?'

'I have work to do,' Phillip replied.

'Thank you, but we are expected at home,' Rupert refused too. Were they rejecting her?

'Well, I will celebrate with you,' Drew stated. Harry let go of her hand and turned to face Drew.

The woman who had not yet spoken came forward and touched Charlie's arm. 'Congratulations.'

'Thank you.'

'It is a strange feeling, isn't it? When things are so hurried.' The woman smiled in a way that implied empathy and almost a conspiratorial nature.

'Yes.'

'It is quite hard to believe it at first. My marriage to Rupert was a very long time ago, but we are happy even now. You must not fret too much as things settle. They will settle.'

Harry had said they'd married after a scandal. Charlie could not imagine the scandal being anything very great. Her husband had a posture that implied he thought himself better than the rest of them.

The woman turned away, but her words had left Charlie more unsettled. If this man was an earl and acted so proudly, Charlie could not imagine how the dukes in Harry's family might react to her.

Harry looked back at the vicar. 'Thank you.' He took some money out from his pocket and gave it to the minister.

A bitter taste flooded Charlie's mouth as a sour, sickening memory filled her mind. Harry was right, he had unlocked her mind last night. The vicar in the church in the village had accepted money from Mark. The church and God had not turned their backs on Mark.

There were no morals in this world. People said one thing

125

before others, but did not abide by their words in private. Liars. Priests and officials and do-gooders. They all lied.

'Come along, newly weds. John will have a good bottle of champagne in his cellar that we can break open for you.'

Harry held her arm as they walked back down the aisle, with Drew walking on Harry's other side and the others ahead of them. Harry picked up his hat which contained her gloves before they walked out of the church.

They said goodbye to the others in front of the carriage. Meredith leant and kissed her cheek. Phillip gave her a shallow bow and Rupert a very stiff bow. Then the men shook Harry's hand.

Drew touched her arm. 'Do not mind them. Harry has a very generous, wonderful family, his parents behave as though they are mine. You must not measure them by these stiffer members of Harry's relations and do not be nervous about meeting the rest of them. What I have learned is to be honest with them and then they are both honest and good to you.'

He had seen and understood her expression and divined her concerns. She had thought herself good at hiding her thoughts. Perhaps she would need to get better if she was to spend the next weeks with Harry's family. She had no desire to let them know if they upset her, nor to be honest with them, because if they decided to be honest with her in return she knew what his father thought and she did not wish to hear it said to her face. She had lived with that and she'd run away from it.

Harry turned and took her hand again. 'Up you get.' He handed her up into the carriage first, then climbed in and sat beside her. Drew sat opposite them, as he'd done on the way there.

'I have never had any patience for Rupert. The man is too starched,' Drew stated.

Charlie looked at Harry. He smiled broadly, not at all angered by his brother-in-law's bluntness. 'He is Rupert. He is not raucous like us, that is all.'

'I am not raucous any more. I am still not like him.'

'But you once were raucous. It is in your nature. Papa said many years ago he was closest to Rupert. They used to go about town together—'

'Your father has never been raucous either,' Drew scoffed.

Harry made a dismissing sound. 'Precisely. But Uncle Robert was. Papa always says he was forced to be sensible because Uncle Robert was so irresponsible.'

Drew laughed. 'That is his excuse. But I like your Papa staid, it suits him. It makes him a solid pillar to lean on when I have need of his support.'

Staid. She pictured a man similar to Rupert. Sober. Grave. As she saw the accusing words he had written. She did not want to meet Harry's father.

Harry smiled. 'Something happened to stop Rupert being close to either of them, though. He's never visited even when Papa and Mama are in town. He speaks to them at balls and he talks to John because of course they see each other in the House of Lords, but he is always colder towards Mama and Papa.'

'Yet he came today …'

Harry shrugged. 'He would probably have been too embarrassed to refuse when Phillip asked him directly.'

'I suppose.'

'I liked his wife,' Charlie said. 'She said some kind things.' She wanted to take part in their conversation, she hated to feel shut out.

Harry looked at her. 'I think Meredith is more relaxed. I think her nice too, although I have rarely spoken to her. As children we never mixed much with that side of the family because of whatever occurred which made Rupert cold towards Papa.'

The carriage took them back to the house, where they ate luncheon as Harry had planned, only now his brother-in-law had joined them he and Harry talked as Charlie looked from one to the other.

It did not feel as though she had just married Harry. It felt as though she was in a pantomime. She had met an earl and now she was sitting in a huge duke's townhouse, with ornamentation everywhere, eating the food from a duke's kitchen and drinking his champagne, and her bridegroom was his brother. She could still not picture her Harry from the seashore as a noble man – an earl's grandson on his father's side and on his mother's side a duke's grandson and brother.

They climbed back into the carriage at about two. It carried the trunk of clothes Harry had bought for her on its top and it held Harry's things in its boot, which Obsidian was tethered to, and Ash awaited them inside. She appeared at the door, her tail wagging.

'Hello, girl. The children are going to love seeing you again.' Drew patted the seat to encourage the dog to jump up next to him.

When their journey began Charlie looked out of the window as the men talked; as they had throughout luncheon.

Though, Harry's fingers weaved through hers and held on to her as he spoke.

Did he realise that she already felt left behind? But they would be going to India and he had chosen to marry her, he did not want to leave her behind, that was why he'd asked her to marry him.

But the weeks with his family were going to be hard.

~

When the carriage passed through the gates on to John's property, Charlie turned. 'Harry,' she said in a low, concerned whisper.

He'd been talking to Drew, her words interrupted their conversation. She'd paled and her eyes were wider. She turned away and leaned forward, looking back at the gate.

Nothing could be seen of John's house, it was still a mile or two away.

The carriage rode on through the park land as Charlie turned to look at him again, her eyes expressing horror.

He smiled and said quietly. 'I did tell you John was a duke.'

'But, Harry …' The tone of her voice said she had not imagined this.

No, he supposed it was unimaginable for someone who had not lived this life.

'There is no need to be concerned.'

'There really is not,' Drew added. The carriage was too small for him not to overhear and become involved in their conversation. But he had grown up in and around such places too. It would never have seemed frightening or threatening to him. Last night Charlie had told him she grew up in one room, with only a curtain to separate her bed from her parents' bed.

'You are my wife,' Harry reminded and reassured. 'I will be with you.' The word wife shocked him a little. He'd not said it aloud until now, but it was true. He'd taken a wife after all the years he'd said he never would. The thought made him smile.

'I shall be there too. If you feel overwhelmed, you may run to me too.' Drew sought to be helpful.

Harry's eyes remained focused on Charlie. 'He is not jesting. Drew's sister, Caroline, Caro, my brother's wife, will tell you Drew and Mary provide a very reliable bolt hole if you are ever in trouble.'

'Is Caroline the Duchess?' Charlie asked.

'No. Caroline is Rob's wife, my elder full-brother's wife.'

'And my sister. Katherine is the Duchess. John's wife,' Drew explained. 'But Kate is a quiet and pleasant woman, not at all stuffed and pompous like Rupert. You have no need to fear her.'

'Though John may seem pompous, he is not either, not really,' Harry added.

Drew laughed. 'No. I constantly see the side of him that is more relaxed, especially when it is only a small number of us with Katherine and the children.'

'Your family are going to confuse me.'

'But you will manage with them.'

'We will make sure they are all especially nice,' Drew confirmed. 'Although it may take them a day or so to get over the fact that Harry has married you.'

Charlie's fingers tightened their grip on Harry's hand.

Damn. Drew had said the wrong thing. He obviously had not heard a word from John on the subject of Harry's latest misdemeanours. Charlie had taken Drew's words to mean that people would be upset that he'd married *her*, not that they would simply be shocked that he had married at all. 'I have told them numerous times marriage was not for me. They will be amazed you have converted me to the idea.'

She nodded, but the movement was awkward and the look in her eyes uncomfortable.

He must stay at her side when they reached the house. She would need him near her. They would be there soon.

He looked at Drew, who'd realised there was more to Harry's hurried marriage than had been said.

Harry would never answer the question that was in Drew's eyes. Charlie's past was just that, past. She deserved to be able to leave it there. But perhaps that was what concerned her most – walking amongst his family with the past nipping at her heels as Ash nipped at Obsidian's if she did not move fast enough. He was going to have to work out how he could cut Charlie free from it, from the memories. Perhaps India would do that? Perhaps a change of country would help them both.

They looked out of the windows and didn't speak for a moment. Then he looked at Drew. Harry was not in a mood for silence. 'Will Mary and the children be here or are they at home?'

'They should be here. Mary was bringing the children over to spend the day with the family and Rob and Caro are here too. So you may announce your new situation to your entire family at once.'

Lord. He had not thought about this from Charlie's point of view. If everyone was in one room there would be a lot of them. She would be overwhelmed. But, then, the news must have already reached here. John must have spoken. There should not be too much surprise or fuss in her presence. He expected all the fuss to be made behind her back.

The carriage drew to a halt on the gravel outside John's beast of a Palladian country mansion.

Harry looked at Charlie. She'd become statuesque, her lips were stiff and her expression fixed as she stared out of the window at the huge, pale stone columns that held up the portico.

The area about the carriage became busy with servants and grooms.

A footman opened the door. Harry looked at Drew, telling him to go first. Ash jumped down with Drew.

Harry looked at Charlie once more. 'You are a brave woman. You have proved that a million times over, I am sure, and this will not be the hardship it feels, I promise.'

He climbed out then, and kept hold of her hand to help her down. 'Chin up,' he whispered lastly.

The doors of the house opened as they crossed the gravel, her hand clinging to his. Drew was ahead of them, walking quickly. Mary was the first out and she hurried towards Drew, then wrapped her arms about his neck. They kissed as though they were the newly wedded couple.

'Uncle Baba!' The children followed, not running towards Drew but rushing at Harry.

He let go of Charlie's hand, grasped Iris's midriff and lifted her high. 'Hello, Iris, you little diamond, you.' She was getting tall like her brother. He turned with her once, then set her down. She was getting too old to be thrown around.

'Uncle Baba!' George, Drew's eldest son sought Harry's attention.

Harry held out a hand to George. George was definitely getting too old for silliness. George shook his hand with a grin.

'I have brought Ash home for you, Iris.' The dog was already pacing about the children, seeking attention, though she could probably not remember them. She had been a puppy when they'd left.

'Can I see your sword?' George asked.

'No. It is too sharp. It is not a plaything, George. Now where is your brother?'

'In the nursery with the other little ones,' Iris answered.

Little ones … it did not feel so long ago that she had been little.

'Harry.' He looked at Mary when she called to him. Her gaze turned to Charlie. The look asked, who is she, and it implied Mary had no idea. If John knew the information, then it had not reached Mary. She came over and embraced him, her arms encircling his neck. 'What have you been up to now, who is the woman?' she whispered in his ear, voicing the question she'd already asked once with her eyes.

'Have you brought us anything?' George asked as Mary let Harry go.

'I have, George.'

Harry walked back to Charlie, he had already broken his oath and left her standing. She was rigid and unsmiling. He set an arm about her waist. 'I have brought you a new aunt. This is Charlie, Charlotte, my wife.'

'Your wife,' Mary's voice came out in high pitch of surprise and yet in the exclamation was a lilt of accusation too. Charlie's muscles flinched.

Harry looked at the children, leaving Mary to get over her surprise and cease staring, as though Charlie was an oddity in a fairground. 'Iris, George, meet your new aunt.'

'Auntie Baba?' Iris asked, as she patted Ash.

Perhaps not that. 'Auntie Charlie.'

'Hello, Auntie Charlie?' Iris bobbed a childish curtsey with her palm resting on Ash's head.

'Hello, Auntie Charlie.' George bowed.

Drew watched them with the smile of a proud father.

'Hello,' Mary echoed, finding her voice and stepping forward.

Charlie's hands had hung at her sides, but Mary took hold of them then kissed Charlie on both cheeks. 'You must come in. You must meet our parents and brothers and sisters. They are all going to be so surprised.' Mary kept a hold of one of Charlie's hands and pulled her out of Harry's embrace.

Drew sent Harry a smile and a one-shouldered shrug as the children grasped a hand each and pulled Harry into the house behind Charlie and Mary, leaving Ash to be cared for by the grooms.

'Uncle Baba!' Rob's daughter Sarah was at the top of the stairs. She came running down as he crossed the hall in the possession of George and Iris. Sarah was a sweet fey little thing like her mother, not Rob, with pale-blonde hair. She had been six on her last birthday.

She embraced his middle. He settled a hand on her shoulder. 'Hello ha'penny.' That had always been his nickname for her because she was so small.

A footman took his hat and Charlie's bonnet.

Mary glanced over her shoulder as she started climbing the stairs, leading Charlie ahead of him. 'Mostly everyone is in the drawing room. Katherine has just had tea served. It is only Jemima and Georgiana outside with Gerard, they are playing badminton.'

'Who is here?' Harry asked as Sarah claimed his hand and pulled him on. Iris still hung on to his other hand, while George walked on with his father's arm about his shoulders.

'All of us and all of Uncle Robert's family.'

'Henry and Susan too?'

'Yes.'

'The others arrive in three weeks,' Drew added. 'For a summer ball.'

He was home. Even though John's property had never been

his home. There was always this mass of people in his family and the sense of camaraderie. That was the feeling of home that he'd known as a child and found replicated in his early days in the army.

Yet his life here and the way of the army were worlds apart. Here there was affection too and open, tender hearts. The last time he had joined his family had been immediately on his return from the Crimea and then it had been very difficult to step back into this. He'd felt alone amidst the crowd as memories had clouded and haunted his view of life. It was hard to carry around the guilt and the images of battle in a room of people who loved openly and lived with a simplistic view of right and wrong.

But now …

Charlie looked over her shoulder at him as she walked up the shallow steps. He was not alone this time. He would not speak of his army life here because he knew the two lives should never collide – but he had found a woman to be his companion, who seemed to understand the soldier in him. She had memories that held her apart too.

He smiled encouragement at Charlie.

She looked ahead.

This was grander than John's London house and it was not draped in dustcovers, her humble background made her feel intimidated by all this splendour.

He sighed out a breath. He would free himself from the children when he reached the drawing room.

The drawing room was busy, although the long room was not as full as it was when all his mother's family were here too.

Drew looked at him and raised his eyebrows, saying, how are you going to tell them?

He let go of the children's hands. 'Excuse me, girls, I have something to do.' Then walked over to Charlie as Mary let her go.

He wrapped an arm about Charlie's waist as he looked across

the room. His sister, Helen, noticed him, and his cousin, Sarah. They had been talking to one another. He sent Helen a crooked smile. Then caught his cousin Henry's eye. People's gazes turned to him like a whisper passing across the room. He could not see his father, though, nor John.

'May I have your attention, everyone!' He shouted in the voice of a man who had called men into a charge during war.

'Harry!' Jennifer, his sister, who had not noticed him, cried out, turning to hurry over.

'No wait.' He lifted a hand to stop Jennifer's approach. 'I have something to tell you.'

The faces in the room became serious as every gaze turned to Charlie. None of them appeared to know who she was. John had kept the news to himself and left this moment for Harry.

'This is Charlotte, Charlie, and this morning she became my wife. So there, now you may tell us how pleased you all are for us.'

Poor Charlie was rigid-backed and stiff-faced in the style of the pillars that held up the portico outside as everyone rushed towards them like a frothing wave rolling on to the shore.

Charlie did not even try to smile.

'Harry, you scoundrel.' He could not keep a hold of Charlie as Jennifer wrapped her arms about his neck and kissed his cheek. 'Congratulations.'

Helen was next. 'I never thought you would marry. You have always been so against the idea.' He was hugged and kissed again.

Then their husbands, the Paget twins, shook his hand. Helen had married Lord Paget, the Earl, the eldest by less than an hour, and six months later Jennifer had claimed his twin brother. Beyond them he saw his cousin Henry walking towards him, accompanied by Uncle Robert, Harry's father and John. His mother came towards Charlie as the girls welcomed her to the family.

Harry could see from his father's expression that he had known about the marriage. He and John were the only people who did not appear surprised.

Henry gripped Harry's hand, then embraced Harry with the other arm. 'Bloody hell, you discovered a woman who has entranced you. You've always said never and you have said it often.'

His father and John stayed back as his cousins and his brothers, Daniel and David, came to shake his hand and laugh at him for catching himself in the noose he'd always sworn he'd avoid. Uncle Robert and Aunt Jane added their felicitations and then Katherine was the last to wish him well, she hugged him and kissed his cheek as his sisters had done. Then she turned to Charlie, who his mother still stood beside.

'May I have a word with you?' his father stated. John stood beside him, his eyes holding the accusation Harry had known would come.

Harry glanced at Charlie, his mother would make Charlie feel welcome, she would manage.

His father raised his hand, encouraging Harry to walk ahead. Lord. It was like being marched out under guard.

'We'll talk in the library,' John said, as they reached the landing.

Harry walked downstairs with one hand resting on the hilt of his sword.

One of John's footmen moved to open the library door for them to walk through and when they were all inside the man shut the door.

Harry stood straight, with the palm of his right hand still resting on the hilt of his sword.

'You married her …' John said, the accusation brimming in his voice challenging Harry's sanity with his outrage.

'Yes.' Harry let his answer ask what was wrong with that?

'For God's sake, why?' his father reproached.

'Why not? I think it is my choice who I marry.'

'Except, I know where this began. She was a man's mistress

and you were with her in his house. The scandal is running through the clubs in London. You asked John to pay for the woman and then, in the next moment, you are married. Why? Because John would not give you the money? I thought you had outgrown rebellion, Harry.'

He widened his eyes at his father, in censure. Whatever Charlie's background she was now his wife. 'Do you think I would marry her to spite you?'

'You cannot use a woman like this. If you knew what you have done …' John said in a more ominous tone, as though Harry had committed the worst sin in the world.

'Papa, you told me again and again to think about the lives of women who choose to be paid for their favour. I understand now. Charlie deserves this. I did not marry her to spite you. It is right, that is all. Do you think I would be that foolish to commit myself for such a shallow reason? I have been posted to India. I am due to leave in six weeks. I want her with me.'

His father stared at him. 'And that is what she wants?'

She'd had little choice, but. 'Yes.' He thought so.

John stared at him. 'One never knows if you are serious, Harry, or being dismissive. God, if you knew the truth in this …'

He knew well enough. He did not need John behaving as though he was the authority on life. Harry had seen things John could never imagine. He looked at his father. 'She is terrified of you all. She comes from a poor family. Do not insult her and do not blame her. Please?'

'We would not treat her badly. You simply cannot realise the impact of this,' John said.

'Of course I know. I have married her. I will be living with her. I am being sent to India for my sins towards a retired officer and I would do everything again if I had the same chance.'

'She has a bruise about her eye …' his father said, in a low, cutting voice that questioned why.

Damn. Harry had become so used to looking at her with it

137

he'd forgotten about it, but then his mind had been focused on marrying her. Perhaps that was why everyone had stopped and stared for a minute before greeting her. God, and no wonder Rupert had been so starched. 'The man she left did that. You should be praising me as the heroic son you have always wanted, not berating me.'

His father swallowed and his skin coloured red.

He hardly ever blushed.

Harry looked at John, expecting approval. His brother was a holier-than-thou Puritan. Harry did not receive approval. John looked ... odd. He was paler and he looked as though he'd eaten something bitter.

'You had better treat her well. I would like to stay here until I join my new regiment in four weeks, but if you do not accept Charlie, I will go and God knows when I will see you again. I might be in India for years.'

'Harry,' his father walked towards him, finally recognising what his going to India meant and he was embraced. 'I *am* proud of you.'

They were words often spoken to Rob or Mary or the others, but rarely to him.

He held his father and breathed in the smell of his cologne. It was strange things like that which had hovered in his mind in the time he'd endured the nightmare of the Crimean War.

'Do you love this woman?' his father asked as he let Harry go.

Love. He did not answer. He had not allowed himself to think of love. He had kept his heart hard. If his heart became soft again how could he walk away from his family once more, probably for years, and how would he live with the guilt in his head.

John sighed, his eyes saying that he was still unhappy.

When Harry was on the other side of the world what John thought would not matter. But Harry hoped he did not make it uncomfortable for Charlie while they were here, and if he did then Harry would ask Drew if they could stay with him.

Harry looked at his father. 'May I go back to her now?'

'Yes.' His father turned and opened the door.

John caught hold of Harry's arm. 'Do not mention to anyone the name of the man she was with.' The statement was a whisper he did not want his father to hear.

'Why?'

'Do not risk trouble that does not need to befall us.'

What had John heard? But he could not ask John to explain as his father held the door and was waiting.

Harry turned and walked out ahead of them. Poor Charlie would be upstairs as alone as he'd felt the last time he'd returned. He climbed the stairs two at a time, his hand on his sword hilt again to stop it swaying. He'd take it off in a minute, but not near George or John's sons.

Charlie was sitting on a sofa flanked by his mother and Katherine. He hoped she had not been grilled. *Where did you meet? When?*

Charlie looked up at him, her eyes speaking her plea to be saved.

He looked at Katherine. 'Is there a room we can retreat to? It has been a long day and we would welcome the chance to rest before we change for dinner.'

She stood up and beckoned over one of the footmen who'd waited at the edge of the room. 'Show Captain Marlow up to his room please.'

'But before you go, you must let me say my congratulations, Harry.' His mother stood and her arms wrapped about him. He held her in return. 'You are a bad boy,' she whispered into his ear. 'It was cruel of you to marry without me there.' The words were not said unkindly, but they were genuinely meant. He had deprived her.

He ought to admit, though … 'Rupert and Meredith were there. They were in town. Phillip invited them—'

'Phillip was with you?' Katherine asked with a pitch of envy.

'Phillip, Drew, Rupert and Meredith.'

'You should have come here and fetched us,' his mother chastised.

'And then everyone would have wished to be involved and a fuss would have been made.'

She did not answer, but their embrace ended.

'Will you excuse us?' He nodded at his mother, then Katherine, then caught hold of Charlie's hand.

Chapter 10

Charlie clasped Harry's fingers as though she was drowning in a river and he was a rope someone had thrown to pull her to safety. All these beautiful, well-dressed people. Wealthy people. Noble people.

What had she done?

This was not a world she should be in.

Why had Harry asked her to marry him?

His father and his eldest brother had taken Harry away within moments and they had not spoken to her or looked happy about Harry's announcement. They had looked uncomfortable when they'd returned. They did not want her here, they knew her past. But they could not have told anyone else, everyone else had spoken to her. How long would they keep the secret?

Uncle Baba, the children had called Harry. He'd told her about the nickname and that his family had deemed him the naughty one, the one who liked to cause trouble. Had he married her because he wished to contradict his father's words? He had received the letter and then proposed.

She hung on to Harry's hand as they followed the servant up another flight of stairs. Their room was at the far end of the hall on that landing. The walls were covered in a paper decorated with green vines and the ceiling had gilded plaster-work.

Harry let her go. She walked further into the room as he thanked the servant, then shut the door.

When he turned, he sighed.

She looked back as she heard it.

'Now you may breathe, Charlie.'

She did, her lips parted and she drew in a deep breath; she had not even realised she had not been breathing properly.

'Sorry I left you. But it was better I let John and my father have their say. I knew they would not approve of our rushed marriage.'

'Do they hate me?'

He walked quickly across the room and held her.

She clung to him, her fingers curling into the cloth of his coat at his back.

'They do not hate you. It is me they are angry with and the bruise about your eye raises questions. I had forgotten about it myself, but if you think people have been looking oddly at you, you must remember that.' He let her go and instead held her hands. 'This is not the wedding day I would have chosen for you. I am sorry. But shall we take a while to recoup? Shall I ring for a bathing tub and hot water?'

She nodded. In this room, she could pretend that it had been like the days in the inns – as it would be again when they left for India. She only needed to survive this intense weight of unworthiness and guilt for a few weeks.

Yet weeks ... Days would be easier, but weeks...

It felt as though she was walking along the High Street in her village, when everyone had stared and instead of others doing it, her own mind shouted the names that people had called her and threw the stones that people had bent to pick up and hurl at her.

'Come back to me,' Harry said in a quiet voice.

She had been lost in thought – fear.

He pressed a kiss on her lips. 'I shall ring down.' When he turned away he began unbuckling his sword belt.

She turned away too, uncertain what to do, and walked to the window. No. She could not pretend this was a room in an inn. When she looked out of the window she saw a landscape that was perfectly laid out, as though it was the view in a painting. There was a huge lake with a weir that flowed under a bridge and perfectly placed trees in the meadows about it.

Harry wrapped his arms around her waist from behind. He'd taken off his gloves.

'My wife. I like the word.' He kissed her neck. 'Did Mama interrogate you?'

'Yes.'

'Sorry.'

She did not say more. She had avoided the questions as much as she could and said nothing about her family or where she grew up. Her head rested back on Harry's shoulder as he bit her neck then kissed it again.

She and Harry had this sense of closeness and attraction, no matter what.

Someone knocked on the door. Harry's hands fell away and the warmth of his body left her.

She turned and watched as he opened the door and spoke with the servant. Then he shut the door and turned back, looking at her. 'The bath and the water will be up directly; they keep water warm here. You do not make a duke wait if he wants something.'

He began unbuttoning his coat. She noticed her trunk had been placed in a small room adjoining theirs. The door was open and she could see her trunk in the corner. Beside it were his things and on top of them were his hat and her bonnet. It must be a dressing room.

Her heartbeat raced with the desire to run.

'Charlie ...' he said her name as though he'd thought her mind

143

was wandering again. 'Do not be afraid of them.' He stripped off his coat.

But she was afraid of his family.

The door was knocked on again. Harry walked into the dressing room and laid his coat down on top of the trunk beside his other things, where he'd put his sword too, and came back in to open the door.

The servants brought in a large copper bath, lined it with a linen cloth and then filled it with water. They also brought soap, cloths and towels. Then they were gone again.

'Let us open the window. It's warm in here.' Harry walked past her to do it. 'I'd rather be swimming in the lake, but we might cause some outrage if we did that.'

He turned then and his fingers started releasing the buttons on the back of her dress. 'You are joining me, aren't you?'

'Yes.'

She felt better when she was sitting in the water with him, between his parted legs, resting her back against his chest. His arms were about her and his fingers were threaded in between hers. He lifted her left hand and held it up so that the sunlight caught on the ring.

She could sense him smiling.

He was happy. That was a good thing. They had promised each other happiness. But she wanted it too.

She sighed out her breath.

When he'd had enough of bathing, as she stood in the bath he wrapped her in a towel, then lifted her out and carried her to the bed, where he kissed her everywhere. Then she kissed him everywhere before she climbed over him and made him even happier.

But he said they must go back downstairs afterwards to join his family again.

Her heart pulsed in a hard, heavy beat as they dressed.

He kept a firm hold on her hand as they walked down and as

they stood in the drawing room she met his youngest sisters and his cousin Gerard, who had been outside earlier.

When his sister-in-law Katherine, the Duchess, and his mother, Ellen, came to speak to her she could not take her eyes off their jewellery. Their necklaces held layers of gemstones. She had thought the things the Colonel had bought her were pretty and extravagant, but now she saw that they had been cheap and gaudy compared to real jewels.

When they sat at the table she was in between Harry and his brother Rob.

Rob spoke to her pleasantly. Yet she had a feeling that Harry's family had been talking about her before she'd come down. There was an atmosphere of caution at the table. Did they want an explanation for her bruised eye? She saw some of them glance at it when they spoke to her.

She watched them too. There were a number of couples and at times they talked exclusively while other conversations flowed across the table.

Most of it excluded her. But even if she could not participate, there was one thing she was skilled at; she could smile for hours and bear anything and pretend she was happy.

It is only for four weeks, she told her silly head. It was not long. She would make her cheeks ache with smiles in those weeks.

Katherine stood a short while after they had finished eating, then Harry's mother stood and his Aunt Jane and his sister Mary, and it was like a wave flowing down the room. Harry touched Charlie's hand. 'I will be as quick as I can.'

As every woman had stood, she supposed she must have to stand too. When she did, the women started walking from the room. Oh. She was to leave Harry…

She swallowed, then stiffened her smile and remembered the nights when she had served Mark's friends with drinks and cigars. That was her only marker for understanding how to behave here.

The women returned to the long drawing room, which was

full of red velvet and dark wooden furniture, huge portraits and more gilded plaster. This world, this place, was the gilded edging on Harry. She had met the solid, plain, bear oak of the man in Brighton, but here…

'So how long have you known Harry?' Helen asked.

Charlie turned, met Helen's gaze, and forced her voice to stay steady. 'For a few weeks.'

As Charlie answered, Harry's female cousins walked across the room, as though they had been desperately awaiting the moment when they could question her.

'Sit, Charlie.' Helen patted the end of a sofa as she sat there too. Then Harry's sisters and cousins gathered about them while Harry's mother, Ellen, and Katherine, who had already asked these questions, stood across the room talking with his aunt.

'Tell me where you met?' Helen prompted.

'Yes, where did you meet him?' The youngest, Jemima, pressed too.

'At the seashore. I saw him everyday throwing a stick for his dog.'

'Did he spot you and come and talk to you?' Someone else asked.

'No. I spoke to him first.'

'Oh, that would have polished up his ego,' Mary answered.

'Did you go to assemblies?' Georgiana asked.

'No, but we walked out together, along the front, with Ash.' These women were so very different to her. Those who were married must have met their husbands at balls and been courted on carriage rides, in the way of a penny romance novel.

When the men entered the room, Harry came over to Charlie immediately; he walked behind the sofa and set his hands on her shoulders, then he leant down and kissed her neck. It was an excuse to whisper in her ear, 'How are you?'

She touched his hand as it rested on her shoulder and glanced up to smile. The smile was such a lie, more of a lie than any she had told the women about how she had come to be his wife.

They retired to their room before anyone else had and he asked about what had been said to her as they walked upstairs. She told him the answers she had given so that he could say the same.

In the bedroom, immediately after he'd shut the door, his hand braced the back of her head, and things became as they had been in Brighton as his fingers clasped in her hair and he kissed her for a long while.

Her hands held on to the upper arms of his coat as the world swayed about her like the sea and the room became an island.

Once they were undressed, she lay on top of the bed, with the breeze of the night air sweeping through the window they'd left open, caressing her skin, while he lay over her pressing into her body with a skill and gentleness that made every sinew in her body ache with pleasure.

She spoke to him afterwards, as she was wrapped in his arms and when he asked if she liked his family, she said, 'Yes. But I am not sure they all like me. Your father and the Duke have not spoken to me at all. I think they *must* hate me.' She could not hold the thought in; the words in his father's letter hovered in her mind like a bird of prey waiting to swoop and strike.

He stroked her arm in reassurance, and yet his muscles stiffened and she imagined it was with the instinct of defence; the reflex had been the same when he'd been suddenly woken. 'They do not hate you, I promise. They are angry with me. They have delicate constitutions when it comes to anything that I do. Remember I spent years upsetting them as the naughtiest in the family when I was younger. I will speak to them.'

~

When they sat at the full breakfast table the atmosphere was more informal than the dinner table. It made the conversations louder and more animated as people discussed how they intended to

147

spend the day. A ride became the favourite idea and the majority of the men and some of the women said they wished to ride.

Charlie looked at Harry. His lips were closed, but she knew … He was a cavalry man.

'Would you like to join them?' she asked in a quiet voice.

He looked at her and his lips parted in a smile that said he'd been caught out. It was like one of the unsure smiles he had given her in the beginning. 'Yes, and I am thinking Obsidian has not been ridden for days.'

'I cannot ride.'

'I had guessed, Charlie. When we reach India, then I will take some time to teach you?'

She nodded, but India was not now and so she could not ride and she would have to stay here and let him go. She nodded again and put on her fake smile. It would be easy to make him happy. She had spent seven years making Mark happy – what of her, though? 'But for today you must ride if you wish and you must ride if you wish all the time we are here.'

He gave her a different smile then, one that said thank you, before he looked away and joined the conversation.

After the riding party had left she returned to their room before any of the women left behind had chance to gain her attention, and the Duke had remained too and he simply scared her. He had looked at her and not spoken, before turning away to go about his business.

Once in the room, she climbed on to the bed and lay there to await Harry's return.

After only a moment, someone knocked on the door. She did not answer. She was hiding here.

It was knocked again, then a man called, 'Mrs Marlow! There is a gentleman caller to see you, a Mr Cotton! He says he is your brother!'

Charlie sat up. Rodney … Oh goodness. She scrambled off the bed and ran to open the door in her stocking-clad feet, with her hair probably untidy, having been crushed on the pillow. She had given her family her address here and Rodney had come. 'Where is he?'

'In the stable yard, Mrs Marlow.'

Because, of course, her brother would not be allowed inside this grand house.

'Wait a moment.' She turned away and put on her half boots, the boots she had gone to Harry wearing, not the dainty shoes that Harry had bought her. 'Show me.'

The male servant walked before her at a steady pace, leading her to the landing on the first floor, but then he opened a door that was decorated to match the walls, so it was almost hidden. It took her in to the servants' stairway. She followed him down, one hand on the wooden rail as her other hand held the skirt of her pale-yellow muslin day dress, with its pattern of small daisies.

When he came to the bottom of the stairs the serving man followed a long flagstone-paved hallway. It contained dozens of servants, walking one way or another. A couple of the servants recognised her and bowed their heads or curtsied, but there seemed a bit of confusion in the corridor over how they should treat the interloper in this noble family.

At the end of the hallway she could see a door leading into the stable yard and when the man opened the door she saw Rodney.

He was holding his cap in his hands, standing a few feet away, a lone auburn-haired man, with a scruffy ginger beard, in the middle of a giant square surrounded by stables.

'Oh Rodney!' She rushed at him and wrapped her arms about his neck. It was a home-coming she had never expected to happen. He was taller than he had been and broader. He was a man and not the youth she'd left behind. He smelled of labour.

His arms only came loosely about her in return, for a moment.

She stepped back and looked at him holding his arms. She had longed to be held tightly. Home. Her brother. It had been so

149

many years. Every moment of the happiest times of her childhood filled her head. She had longed for so many years to see her family again.

Her brother was here. Before her. He had come.

An emotion of relief and joy washed over her as she looked at his so-familiar face, even though he looked older.

He'd worn his Sunday suit to visit her and he looked very smart, as smart as she had seen a man look before she had come here. But he was not smiling as he looked back at her and his eyes did not express any joy.

'What is it? Did you come to wish me well?' *Smile for me, please, because I have been struggling to smile for myself.*

'What 'appened to y'ur eye?'

Oh, her eye. Of course he was not smiling. Of course he looked concerned and as though he was judging something. 'An argument with Mark before I left.'

He swallowed.

The house servant had disappeared, which meant she could not turn and say may she invite Rodney inside and all of the outdoor servants in the courtyard were focused on their work, though they occasionally looked her way.

'Shall we walk?' She let go of him as his hands gripped his hat.

'No, Charlie. I came … I just … I am … I only need …'

Why was he struggling with the words of a greeting? Spit it out, Rodney! She wanted to yell, as Mark would have yelled at her if she had stuttered.

'I need you, that is y'ur 'usband, to pay the Colonel.'

'What?' The words struck her with a hard slap. In her memories of the past she recalled her mother's hand in her hair as her head was dunked into the cold barrel of rain water. Her mother had used to do that when Charlie had done something wrong as a child.

'I need y'ur 'usband to give the Colonel the money 'e 'is askin' for.' It was said in a deep tone that refused emotion.

'Why?' He had not even asked how she was. He had not even come here to see her but to ask for money.

'Colonel 'illier wants 'is money back. 'E is throwing us out of our 'ome or …'E said 'e'd take Ginny in y'ur place.'

No. 'She is twelve!'

'That she is, Charlie. Ask y'ur 'usband to pay or y'u must go back to 'im. I will take y'u back.'

'What? I am married now. Do not be absurd.' A darkness came over her, as though something had covered the sun. Rodney did not care for her happiness; he had come to wish her back where she had been – in misery.

'That cannot matter. Would y'u 'ave 'im 'urt Ginny? Or our mother? Or leave my Martha and my baby with no 'ome?'

No! The word screamed inside her as her hand lifted and she struck him on the side of his face. The cracking sound of the impact echoed back from about the stable yard as tears gathered in her eyes. Then she shook her head as she stepped back.

She had always believed in the years that she'd spent with Mark that her family loved her, that there were people who loved her. She had sacrificed herself so they would not suffer because of the error she had made when she had accepted the ride in Mark's carriage. She had gone to Mark so that Ginny would not wail with hunger and her mother would not cry for fear of how they would survive and her brother would not shout in distress over how he was supposed to support them all.

Rodney did not love her. He was thinking of himself. He could work. He could move out of his home and rent another and work to support the others.

'Go away,' she said in a low voice that was husky with pain as he cut her heart in two with the swing of an axe. 'I will not go back there.' She turned away, swallowing the choking sound of tears before he could hear it and walked with quick strides towards the house, her legs slicing at the layers of her petticoats.

'Charlie.' He had run after her and his fingers closed about her arm in a grip that stopped her flight. 'Get us the money then, so 'e will leave us alone. 'E said five hundred.'

Across Rodney's shoulder she saw one of the grooms, who had been glancing their way turn and come towards them.

She pulled her arm free. 'Harry does not have the money. He is not rich. It is his family who have wealth, not him.'

'Then ask him to beg for it if y'u will not go back.'

She stared at her brother, unable to believe what he'd asked her to do. The images she'd been seeing in her head over these last hours flooded her mind; people spitting at her and calling out names.

She had lied to herself as successfully as she had learned to form false smiles. Rodney had not been there then. She could see it now. He'd never defended her. He had never comforted her. He had not even been angry with Mark. He, and her mother, had only ever been angry with her when it had happened. They had blamed her.

She had only received three short, terse, letters back from the numerous ones she had sent over the seven years. She had told herself it was too hard for them to write, Rodney was too busy and her mother could not write and then there was the paper and ink to be paid for. But they had not written because they did not care.

She had sacrificed herself for their and Ginny's happiness. She had gone to the man who had hurt her for help, to make their lives better, making hers awful and they had not even appreciated the gift of her life.

Well, she wanted her life back.

The groom reached them. 'Unhand the lady, sir.' He glared at Rodney.

Rodney looked at her as his grip released her arm.

'You had better go, sir.'

Rodney did not move, but stared at her.

'You had better go, sir,' the groom repeated.

She wanted nothing more to do with her brother. She turned and hurried away, leaving the groom to see Rodney escorted off the Duke's property. She wished to walk as far away as she could get. To India. The sense of guilt could not scream at her and pressure her in India. But it screamed again now.

What about her? The words yelled through her head in the battle of denial against guilt and grief she had experienced when she'd been young. She had ended this fight before. Now she wanted to be selfish. And happy. Why was it wrong for her to be happy? But Mark had threatened Ginny.

Her feet took her blindly back through the corridor as tears blurred all the servants that stared at her. She wiped the tears away with the sleeve of the pretty dress Harry had bought her.

In her head the words replayed – *beg for it*. Money. Harry's family had money. But she would never ask Harry to beg from them. He could not beg from the family he loved. It would embarrass him.

She did not care about Rodney. He would manage. He could work. But Ginny … Her guilt screamed of Ginny's innocence in the pitch of Ginny's childhood wails when Charlie's stomach had been hurting with hunger too.

But her … If she begged on her own account, not Harry's, and if she did not tell him, then Ginny would be safe and Mark and Rodney and everything from her past would go away.

At the end of the corridor there was a man dressed in the uniform of the upstairs' servants. 'Where can I find the Duchess?'

The Duchess had not gone out riding and in the village it had always been the women who undertook the charitable acts.

'She is in her rooms. Shall I show you up, madam?'

'Yes, thank you.' Charlie's heart leapt into a pounding rhythm. Harry would likely be cross with her for begging from his family, but what else was she to do? There was Ginny. Poor Ginny. Ginny had done nothing wrong to anyone. Charlie could not let anything happen to her sister.

No. She would suffer this embarrassment. She had suffered far worse. This would be nothing.

Smile. Smile and the guilt would become silent again.

Chapter 11

Charlie stood self-consciously before the door as the man knocked, just as her mother had done as a caller in the village when they had begged for help after Charlie's father's death.

The door opened. A maid stood there.

'Please tell her Grace that Mrs Marlow wishes to speak to her,' the man spoke as though Charlie was not standing beside him waiting.

The maid bobbed a quick curtsey at her then shut the door.

The rhythm of Charlie's heart could hit a nail into a board. Her hands clasped before her waist.

Then the door opened again and it was Katherine. 'Charlotte, what are you doing standing there?' She looked at the man. 'I am quite sure my sister-in-law does not need someone to ask if she might see me—'

'I did not know the way to your room, this man was kind enough to show me.'

'Well, then, thank you for doing so, Frank, but now you may leave us.' She grasped one of Charlie's hands and pulled her into the room. 'I am writing invitations for the ball. You must help me and then we may talk as we work.'

She let go of Charlie. 'Take a seat at the desk.' There were two chairs before the wide desk made of a russet-coloured wood and on the desk was a pile of printed gold-embossed cards.

'They look pretty.' Charlie touched the card on the top of the pile. How did she begin the words to ask for five hundred pounds? It was a vast sum.

'I like them myself. Sit do …' Katherine sat in the chair nearest the window as Charlie accepted the other chair. 'What is it you wanted to speak about?'

Charlie's throat dried up. The words would not come.

'Here. These are the invitations to be written and this is the list of names.' Katherine pointed at them, then reached for a quill, dipped it in a pot and stroked the tip to wipe off the excess ink. 'There is another quill, there.' She moved the tiny ink pot so that it stood between them.

'My letters are not very good.'

'I'm sure they will suffice.' She sent Charlie a smile. 'But tell me what made you look for me?'

Charlie swallowed. She could not do it. The words would not come. It was too humiliating to beg. 'I was unsure what to do while Harry is riding.'

Katherine smiled at her again. 'Well, now I have occupied you. You do not mind helping me?'

She shook her head.

Katherine began writing.

Charlie glanced about the room. She could hear Katherine's maid in a room next door. It was a suite, like the rooms she and Harry had stayed in in London. Only this set of rooms were twice the size of those in the house in London and more lavishly decorated.

There were china ornaments and paintings of scenes of far-off places and a lot of furniture, and there were sparkling necklaces and earrings on one table.

'If I write the next, you could write the one after.' Katherine pointed to the list.

Charlie's attention was drawn back to the task. But as she drew over a blank invitation her mind's eye hovered on the jewellery. The necklaces must be worth hundreds. She reached for a quill as the value of what had been carelessly left on a table continued to whisper to her. She wrote, copying the letters of the name in front of her as Katherine wrote beside her.

'After we have finished, I am going to the nursery. You have not met the small ones yet, you must come with me.'

Charlie nodded, though she had no desire to see the children. She could think of nothing but Ginny.

She left the invitation to dry, then drew over another to be written.

She wrote several as Katherine wrote too and spoke about her children. Charlie said very little.

There had to be a way to obtain the money. Five hundred. The sum spun in her head and the beat of her heart resonated through her body, even reaching to her fingertips as she wrote. The guilt Charlie had not heard for so long shouted in her ears. It had been silenced when she'd gone to Mark. But she could not make that choice again.

Katherine wrote the last invitation, then slid it away. 'I shall have John ask someone to write out the envelopes for us. If you wait here I shan't be a moment and then we can go up to the nursery.'

When Katherine stood, so did Charlie. Then Katherine walked away towards the open door, from which the noises of a maid working could be heard.

The glitter of the jewellery pulled Charlie's gaze back to the table, where the necklaces and earrings lay, so carelessly put aside. There were three sets spread out on the table. She stared at them. Then found herself walking towards them. They called to her. They must be worth five hundred and more.

Her fingers reached out and touched the gem stones, rubies, sapphires, emeralds and diamonds. In the room next door, Katherine spoke with the maid.

Shallow breaths slipped past Charlie's lips as her fingers closed and gripped. Her other hand reached out too and gathered up the necklaces. She had a pocket in her dress. She slipped them into her pocket. Then she looked towards the room where Katherine was. 'I am feeling tired! I think I shall go back to my room! Do you mind if I do not accompany you?'

'Of course not.' Katherine was there at the door, looking across the room.

Her head was full of noise, of anger, guilt and fear. Each voice yelled at her from a different direction as she sensed her skin colour a deep red. Yet she held Katherine's gaze and smiled. She could only think of Ginny. Harry's family had so much; they could spare something for Ginny.

She smiled and bobbed a curtsey.

Katherine smiled too. 'I shall see you at luncheon, then.'

'Yes.'

As Katherine went back into the other room, Charlie hurried across the sitting room, her heart racing. Once she was in the hall, she lifted her skirts and ran to her room, and there she looked through Harry's things. There was a small amount of money. She took his pistol too and wrapped everything in her cloak. Then she rushed back downstairs.

No one was in the main hall. The servants must all be serving the family elsewhere.

She turned the round handle on the giant door and walked out, leaving it for someone else to shut. The road must be a mile or more away, but she did not know how to find her way to anywhere without walking back along the drive and so she walked that way. However when she thought she was out of sight of the windows in the house she lifted her skirts with her free hand and ran again, hoping the riders would not return this way.

~

When Harry dropped down from Obsidian's saddle on to the ground, he looked about everyone, trying to see his father. It had been good to ride in a large group again when it was only for pleasure, and yet he'd wanted to speak to his father about Charlie and he hadn't had the chance.

'Papa!' he called out as he spotted his father about to walk inside ahead of everyone else. 'Father!'

He turned and looked back at Harry.

Harry uncharacteristically left Obsidian in the care of a groom and walked towards his father. But he wanted to ensure his father treated Charlie as he should and she was a higher priority than his horse.

The others talked animatedly as they passed his father, exhilarated from their ride.

Harry breathed out a long breath. He hoped this would not be too much of a challenge.

'Harry …' his father acknowledged as Harry reached him.

'May we go somewhere to talk?'

His father's eyebrows lifted, saying why? 'Yes,' he agreed anyway. 'Let's see if John is using the library.'

He was. But he offered to vacate it, saying that he'd use the excuse to go up to the nursery.

Once John had left and the door was shut, his father looked at Harry. 'So …'

'Why have you not spoken to Charlie?'

A frown crunched his father's brow, but he did not answer, he turned away.

'I have never thought you pompous before. She is not what you think.'

His father stared out through the window, as though he sought to avoid the conversation.

Harry had never seen his father run from a conversation before either.

'You have no idea what I think.' He had not turned back to face Harry.

'I think you cannot bring yourself to speak to *such* a woman.

That is how you have termed my associations in the past. But there is a reason she lived as she did—'

'You think I do not know!' His father shouted as he finally turned. It was also unlike his father to shout. His father breathed in, in a way that suggested he fought to regain control of his temper. 'That she has some explanation is exactly what I do know.' His pitch had lowered. '… She has a bruise about her eye that declares it. Why do you think I have hated you sleeping with such women? Because, in my opinion, there is always a reason, a history, these women are never there by choice. They are in that position due to fate or force and *you* have compounded that.'

The words hit Harry hard, he had learned that now and, yes, he had compounded that in the past, and since meeting Charlie it had added to his sense of guilt. But he no longer felt guilty about Charlie, not now she was his wife. 'I wish Charlie to be happy. That is what she deserves and you are making her unhappy by ignoring her.'

'Sorry.' His father's hand lifted and ran over his face.

With the apology his father's demeanour changed and instead of anger there was a defeated appearance in his stance.

'It is not her. It is only that she makes me think of things I would rather not recall. There is a life that goes on away from us which is easier not to contemplate.'

'I know.' His own imagination was broader now. But he could do nothing for the women he'd lain with in the past.

'It is why I have always hated you using such women,' his father said again.

Harry sighed. 'I understand that now. But I cannot change the past. I will change Charlie's future, though. I cannot let you ignore her.'

His father looked into Harry's eyes. 'I have not meant to ignore her. I am just not sure what to say to her. It sickens me to imagine what she has experienced. It is disgust that has silenced me. It is because of the bruise about her eye. I shall force myself to ignore it.'

'Good.' Harry's voice was sharp. *Disgust*. The word made anger bleed into Harry's veins. He'd always been irritated by his father judging him for sleeping with *such women*. Now he was angered because his father was judging those women – and Charlie among them.

A knock rapped on the thick wooden door. Harry looked back as the door opened.

It was John. 'I've been told something I'm sure you will want to know.'

John was now forty-ish in age and had grey at his temples in the same place Harry's mother did. His half-brother was father-like in appearance now as well as could be discerned from the staunch inflexibility of his nature – and the way he had of needing to be the family's protector. Harry would have to have the conversation that he'd just had with his father with John too. He needed them both to accept Charlie.

'Your wife was outside in the courtyard earlier with a man.'

What? A frown pulled at the muscles in Harry's brow. 'Do not be ridiculous.'

John shut the door behind him. Then sent Harry one of his ducal looks that denied all emotion and expressed his authority. 'I am not being ridiculous. A man called here who claimed to be her brother. They spoke together outside, but at the end of the conversation she slapped him, and then he stopped her walking away. My groom interrupted and told the man to leave, then your wife came in and spent the next hour with Katherine.'

It was all said as a matter of fact.

She had been talking to a man who had offended her and then detained her. Anger turned over in Harry's stomach with the sharp twist of a dagger's blade as a strong punch thumped at his chest. Was it one of Hillier's servants?

Yet John had said her brother. 'She has a brother. She wrote to her family from Brighton and gave them this address.'

'He was very much a working man,' John stated. Again it was

voiced as a fact and yet was he questioning her background?

'Yes, her family are poor, as I told you,' Harry said it as factually as John had been speaking. 'She thinks you all incredibly odd and that is making her find it difficult here, I know.' He looked at his father. 'And she thinks you rude. She has said that you both must hate her.'

'I do not hate her,' John said immediately. 'I simply …' He had paled in that odd way he did when Charlie was mentioned or present. 'I do not know how to manage with her here. It makes things awkward. But it is not her fault.'

It was Harry's, then. Well damn them. John was as bad as his father. 'Oh never mind. Please just try to speak to her and make her not feel so terrible while she is here. We shall not be an embarrassment to you for long. I shall ask Drew if we can move to stay with him.' Harry turned and opened the door.

'Harry,' John said.

Harry did not look back.

'Harry. You do not need to go to Drew's.' John followed him.

Harry looked over his shoulder before going into the hall. 'No. You have expressed your view. I'll not have her feeling insulted and unhappy.' He walked out. So many times in his life he had walked away from his father's ill opinion. Now he knew his father's perspective on all of those occasions had been correct – but in this … He was wrong. Charlie might have a past and a story that had brought her here, but why should that influence her future. She had a right to write the story of her future as she wished.

He climbed the stairs with his teeth gritted and his hands fisted against his anger. He went to the drawing room first. There were several of the people who had returned from riding there and Katherine and his mother, but not Charlie.

She had probably been too self-conscious to remain in the public rooms of the house while he had ridden out. She would be in their room. He did not stay in the drawing room, he turned around and walked back out, then climbed the next flight of stairs in a hurry.

Was she afraid? Had she been hurt by this man she'd been speaking to? Her brother … The brother who at nineteen had let his sister, who was a child of fifteen, sell herself.

Harry's strides were swift and his footfalls heavy as he walked along the landing to their bedchamber. He did not knock, but opened the door, his heart pulsing out the rhythm of the drumbeat for a march. She was not in the bedroom. He opened the door of the dressing room. She was not there, but it looked as though she had been there; his things were strewn across the floor, as if she'd been looking for something and throwing things aside.

The items of his clothing and possessions that were scattered over the carpet spoke of urgency and desperation. The pace of his heartbeat did not ease. He leant to pick the things up. His sword rested on the chest, unmoved, on the far side of the room. It reminded him that his pistol had been in the bag, which now had its contents scattered. His pistol and his purse.

He patted the bag. What was left within it definitely did not include either the pistol or his money. Damn.

A bitter taste flooded his mouth as it spun through his gut too. He continued picking up clothes, refusing to believe. Yet someone had been here, talking to her … What had they said?

'Harry.'

He straightened and turned. He'd not shut the bedroom door and now John stood there, looking at the mess and the creased clothes that were clutched in Harry's hands.

'What?' Harry asked.

John walked a few paces forward. 'I am sorry.' His pitch held an ominous note. 'This is not what you will want to hear and I feel awful for thinking it and yet … there was the conversation witnessed outside too and—'

'What? Simply say it. I do not need the preamble to sweeten it.'

'The maid has told me three of Katherine's necklaces are missing. They had been left on the table in the sitting room. Katherine was deciding on a dress for the ball and the jewellery to accompany it. I'm sorry. When your wife visited Katherine in our rooms, she was left alone for a short time. No one has seen her since.'

Damn. Damn. One hand lifted and combed through his hair. It must have been Charlie, and she'd gone.

But she must have walked, she could not ride and the only way she knew back to the road was along the drive.

He turned his back on John and threw the clothes he'd picked up on to the bed, then noticed her bonnet was still in the far corner of the dressing room. She had taken the time to find his pistol and his money, but she had not taken her bonnet. Her actions suggested she had been emotional and not thinking clearly. He refused to believe this was calculated. 'I will find her.'

'I will come with you,' John stated.

Harry turned around. 'No. I'll manage this. You will scare her.' He walked out past his brother. Damn. He wanted to believe her innocent and yet many women *such as her* were not honest. The tainted phrase his father used pulsed disgust into his blood.

If his father was disgusted by talk of such women, Harry was disgusted by his father. And he refused to think badly of Charlie. She was not like anyone but herself. She had been stupid, that was all. There must be a reason.

He hurried down the stairs, then on the first floor landing opened the door leading to the servants' stairs and walked down that to get to the hall, which would take him directly to the stables. The servants were busy taking the family's luncheon up to the dining room and the hall was full of people. He dodged through them as they bowed and curtsied.

She could not have come out this way. She must have left via the front door. It was a wonder no one had noticed. John's servants usually saw everything.

A groom was brushing Obsidian down. Harry asked for

another horse, 'A fast animal, with an appetite for a gallop.' Harry had the appetite, it clenched in his gut, like the moments before the battle cry to charge when all he wished for was to be off and running to silence the roaring words of doubt.

When the horse was saddled, he mounted with a swift single movement. Then clasped the reins tight and led the stallion out of the courtyard, before kicking his heels. Then they were away, riding fast along the verge of the long drive.

She was not on the drive and she could not have hidden because it was all open grassland.

He turned the horse on to the road, in the direction they'd travelled from London, wondering suddenly if he was wrong and he should have brought someone with him. Not John. But Drew or his brother Rob. Rob owed him favours like this.

Perhaps he should have put his sword on?

What if she had gone to meet this man she had been speaking to.

Perhaps she was not even on the road but had arranged an assignation somewhere in the grounds of his brother's property?

Harry breathed out. His heart might be racing but his breath was steady. When he fought, he needed the strength that air gave his muscles and his mind. He'd learned to maintain the pace of his breaths.

He continued riding at a canter. Charlie would not have had time to get much further. He must catch up with her soon.

The Pheasant Inn came into view.

Suspicion and hope snarled up. It was a coaching inn. She might be there and, even if she was not, someone may have seen her on the road.

He pulled the stallion into a trot and held it firm. They had given him the liveliest horse, as he'd asked.

But he had not asked for a lively woman. He had not asked for any woman – but he'd gained a lively wife; the wife he deserved for his former sins.

He stopped before the inn, swung a leg over the animal's rump and dropped to the ground, then walked the animal under the arch into the yard. A coach stood in the centre. A coach for paying passengers.

He breathed out steadily as he looked for a groom. A young lad caught his eye and came forward. 'Hold my horse for a moment.'

Harry walked towards the carriage, not wanting to believe and yet … He clasped the coach's door handle, turned it and opened the door.

She was there, sitting in the far corner clutching a cloth parcel. Her rolled-up cloak. He presumed it contained his pistol and his purse, if nothing else.

What was this? Why was she here? What had it do with the man she had spoken to? Was she making a bloody fool of him?

'Get out.' His voice was bitter and accusing. 'Get out!' he shouted when she did not move.

But this seemed so unlike Charlie? Yet what did he really know of her?

She was like a deer, sitting in her corner, frozen, as though if she did not move he could not see her. The deer was always seen by the human eye, there was no hiding. The instinct simply made the animal, or a human, an easier target for a shot.

He knew hardly anything of her. He had known nothing of her history until the day before they had married and it could have all been a damned lie.

'Out!' he growled at her, reaching in and clasping her arm. 'Come on. Come out. What the hell do you think you are doing?'

'Sir …' A man in the uniform of the coach company approached. 'Please unhand that woman.'

'This is my wife. I will handle her as I wish,' he snarled at the man, then looked at Charlie 'and she is coming home with me to explain just why she felt the need to run away.'

There was one thing he did know for certain; that Hillier had hit her and thrown her out of his house. But why, then, had she chosen to steal from the family of the man who had helped her, instead of asking him for help!

Because she was desperate. The answer whispered at the back of his head. The state of their room had spoken of that. But he was damned well desperate now. Desperate to understand –

Charlie stumbled as Harry started walking, pulling her along beside him. There was a crowd gathering about them, a crowd that might become a mob if Charlie uttered one word of complaint. She did not speak, but her skin burned a vivid red.

Damn her. How could she have done this?

He'd been telling his father and John that they were wrong, and she had done this. How was he supposed to help her when she had done this?

He picked her up by the waist and put her up on to his saddle on her stomach as she still hugged her precious parcel of stolen things. She deserved to be taken home like that, but he was not a cruel man like Hillier. 'Grip the saddle, lift your skirt and slide your leg to the far side.' She did so, struggling to balance as she held her rolled-up cloak.

He gritted his teeth and set his foot into the stirrup, then pulled himself up and sat behind her, with his hips up against her bottom. Now he must ride home in this frustrating position when he was angrier at her than he had ever been at anyone.

'Good day, all.' He touched his fingers to his forehead in a mock salute to their audience.

His brother was going to kill him for this. There would be a rumour flying about John's estate within hours. His violent younger brother had returned from war to treat his wife so brutally she had run away.

He did not speak as his hips rocked forward against her bottom, in a rhythm that had a sexual undertone, but it was only to tell the horse to walk. The horse walked out of the courtyard and into the road. Then Harry lifted into the rise and fall that told the animal to trot. Charlie was hanging on to the stallion's mane. He still did not speak because he was too angry to say a word. Why? The word was spinning, shouting and yelling a charge in his head. But if he spoke it now he would scream the question at her like the army officer he was.

His calves gripped the horse as he lifted his body and pushed his weight down into his heels, telling the stallion to canter.

Charlie bounced about on the saddle, indecorously, but she was safe enough, his arms were about her and his body behind her. She did not try to speak either. If she had done he would have told her to be quiet anyway.

When he reached John's he did not ride before the house but rode the horse and Charlie towards the stables. But for goodness sake he had to speak to her at some point and if he lost his control and shouted at her in the house John would hear of it from his servants and he did not want John to think badly of her. He had desperately wanted his family to learn to like her – and then she had done this!

Damn.

He turned the horse off the drive.

Charlie tried to twist and look back, but the horse's movement was bouncing her about too much.

He drew the horse to a halt in the area beside the stables, but with enough distance that they would not be heard and in a position where they might not be seen from any windows in the house or the stable block.

He wrapped an arm about her waist. 'Move your leg across.' She pulled her skirt and petticoats up out of the way, her rolled cloak clutched to her chest in her other hand. Then lifted her leg over.

He continued holding her waist and half-lowered her to the ground before letting her drop. 'Do not run,' he ordered.

She stood looking up at him, her cloak – his pistol and purse – and perhaps Katherine's jewellery – now clasped tight against her chest with both hands.

He swung his leg over, then dropped to the ground.

The anger in his chest was a volcano waiting to explode. He did not understand. If she took a step wrong it would erupt at her with fire, flames and rivers of molten lava. He walked the stallion to one of the carefully positioned to look informal trees, and tied the reins to a branch, fighting the temper inside him.

What was he to do about this?

He'd lost his regiment – lost his position – he might have been angry at his father and John but he had no wish to lose his family too. He could not stand to be put in a position where there was a need to decide permanently between her and them. Half of him did not care for whatever reason she would give him. No reason felt that it would be good enough. Why had she not come to him if she was in trouble, instead of running? He had helped her, believed in her and … Another word hovered at the back of his mind like a wasp waiting to sting. Love. He had fallen in love with her, and she had done this!

Why?

Because she had lied and he had been used … The words were there as doubt inside him. Because she had run and raised them. But they simply did not fit with the woman he'd come to know. Then why?

She was watching him.

'Why did you leave?'

She did not speak. It was a wrong step. His volcano spewed out its lava. 'How dare you? You have made me look a fool! I was defending you before my father! Who was the man you spoke to?' Each sentence was shouted at her as he took step after step towards her, until he was a foot in front of her, glaring at her. 'Did you steal Katherine's jewellery to give it to that man? If you needed money for some reason, why instead did you not come and tell me?'

Her back had stiffened and her chin was high in the posture he imagined would have been her armour on the day she had gone back to Hillier at the age of only fifteen.

The thought shook the anger from him as if someone had grabbed at his shoulders. Damn it. He saw the image of her the night she had come to him for help. 'Please, tell me who the man was, Charlie? And why, instead of waiting to speak with me you took my pistol, my money and Katherine's jewellery and ran away?'

She breathed out, but did not relax her posture at all. 'It was my brother.'

'I heard he said he was your brother ...' Perhaps his tone implied disbelief, but how could he just trust her now? She had made herself un-trustworthy.

'He was my brother.'

'And he asked you for something. Money?'

She shook her head, but her blush told him she was lying. 'Charlie. He asked you for something and you cannot have been happy because you were seen slapping him and he was seen detaining you ... I am not a fool. Do not treat me as one. Tell me the truth.'

Her eyes stared at him, in an odd way. It was not challenge in her eyes, but – 'He asked me to go back.'

'Go back where?' No. Even as he spoke, he heard the answer in his head. Hillier's. Why?

'To Mark.'

'Why would he ask that of you? Was it not your brother?' He did not understand.

'It was my brother; I told you.'

The words stunned him. Her brother was a cold-hearted bastard. It had been one thing not to do enough before, when they had both been young. But now ... To ask her to go back. Why?

He cupped her elbow in a gesture that must tell her how much he cared, no matter that he'd shouted.

Why had she not waited to speak to him? Did she not trust him? He had done nothing to deserve a lack of trust from her.

She had gone to him in Brighton and he had helped her. Yet now there had been another option, the jewellery she could sell ... He'd thought she cared for him too, though. But they'd never spoken of feelings. They both had hearts encrusted in stone, hearts that needed to be protected and hidden from the truth, talk of feelings had not been wise. 'Why? Charlie, I do not understand.'

'Mark is going to throw them out of the house: my mother, sister, Rodney, his wife and his child or ...' her voice softened and she no longer looked into his eyes but to the right of him.

'Or ...'

Her gaze came back to his. 'He wants my twelve-year-old sister to take my place.'

'God!' The anger charged into his blood again. 'Why did you not wait to tell me? Did you think I would not help?'

'How can you help me? I want to give him the five hundred pounds. I want to pay him to leave me and Ginny alone.' The defiance that had been in her body now resounded in her voice.

'And you took my pistol.'

'Because if he does not agree and he tries to make me stay, then I will shoot him.' Tears caught the light and sparkled in her eyes.

His hand lifted and braced her cheek. 'You should have waited until I came home. You should trust me.'

'I wanted to ask Katherine. I thought a duchess ... she must undertake charitable acts ... but I did not know how to begin—'

'Then you saw her jewellery and so you took it.'

'I did not plan to.'

'I'm sure.'

'I need to give him money.'

'That is not the only answer. Let me deal with it.'

'But what about my sister?'

'I will manage it. But for today let me take you back to the house. You are upset and it is late. Tomorrow I will travel to Brighton.'

171

'I need to help Ginny, it cannot wait. I need to go. She will not know you.'

'You are overwrought and anxious. I told you, I will travel tomorrow. But today let me take care of you. Tomorrow will be soon enough. I promise. Hillier must know your brother has come to you and is trying to raise the money. I will go to Brighton and stop him from hurting your sister.' He held one of her hands.

Her large eyes stared at him.

'Charlie, promise me you will leave this to me.'

She nodded slightly. Her fingers still clutching her cloak.

'I will walk you back.' He untied the horse and then walked both Charlie and the horse back to the stables. Ash was there, not within a stable but in the courtyard. She ran towards them, barking with excitement.

Curse what John thought about a dog in his house. Ash was a part of Harry's family.

A groom took the stallion. Harry tapped his thigh, telling Ash to come to heel.

In the hall he told one of the maids to have laudanum, tea and sandwiches taken up to his room. Charlie could not have eaten since breakfast.

When they reached the room, he took Charlie's precious bundle of stolen items from her and put it aside, then made her sit in a chair. Ash sat beside her.

Harry sat on the bed. 'We are even. I do not like your brother as you do not like John. He had no right to come here and tell you that. It was cruel.'

'But if he had not come, I would not know that Ginny is in danger.'

'But he should have resolved it without coming to you.' Her brother was her sister's guardian. No man he knew would even contemplate letting his sister be taken in such a circumstance. They would do whatever it took. But then every man he knew had the financial resources to fight with. But she had said her brother was a blacksmith now, hadn't she? He was not without the ability to simply move to another village.

A knock struck the door. Harry rose. He took the tray from the maid, then set the tray on the bed and removed the plate of dainty sandwiches. 'Here. Eat. You must be hungry. I'll pour you tea too. But after you have eaten you are to take the laudanum and sleep.' Perhaps he was being too directive and yet there was a need screaming in him to keep her safe. God, so much had become tangled up in his mind today – past and present. Peace and war. Death and life. He felt quite sick.

He watched her eat and drink as he ate a little himself. Her hands trembled the entire time.

He believed that had she reached Brighton with his pistol in her possession and worked out how to use it, she would very likely have shot at Hillier. He doubted Hillier would have let her walk away again. Then she would have been hung.

For seven years, though, she had lain in a bed with Hillier, shutting off the hatred and hurt from her heart.

He did not want her anywhere near Hillier's. He wanted her safe here and that man out of her mind. That was what she needed. Tomorrow, when he had had chance to right things with his family he would feel happier leaving her here in their care. But today he only wanted to give her some escape.

He helped her undress down to her chemise and drawers and then gave her the dose of laudanum to drink.

'I don't want it, Harry.'

'Take it. It will calm your nerves and help you settle, that is all.' God, there had been times in the Crimea when his men had needed such a potion of comfort, but there had been no medicines to ease their misery. He could ease Charlie's pain with the drug.

She drank from the small bottle, then set it down on the cabinet beside the bed and lay down. Her eyes looked at him as he sat in a chair watching her.

'I will stay until you fall asleep, but when you wake, if I am

173

not here, do not worry. I am going downstairs to plan my journey to Brighton. Trust me, remember I have made a promise and I will keep it.'

She bit her lip, giving him no verbal response, as she continued to look at him.

What was in her mind?

He'd given her the laudanum because there must be images in her head. Like war, there would be flashes of memory, visual and sensory recall. He knew they were there in her head because the state of this room had expressed panic and those memories had made her take his pistol.

Her head rested on the pillow as they looked at one another for a long while, without talking.

He ought to ask what was in her thoughts. He had told her once that she could talk to him about her past and yet today he was a coward. He did not really want to see the things she would remember any more than she would want to see his memories.

Her eyelids looked heavier as they closed and opened and then they finally closed as the laudanum took effect.

'I wish you would go now,' she whispered before she fell asleep.

Harry waited for a moment, so that he would not disturb her. But then he rose, walked across the room to her makeshift parcel and unwrapped it. Everything he'd expected to see wrapped up in her cloak was there. He breathed out. Then looked at his sword. He walked over and picked it up. He wanted to trust her and yet he knew how confused a mind could become when it was in the grasp of traumatic memory.

He left the room with his sword, pistol, purse and Katherine's jewellery.

Chapter 12

As Harry walked down the stairs, Katherine's jewellery was clasped in his left hand and the scabbard containing his sword was gripped in his right, while the barrel of his pistol was down the back of his trousers and his purse weighted down his coat pocket.

Lord. He'd never imagined that he would feel so ashamed before John, but there was nothing to do other than accept and face this. Yet the pain in his heart at the thought that Charlie would choose theft over trusting him, and that John would know it … It embarrassed him. This was his fault. Some error he had made in his dealings with Charlie. What?

What had he done wrong?

A confused feeling of guilt was setting his mind into a downward, uncontrollable spin into darkness. Into a darkness where the battlefield of ghostly cannon and rifle fire awaited him.

He breathed slowly, pushing away the sounds and emotions.

It was the time of day when everyone dressed for dinner. He hoped John and Katherine would be in their room, alone, so that he might manage this privately.

He lifted the sword and tapped on the door with its hilt.

The door opened.

'John.'

John held the door wide, but stood in a way that barred the entrance. But his rooms were probably the only space John had in which he need not be a duke, just a man. Harry would have set up a barrier too.

'Harry.' John stood in his evening shirt and trousers, with his neckcloth hanging loose, as though he had been just about to tie it.

'Here.' Harry held out the jewels, opening his palm.

'God.' John stepped back and let go of the door, not taking the jewels but, by his movement, encouraging Harry to go in.

Harry did so. John shut the door behind him.

There were no servants in the sitting room. John took the muddled jewellery from Harry's hand. 'She had them, then,' he stated the obvious as he put them on a table. When John turned he met Harry's gaze and asked, 'Why?' But without accusation.

'She believed she might pay for her freedom with them.'

'Her freedom ...'

'Hillier does not want to let her go. Her brother called here to beg her to go back. Hillier has threatened her family as his threats towards me did not work.'

'Good God.' John had paled again in that odd reaction he had to Charlie.

'Stop judging her, John. This was not her fault. He tricked her into sharing his bed when she was fourteen. It was rape. But then she was rejected by her entire village and her family were starved to the point she chose to go to him, the man who had assaulted her, so that her little sister would be fed and her mother and brother happy. She spent seven years with him. Please be kind to her.'

'Of course we will be kind to her.' Harry looked across to see that Kathrine had come out of the bedchamber and was standing at the open door. He had not even considered who might be in there. His mind was failing.

'You should not have heard that.'

176

'She knows more than you do,' John said on a low breath. He had been cryptic from the moment Harry had brought Charlie here, it was becoming annoying.

'What do I not know?' He had experienced the carnage of a battlefield and the casualties of war. He knew about a dark side of life that his pious brother had never journeyed into.

John shook his hand and did not answer, then turned to take the jewellery over to the safe.

This was a sorry, pathetic day.

John opened the safe and put the jewellery inside it.

'Hillier is threatening to throw her family out of their home,' Harry continued. 'He owns the house they live in, or he has threatened to take Charlie's twelve-year-old sister in Charlie's place. Charlie is desperate to end this.'

'Why did she not ask me for help?' Katherine enquired, walking further into the room. She was dressed for dinner.

'She came here to do so, but did not have the courage. Then she saw the jewellery and she was desperate, Katherine. I'm sorry, she just took it.'

'Tell her she need not feel sorry, nor guilty, I understand and she is forgiven.'

Harry nodded.

'And her family may come here. I will find a cottage on one of my estates. They may choose which. But wherever they go I shall make certain that Hillier cannot find them.' John said Hillier's name as though he knew the man. He could not, though. Hillier would not mix in the circles that a duke did. 'She has no need to worry. Tell her that too. Shall I send someone to fetch her family tonight?'

Lord. Harry walked forward with a sudden surge of emotion, lifted his arms and wrapped them about John, his sword pressing against John's back. Harry had been trained for battle, he had survived battle, he had not been trained to manage this. 'Thank you.'

John held him too. 'You are not alone, little brother. You must never think you are.'

He had felt that it was so when he had joined his family last time. But no, even with all the nasty words of guilt in his head and all the memories his moralistic family would abhor, he knew he was not alone. Different from them now. But never alone.

John let him go and his hand slipped across Harry's back, touching the handle of his pistol, which protruded from the waistband of his trousers beneath his coat. 'You are well armed. Did you expect to be accosted on your way downstairs with Katherine's jewellery.'

Harry smirked at John's humour. 'Charlie had taken my pistol with her and in her current state of mind I do not trust her within reach of a weapon.' Harry breathed in, 'and nor do I trust myself. I want to ride to Brighton now and kill the man.'

'I wish that we could do it,' John answered.

'What?'

'I said I would gladly join you in the exploit, but I do not fancy hanging within the year and nor do I want to lose my brother. Give me your weapons.' John held out a hand.

Harry laid the scabbard containing his sword on to John's palm. Then John held out his other hand as Harry lifted the pistol out of the back of his trousers. He handed it over and breathed out. 'Will you keep my purse in your rooms too? I do not trust her with money either. She might decide to make another run for Brighton.' Because nor does she trust me.

'Where is Charlie now?' Katherine asked.

'Asleep in our room. I gave her laudanum. She should sleep for a few hours.'

'Do you wish me to go and sit with her?'

He shook his head. He had no idea how Charlie might react to others if she woke. 'She would probably rather not face you now. But I am going to go to Brighton tomorrow and see if I can stop Hillier without shooting him or slicing my sword through him.

Please do not let her into your room so she is not tempted again, and tell the others the same, Kate, and watch over her for me.'

'I will come with you,' John stated.

'No. I would rather go alone. You may help, as you said, send people to fetch her family and bring them here. Thank you.'

'Where do they live?'

Damn. 'I do not know. So it will have to wait until the morning when she wakes and can tell me the address.'

'We should go down to dinner,' Katherine said. 'Everyone will be waiting.'

'You will have to excuse me. I am not in the mood to give people fake smiles and talk polite nonsense to pretend all is well.'

Katherine came forward and touched Harry's arm in a gesture of sympathy and understanding. 'I will make up some reason why you are not there. You are only two days' married, you have a good excuse to want to be with your wife.'

Except that he could not stomach being with his wife at this moment.

'Do not worry,' John added.

He bowed his head at Katherine and then to John, in the way he had of dealing with his brother that was far more usual than an embrace. 'Thank you. I will speak to you before I leave tomorrow and tell you where her family live.'

John nodded.

Harry turned away and let himself out of the room as the two of them returned to their dressing room.

He ignored the opportunity to return to the bedchamber and walked downstairs. The laudanum would have knocked Charlie out. She would not know if he was there or not.

The footman who stood in the hall looked up. Harry did not meet his gaze, he ignored him as he walked on down the last few steps. Then ignored the noise of conversation coming from the drawing room and instead turned to the library. He knew where John kept his cigars and decanters.

He let himself into the library and shut the door on the footman. A full-length portrait of Katherine looked down on him from the far wall as he walked across the room. He had always deemed John self-righteous, yet his brother had a good heart – and a good wife – which probably revealed more of the truth about John than anything that came from his mouth.

Harry lit a cigar, selected a bulbous glass, then he picked up the decanter of brandy by its neck and carried it and the glass back out of the room. The easiest way into the garden was via the drawing room, but that was currently full of the people he wanted to avoid and so he went to the front door and stopped, waiting for the footman to open it.

The man came forward and did so.

'Thank you. But please do not tell anyone where I am.'

The man nodded.

Harry walked out.

The problem with John's grounds was that they were too open. People could see you from the windows easily, with everything being meadow.

He walked towards the lake. Hopefully his family were all too busy talking in the drawing room and they would not see him walking away.

He lifted the cigar to his lips and sucked in the smoke, thinking about Charlie sharing cigars with him. There was an issue, a problem with this. The woman had done it. She had smashed the stone from about his heart and now she was within it.

It was as though she had come into his life to make him learn everything he had refused to accept from anyone else. He cared beyond any perception he had held of that emotion. Love … It was clawing at him and tearing him apart and she appeared to be such a strong woman – when she was not strong at all. The woman who had boldly watched him in Brighton and smoked cigars and laughed over a glass of whiskey was a ruse. Inside, he knew, she was still that hurt fourteen-year-old girl, a girl he did not know how to help and who did not trust him.

The only experience he had to apply to this was what he had learned from the men he had been in charge of. Lessons learned from the things he had done wrong. Mostly, day after day he had held his sword high and called for them to race to their potential deaths, not saved them. But once he had tried to save a man. He had failed.

He did not want to fail Charlie. He had to help her mind heal.

When he was quite a few yards away from the house, he stopped just beyond the brow of the hill and sat down, he hoped in a position where no one on the ground floor of the house might be able to spot him. Yet if Charlie looked out of their bedroom window she would be able to see him.

With his cigar hanging from his lips, he poured a glass of the brandy, then set the decanter down in the grass and with his free hand unbuttoned his coat. His elbows rested on his bent knees.

His family was a myriad of love matches, he ought to have been prepared. He ought to understand, yet he had never realised how much pain came with love, love had made him stand in Charlie's shoes and look through her eyes and he had seen a different way of life that he'd chosen to ignore before. That world … That world appalled him. He wanted to right every wrong that had been done to her. To take his revenge on Hillier, her brother, her mother – the whole damn village full of people who had hurt and forced her into a foul choice.

He shut his eyes as his mind cried 'charge' and the thunder of the horses' hooves and battle cries roared about him as cannon fire boomed through the air.

His free hand lifted, he saw blood on it, blood from the past, but ignored that and let his hand comb through his hair. It was a gesture that implied his inability to do what he wanted. That was what was hurting, that he would, for the rest of his life, have to know what he knew and do nothing. Thank God he would be in India.

He sucked on the cigar and thought of Charlie and drank and

watched the sun set. Trying not to think of Charlie with Hillier. Trying not to remember the war. Perhaps he should have dosed himself with laudanum rather than her? Whose demons was he fighting?

'Harry! What are you doing out here?'

Damn. The sun was only peeking over the horizon, drawing a line of orange across the lake. He turned and rose, serenaded by the chorus of the evening's crescendo of bird song. He must have been out here for a couple of hours or more, entirely lost in thoughts of the past and the future.

Three people walked towards him from the direction of the drawing room and he could see that the French doors were open. He must not have been as out of sight as he'd hoped and yet his scarlet coat was probably a beacon in the sunset.

It was Rob, Drew and Henry who came towards him. 'What are you doing?' Rob repeated.

'Drinking,' Harry stated in a slurred pitch.

'We were told you and Charlie had hidden away,' Rob said, as they came closer.

'So what the hell are you doing out here alone?' Henry added.

'Sulking,' Harry answered, then laughed at himself. It was a sorry sound.

Rob frowned. 'Have you two argued?'

'Not as you might think.' He lifted his glass. 'If you had brought glasses you could have joined me.'

'You are drunk,' Drew laughed.

'Sometimes in life it is better to be drunk than sober. Liquor silences the world.'

'Well, I will join you in silencing it. I am not averse to drinking from a decanter.' Henry walked past Harry and leant down to pick the decanter up.

Harry smiled and shook his head. He and Henry had spent years together getting drunk regularly – and bedding whores too – but those were the sort of memories he was drinking into silence.

'Shall we sit with you?' Drew proposed.

'As you desire.'

Rob slung an arm about Harry's shoulders, turning him back to face the lake. 'What is distressing you? You must talk about it. I owe you a debt for the times you have listened to me, so you must let me return the favour and pour out what is troubling you.'

'Sit and talk to us,' Drew said.

This was what his family did. When someone needed aid, they rallied. He would not be surprised if John had been the one who'd spotted Harry and sent the others outside with some carefully posed hint.

The four of them sat then, in the long grass, the scent of clover rising on the cooling night air around them as the sun disappeared beyond the far bank of the lake. There was a bright moon; they could see easily.

'Is it the war?' Rob asked in a quiet voice. 'You have been different since you returned.'

He'd known that it had been noticed. Lord. 'I wish it was only that.' Which was a terrible thought. The memories pierced his head even as he said it and yet there was a vision of Charlie with the scarlet bruise about her eye too.

'If not that, what is it, then?' Drew asked as he accepted the decanter from Henry. He drank from it.

'Where is Charlie?' Henry asked before Harry could answer.

'Sleeping.' Harry finished the brandy in his glass, then held his glass out to Drew so he could refill it. Rob did not accept the decanter when Drew offered it. He passed it back to Henry.

'Does anyone wish for a cigar?' Drew offered. 'I had the foresight to bring some out.'

Harry smiled. 'Thank you. Is this the cavalry charge coming in to save me?'

'Do you need saving?' Drew asked, as he pulled the cigars out of his pocket.

Harry looked at Drew and caught Henry's and Rob's gaze too. 'Yes.' It was strange to admit it. He had always been the one boosting their spirits in the past.

'To begin with, tell us why you are not upstairs with Charlie?' Rob said in his honest way that cut through everything anyone else would hide with subterfuge.

'Because I do not feel able to face her.'

'Why?'

He looked at them all. He and Rob had always been different and yet always friends and he had once stood beside Rob when Rob had shot a man to protect Caro. Then there was Henry. Henry had been his closest friend and confidant for years, and Drew, Drew was his older brother as much as John or Rob, just not by blood. 'She left another man to come to me.'

'The instigator of her black eye ...' Drew stated, before taking another swig of the brandy.

'Yes.'

'And ...' Rob pressed.

Harry focused on Rob. 'He wants her back.' Rob would know what that meant. That was why he'd shot a man for Caro's sake.

'What are you going to do?' Rob asked.

'That is what has led me away from her and left me sitting out here. I know what I want to do. I want to kill the man, but that is not an option. I would be standing before a firing squad if I did that. So instead I must find a way to talk sense into him.'

'And you think he will listen,' Drew said. 'He cannot have done so, so far, if he is threatening her.'

'Then there is only one answer. We face him together,' Henry declared.

Harry actually laughed. 'You would have us track the man down like a posse, shouting 'hang him high'. Like a witch hunt ...'

Henry and Drew laughed.

184

'And drag him out of his house and parade him down the street as a villain,' Rob added.

Drew handed Harry a lit cigar.

Harry wrapped an arm around Rob's shoulders. 'I am gratified by your outrage. But this is not your problem and you are now a politician with a reputation to uphold, you cannot drag the man out of his house.' He chuckled. The liquor and his friends were working their charms. 'But you may drink with me and help me drown my sorrows out of sight from anyone who cares about your upstanding nature.' Harry reached over and grasped the decanter from Drew's hand then held it up before Rob.

Rob smiled and took it. 'For the sake of the brother whom I love.' He drank from the decanter.

Love. The word lanced Harry, twisting in through the cracks Charlie had allowed to form, making a way into his heart. He had loved his family carelessly, without thought, when he was young. Now love seemed to hold a heavy price. It hurt. It was not thoughtless or careless, it absorbed everything.

'I may, and will, ride there with you.' Henry stated. 'No matter what we do when we arrive. Even if it is to simply tell him he is a reprehensible man.'

Laughter erupted from Harry's throat, as he imagined them standing before Hillier, side by side, and waving fingers of aggression to tell him what a bad man he was. It was the sort of tomfoolery they would have got up to when they were young.

'And I will travel with you,' Drew added.

Harry recalled the anger that had erupted from his throat at Charlie. He should not have railed at her this afternoon. This was not her fault. She had simply been as bewildered for an answer as he was.

Harry sighed out a breath. He was too drunk now to plan for the morning at all, but he would not deny himself the company on his journey to Brighton.

John had offered too, but like Rob, John could not become involved in anything sordid and yet the power of a duke ... what might that do to bind Hillier in some sort of chains? He must consider that when he was sober.

Chapter 13

Charlie rose. Her mind was spinning from the laudanum and it made the room sway as she stood. She had dreamt of the day she'd accepted a ride in Mark's carriage. She had dreamt of the parlour in his house and the cake and the kiss and his hands touching her and every painful thing that came next. She could not allow her sister to suffer it.

She laced her corset before her and tried to turn it and tighten it, but it could not be done. She rang for a maid. A man came first. But she sent him away to fetch someone to help her dress.

She had to go to Brighton.

She could not let it happen to Ginny.

Years ago she had sacrificed everything so that Ginny could be happy.

Her gaze turned to the window as she tried to guess what hour it was. Her limbs felt heavy with laudanum as she walked over and looked out. She had not drunk the full dose in the bottle, but even so the drug had dulled her mind. She needed to think. The sun was already setting, it barely showed above the horizon.

When she looked down she saw Harry. He was sitting on the grass, surrounded by three of the men in his family. He should have gone. Instead he was sitting there drinking.

He had promised tomorrow, but tomorrow might be too late and if she told him that she was going he would make her wait. She could not wait.

A knock struck the door.

The muscles in Charlie's body jumped.

'Mrs Marlow ...'

It was the maid.

'Come in,' Charlie called. 'Please help me dress quickly,' she said as the woman came into the room. 'I want to go downstairs and join my husband.'

Her heart beat with the same sickening pace as it had done the day she had walked from her home to the Hilliers' house, to offer herself in exchange for charity to be given to her family.

This time, when she left the house she had nothing bar the clothes she wore and again she left unseen through the front door as the servants were all engaged in clearing up after the family's meal, or serving them in the drawing room. She did not walk along the drive, though. When she had told a woman at the inn this afternoon that she had come from the Duke's estate, she had been told of a quicker way across the park to reach the village, her marker to finding her way was a tall folly.

She looked for it on the horizon and saw it in the distance, peeping above a copse that was crowned with moonlight. She ran towards it, the skirt of her dress clasped in one hand. She hoped the ticket to Brighton that she had bought this morning would be honoured.

~

Harry rose with the sun, in the way of a soldier on campaign.

He had slept in his clothing, as he would have done on campaign, too, on a sofa in the library so that he would not disturb Charlie.

The clock across the room chimed five times as he stood. His mind was heavy from the remnants of liquor. He ran a hand over his eyes, stretched and then decided to go upstairs and check on Charlie. He did not go into the bedroom, though. Instead he decided to freshen up first, it was still very early. He opened the door of the washing and dressing room that was beside their bedchamber and went directly in there.

He pushed his braces off so that they hung down from his waist, then stripped off his shirt and made use of the jug of water and the bowl on the washstand to freshen himself and shave. Then he pulled a clean shirt over his head and tied a neckcloth about the collar. After he'd slid his braces back on he picked up his coat. The man in the mirror looked more like a soldier as he slotted the brass buttons into their holes. He leant then and opened the connecting door. Ash came through it before it was very wide, but there was no sound beyond her movement. He shut the door again without looking inside. If Charlie was still asleep, he ought to leave her. He would go for a ride and take Ash out for an hour or so. Then he would wake her.

When Harry walked into the courtyard, he faced a place full of activity. The grooms and stable lads were putting out the feed for the horses.

'Shall I fetch your horse, sir?'

'No need. I will fetch her myself.' He walked past the man who had offered to help, to the stall Obsidian stood in. Obsidian had heard his voice and looked out. 'Hello girl.' He patted her neck as he opened the stall. When Obsidian's head turned, he kissed the animal's muzzle. Truthfully, if he had a first love, it was Obsidian. She had brought him through a war and yet it was Charlie who had made him understand love as no one else had.

Harry put on Obsidian's bridle and then her saddle. Then led her out.

A groom came forward and held Obsidian's reins as Harry mounted, not that he had need of the help. He thanked the man with a lift of his hand as the man tilted his cap, then Harry walked the horse out of the stables and broke the animal into a gallop.

When Harry returned to the house it was two hours later. The ride had been stimulating and his blood was racing. He was ready to go to Brighton. He just needed Charlie to tell him her family's address and then he would go.

Ash ran ahead across the lawn, as exhilarated by their exercise as Harry as they walked from the stables around the back of the house towards the drawing room.

Ash had saved him from madness when he'd returned from the Crimea, another moment when his family had rallied and found the solution for him. But he would not take Ash to India. He would leave the dog with Drew and with Iris, who had named her. He would not subject a dog to weeks on a ship. Yet Obsidian … He wanted to take her.

All these thoughts tried to smother other thoughts as the ride had done. But regardless, all he could see in his mind was Charlie's face as she slept, while all he could think about was what had happened when she'd been so young – and it had affected her so badly she would steal a fortune from the family of the man she had run to for protection.

By the time he reached the house the stimulation that had been in his blood after the ride had stagnated. His mind was muddled and twisted. When a soldier's mind needed order.

Now perhaps he saw what his family had seen in him when they had given him Ash. When someone was hurt in the flesh … Damn. He thought of men who had been hurt in the flesh. There should have been treatments that saved them. But when someone was hurt in the mind, there were no treatments. The only answer was strength to fight and battle through.

He walked up the steps on to the terrace. Then remembered that his family might be about the house now.

He hesitated. Ash sat.

But Charlie was in there, and she might be awake too.

Love held his heart in a fist.

As he walked towards the French doors his hand lifted, in anger and frustration. He wanted to hurt the man who had hurt her. He punched out and his fist hit the wall. The strike shot a sharp pain up his arm and ripped the flesh off his knuckles.

He shook his hand out as his left hand turned the handle. Glad that he had the pain to distract his thoughts now.

'Harry, why on earth did you do that?' His mother pulled the door open, then stepped back to let him and Ash in. She had been in the drawing room alone. The writing desk was open and there was paper there and a quill in the ink bottle. She must have been writing a letter.

She held the hand he'd wounded in a careful way that braced his palm but avoided his knuckles and drew him across the room to a chair. 'Sit,' she ordered.

Ash did so, as though his mother had ordered her. Harry laughed with a dry, hollow sound. He did sit, though.

'Why would you do something so silly? Look at your hand.'

He saw it and felt it, but it was only grazed skin, he'd not broken any bones – he'd not been raped, violated and assaulted for years. He had not lost a limb and lain in agony for days as his flesh had rotted.

'Do not move,' she told him, then turned away.

He did not move. He was too distressed and confused to move.

She returned with a decanter and a glass, put them down on a low table beside the chair he sat in, then took a handkerchief out of her pocket. She put that beside the liquor as his hand started dripping blood on to John's carpet.

She moved a chair then so she could sit opposite him. 'Let me see.'

He held out his hand. She gripped it and looked at the scuffed and torn skin. 'What is this about, Harry?' She reached over for the liquor and held the glass beneath his hand, then tipped the liquid over it.

He tilted his stinging hand so that the liquor ran into the glass, now tainted with blood. 'I thought you were going to pour me a glass for my nerves.'

She looked up and shook her head, her pale-blue eyes saying that she had not found him amusing and she was still angry with him for injuring himself.

The open wound stung like hell when she set down the glass. She poured liquor into the handkerchief and dabbed at the grazes to clean the grit from the wall out of the shallow graze.

'Now, tell me, why would you do such a silly thing? I have been worried since you arrived at the house with a wife sporting a blackened eye, when there had been no word to anyone that you were courting a particular woman.'

'Are you very angry with me for not inviting you to the wedding?'

She looked up from her task. 'Of course, you are my son.'

He smiled. 'I am sorry. I wished you there, but there was a reason for our haste—'

'I have guessed that as I said I have noticed Charlie's eye, but that has only made me worry more about the reason for both.'

'I do love you, Mama.' He was unsure why he spoke the words, but they were in his head and in weeks he would sail away and perhaps never see her again.

'I know, Harry. I love you too, even if you were always my most difficult child.'

A sound that was more like a real laugh escaped his throat.

'But now you may stop avoiding my question. Tell me the reason for this sudden outburst of temper that would cause you to hurt yourself?'

Because I cannot hurt the man who deserves it. 'It is Charlie.' His heart, which had been hard but was now entirely soft, aching flesh, wanted desperately to tell his mother everything. 'Papa has always said that if you knew the way I lived my life, you would never forgive me.'

She looked up from her task, her eyes asking why, with a concerned expression.

He wanted to be forgiven. 'I have always used whores.'

His mother's breath caught on the word, with a sharp intake – his father had been right, she was horrified.

'I know it was wrong now.' Harry rushed on. He did not want her to think badly of him, but he had a desire to be honest. 'I realise that women who are paid have probably not had a choice ...' He breathed in, steeling himself. Her gaze moved from his eyes to the expression on his face, and back, as though she sought to judge the truth of his statement and emotion. 'I have learnt that from Charlie,' he said as he breathed out.

'From Charlie ...' Confusion gathered in her voice and her hold on his hand tightened as the handkerchief stopped dabbing at his wound.

'Yes. She was kept by a man.'

'Oh, Harry.' She let go of his hand and sat back in her seat. 'What have you done?'

'Fallen in love.' Yes. That was the truth. He'd been intrigued and charmed and ... 'She approached me. I did not take her from the man in that way. She—'

'I am not angry that you have rescued her. Why would I be angry over that? Oh the poor woman.'

Rescued, it was an odd choice of word, but, yes, he supposed that was what had happened; Charlie had been saved from any more abuse, humiliation and disgrace and the fear of that befalling her sister had led her to steal money, jewellery and his pistol. 'She is still hurting.' She must have felt rescued when they'd left Brighton.

His mother straightened and her body stiffened in a very similar way to the look of defence that Charlie had sometimes.

'I need to help her. I may help her practically, but how do I cope with the thoughts for her? She was fourteen when it began, Mama. It is haunting me more than the war now and it must haunt her ...'

His mother was staring at him with eyes that held numerous questions. 'Just love her, Harry. That is what she will need. A man who loves her regardless of her past.'

'The man she was with wants money and he has power over her family. John is taking them in so they will not be reliant on Hillier, but I am going to go back to – Mama.' She had stood suddenly, and in such a rush she knocked over the chair. 'Mama …' Her hand covered her mouth as she dropped the handkerchief, then her other hand pressed against her stomach.

He saw her stomach convulse as her hand pressed more firmly to her mouth. She was going to be ill.

Harry rose. 'Papa!' he shouted as he started walking across the room towards the door into the hall, to fetch help. His father must be downstairs at the breakfast table, surely. 'Papa!' He yelled again as behind him his mother actually vomited on the carpet that he had bled upon. 'Papa!' he yelled more strongly, using the full depth of his voice.

The door opened as Harry reached it, but it was not his father, it was John.

'Fetch Father. Mama is ill.' Harry turned back as John passed the order on to a servant. There was an ornamental bowl on a half-circular table, which stood against one wall in the room. Harry walked over and picked it up, then returned to his mother, who was still being sick.

She had dropped to kneel on the floor. He knelt on one knee beside her. 'Here.' He put the bowl before her and settled a hand on her shoulder. She had always been slender, incredibly beautiful and serene and kind in nature, and he could not ever remember seeing her ill.

John stood over them, hovering, just as Ash now sat before the hearth, staring at the commotion.

'Your father, Your Grace.'

Harry looked back at the servant who'd announced his father. 'Would you take the dog to the stables?' Then he looked at Ash. 'Go.'

The servant walked into the room behind Harry's father. His mother straightened and turned into Harry's chest, but then his father saw her and realised something was wrong and in a moment she was taken away from Harry's arms and held in his father's. He sat on a sofa with her.

She was crying. The tears ran on to her cheeks in rivers.

'What happened?' his father asked of Harry.

Harry stood as the servant walked Ash away with a grip on Ash's collar. 'I was telling her about Charlie and she just suddenly became ill.'

'Telling her about Charlie …' John's eyebrows lifted. It was a question and an accusation.

'Darling, what is it?' His father's hand lay over her hair, pressing her head against his shoulder.

John stared at Harry. 'Did you say the name?' His voice was low, as though he did not want his father or mother to hear.

'What name?'

'The name of the man Charlie was with.'

'Hillier …'

His mother's reaction was instant, her stomach heaved and she covered her mouth. Harry bent and picked up the bowl, then gave it to his father. Then he looked at John.

John shook his head and did not explain, but walked to the door, then said to someone in the hall. 'Have my mother's maid sent to her room, and Lady Marlow will need sweet tea, and probably laudanum and she will want to retire to her bed, I am sure.' He shut the door before coming back to join their sorry gathering. 'Papa.'

Harry's father looked up at John.

'The man whom Harry's Charlie was with was also my father's Lieutenant Colonel.'

'No.' The shock that hit Harry's father was palpable. The air became thick with the strength of his reaction. He paled and went to move, as though he'd rise and ride for Brighton now, but he could not move with Harry's mother on his lap. His eyes widened and his lips parted. 'She has never said the name,' he said to John. 'How can you know?'

'Mama did not tell me, remember? I know the truth from investigators. They gave me the name.'

The grip his father had about his mother's shoulders firmed in a way that implied a level of protection Harry had seen only when the army had ridden through villages and the men had pulled their wives and children closer. 'And you have known who he was all this time and not said a word?'

'There was no point in telling you. We could have done nothing. It was needless torture to know and be able to do nothing.'

'There would have been a way.'

The conversation flew from his brother to his father, and Harry did not understand a word. *Investigators … known who … she had not given a name.* 'What are you talking about?'

'I will take your mother upstairs,' his father said, sliding an arm beneath her legs, as he braced her shoulders, then he stood with her in his arms.

Harry touched her shoulder. 'I am sorry if I upset you.'

She did not even look at him, her head remained pressed into his father's shoulder.

His father sent him a bitter look before turning away.

Harry walked past them, crossing the room to open the door.

Once they'd gone, he shut the door behind them and looked at John. 'What did I do? Why would the thought of Hillier upset her?'

John's lips pursed, as though he did not want to speak.

'Tell me, for God sake!' Harry was utterly confused.

'Hillier did to her what he did to your wife.' John's hands clasped into fists at his side.

'What?' That was impossible.

'After my father died, Hillier took her in and forced her to become his mistress.'

'She is the daughter of a duke …' The idea was preposterous.

'Grandfather had cut her off when she eloped with my father. She had nowhere to go. It was in Brussels. After the battle of Waterloo. Within hours of my father's death Hillier took her to his home.'

There was a similarity. Charlie had been forced into a desperate situation and she had gone to Hillier. But his mother … The thought was still ridiculous.

'It is true, Harry,' John said. 'If you come into the library, I will show you the file. It is locked in a drawer in my desk.'

'The file … Why do you have papers on this?'

'Because for ten years of my life she was missing and no one would tell me why, so I paid a man to find out. No one would speak of it because she was living, as your Charlie was, for those ten years, kept by men against her wishes, with some freedoms but without freedom because she had no other choice. Now do you understand why Papa and I have told you time and again to leave such women alone? And she will hate that you know this. She did not want me to know.'

Harry could not take the story in. Moments ago his mind had been spinning with the knowledge of Charlie … Now his mother … With Hillier … *Rescue*, she had said just now. 'Who rescued her? How did she escape that life, then?' He still did not believe it.

'Your father. Papa met her and fell in love with her. He helped her.'

If this was true, had Hillier known who Harry was? He'd commented on Harry's eyes that night, the night Harry had thought him interested in men.

God.

'I am going to Brighton.' Harry turned away.

'You cannot do anything stupid. I am keeping your weapons.'

Harry looked back over his shoulder. 'I still have my hands.'

'I should come with you, but if I go I will kill him. It is why

I have never visited you in Brighton. I knew he was there.'

When Harry walked out, Henry stood in the hall with Drew and Rob. Harry's drinking partners of last night. But everything had changed since last night.

'Your shouting disturbed our breakfast,' Henry complained mockingly. 'We have come out to see what the commotion is about. Are you ready to go and causing a scene because no one was here to send you off?'

'What is happening?' Rob asked, more seriously. 'We saw Mama. Was she ill?'

'Yes. I am riding for Brighton in half an hour. If you wish to ride with me, Henry, Drew, I would appreciate your company. But Rob, you are not to come.' He had no idea what he was going to do when he got there, only that he had to go and do something to make Hillier pay for what he'd done to two of the women whom Harry loved.

Pain swept through his chest as the knowledge embedded there, his mother as well as Charlie. God.

'We will have the carriage readied and meet you here in the hall in half an hour, then,' Drew stated.

Harry turned away and ran up the stairs, saying no more, closing his lips on the words that longed to exclaim his outrage and the bitter emotion of betrayal. The world had betrayed him. He had thought it clean and honest. Now he had seen war and come home to discover that nothing was what it had appeared to be.

When he walked into the room he shared with Charlie, he expected to see her red hair spread across the pillows. It was not. The bed was creased but empty. He went to the door leading into the small dressing room, but she was not there either.

'Charlie.' He looked to where her bonnet had been. It was no longer there and her cloak was not on the side where he'd left it.

She had gone.

When had she gone?

He walked over to the bed and touched the pillow. It had no

heat left in it. She had not been in the bed for a while. His gaze caught on the bottle of laudanum as it glimmered, reflecting the morning sunlight. He picked it up. There was still some inside. She had not drunk the whole dose – she had deliberately deceived him yesterday. She had always intended to run away again.

A knock struck the door.

He turned around as hope leapt in his chest. Perhaps she had simply dressed and gone down to breakfast.

He walked across the room. But why would she knock and not walk in? 'Mama.'

She was paler than normal and her eyes shone red from the tears she'd cried, and yet – there was that stiff stance that he'd noticed earlier which was so similar to Charlie's posture as she denied judgement.

God. It was true. She had endured what Charlie had.

'May I speak with your wife? May I see Charlie?'

'She is not here and should you not be lying down?'

'I am recovered. I was shocked, that was all. Your father wished me to lie abed with a fogged mind full of laudanum, but the sweet tea that John ordered was a much better remedy. Where is she, Harry?'

'I have no idea.' He stepped back and lifted his hand, as if to show her the empty room. 'Gone, that is all.'

His mother walked in to look. 'Why?'

'That man has threatened her family and her sister. She tried to go back to Brighton yesterday. I have just discovered she is not here; she might have gone again.'

'To him?'

'To protect her sister.'

His mother's eyes were wide. She had memories too and he had thought when he'd returned from the Crimea that he was the only one amongst his family who knew what suffering looked like and he'd felt guilty for indulging in such a richness of life. But she had known that feeling too. And he had not even thought

– she had seen the wounded men after Waterloo.

'We must find her,' she said. 'Have a carriage readied.'

'There is one ready. I was going myself now.'

'Then I will come. I will tell your father and meet you in the hall.'

'The carriage will be full if you travel too. We will need two. Have them ready a second. But I will go ahead. She will have gone to the coaching inn and I want to check what time she left there.'

After his mother had left, he gathered some of his things and threw them into one of his bags, then went downstairs to find John.

Why had Charlie not trusted him? John would have protected her family. But nor had Harry trusted her. He had not accepted her judgement and desire to leave yesterday. His mother had refused laudanum and Charlie had said she did not want it; *he* had insisted she take it because he had thought it right.

Harry's fingers rubbed at the ache in his temple. He had been confused yesterday and not thinking straight. He had been treating Charlie like a man wounded in battle when she was not that.

Sweet tea…

A cutting painful sound that mocked him left his throat.

He should have gone last night when she had asked. And judging by his mother's response, he should have given Charlie sweet tea and promised to take her with him – he could have kept her safe from Hillier. Except he did not want her in the same town as that man.

A servant directed Harry to the library and he was told that the others were awaiting him outside as he handed over his bag to be put on the carriage.

Some of his brothers and sisters and their spouses and his aunt and cousins were still in the dining room taking breakfast. He hoped they did not come out and he assumed that was why the others were outside, to avoid questions over their departure.

'John,' he said when he walked into the library. 'Charlie has gone again.'

John had been sitting behind his desk, looking up at the ceiling. He stood as Harry crossed the room. 'Your wife is a fool.'

'I do not believe she is thinking clearly.' She was now travelling to Brighton without money for food or anywhere to stay.

'I am leaving to Brighton and Mama is coming with me.'

John's expression stiffened as he walked about his desk. A sense of urgency and concern in his stride. 'Hillier takes advantage of women. That is his way. He took advantage of my father's death and offered Mama shelter, then trapped her. He was my father's superior, whom she trusted. If I were you, I would hold my sword to his throat, then let it slide across his skin as he pleaded for mercy.'

'Or your sword. You can fence.'

'That is a thought I have imagined often. But I am not going to hang for him and nor must you.'

'I will be sensible.' Harry turned away.

'May God and justice go with you. Bring your wife back here and her family if they are there. They will be welcome.'

Harry lifted a hand, acknowledging the words as he kept walking.

It was not only Drew and Henry awaiting him outside, but Rob too.

'You are not supposed to come,' Harry said to his brother as he climbed up into the carriage.

'I may enjoy my political career, but my family come first and you were there beside me in my darkest hour.'

Harry smiled at him. 'Mama and Papa are coming too now. They will follow us and Charlie has gone ahead of us.'

All of them looked at him in surprise.

'I presume Charlie has gone on the paid coach from the Pheasant Inn. I am about to find out.' He did not explain further, but looked out of the window as the carriage rolled into motion.

They had married quiet women, although Caro had a past that had made things awkward for Rob in the beginning, but Harry … well … the rebel of the family had found a rebellious wife.

Chapter 14

The skirt of her dress and the layers of her petticoats swirled about Charlie's legs, blown by a strong breeze as she walked along the seafront. The sea roared up on to the shore beside her. It was angry today and the sound of it had drawn her back from the moment she had climbed out of the carriage. It was as though Harry had never existed in her life and yet she could feel his ring on her finger within her glove. He was real. That had happened to her. She had known happiness for hours at a time.

Then what now?

What would she say to Mark? What would she do now?

She had no money to go elsewhere. No money to return to Harry. She had only thought of coming to persuade Mark to leave Ginny alone.

She strode towards his house, the house she had lived in for years and upstairs was the bed she had lain in with him for years.

Ginny would not be forced to do that.

Her heartbeat thundered so loudly when she saw the house; it deafened her as it pulsed in her ears.

There was nothing in the street that spoke of the sin in that house.

Her hand lifted and her white kid-skin-gloved knuckles knocked.

The door opened and the manservant smiled at her.

Cruel. Mark had been cruel to her. 'Where is Colonel Hillier,' she said as she stepped in. Longing for a pistol in her hand. Harry had probably thought she had not known how to fire it. But she knew. Mark had taught her once when she had been watching him clean his weapon.

'He is in the parlour, Miss. And not to be disturbed. He is with a young woman.'

A young woman … And the whole house had known what that meant and she had hidden in her parlour and let some other poor girl endure what she had sacrificed herself to. Glad that for one night it was not her.

Not any more! No. She would not look away any more.

She turned towards the parlour. The servant moved in front of her. 'Get out of my way.'

'No, Miss. You do not want to interrupt him.'

She did. She did! But …

She knew where his pistol was in his room. She turned and ran up the stairs. Her hands shaking as she climbed. The servant, Jackson, did not follow. Perhaps he thought she had gone to her room. The servants must know that Mark had wanted her back.

The pistol was in the drawer, with powder and bullets. She had everything she needed. She charged it quickly, just as he'd shown her. Then, in moments, she was running back downstairs, only now the hall was empty and there was a pistol in her hand.

Mark's voice seeped through the door of the parlour, in the tone he had that encouraged and urged her to do what he wanted. It was not her in there, but it was another woman.

She turned the handle and threw the door open, holding up the barrel of the pistol and aiming.

The woman had vivid red hair and she turned and looked at Charlie in horror. She was not a young woman, she was a girl.

A girl Charlie had not seen for years. She had thought she might walk past her own sister in the street and not know her. But she knew her. 'Ginny ... Run, sweetheart, run.' She aimed the pistol again as her sister rose from the floor and did exactly as Charlie had said.

Mark's hands lifted, reaching out towards her as if he reached for the pistol that was aimed at his chest. His trousers hung open, and his skin reddened with anger as his arousal tumbled like a broken tower. The tip of the pistol lowered. She wanted to shoot that.

'Now Charlie. Do not be silly.'

No. She would not be silly now. But she had been an absolute fool when she was young. Her forefinger squeezed against the trigger as she heard the front door slam behind her fleeing sister.

~

The pace of Harry's heart was a heavy resounding thud, but his breathing held steady. There was a battle cry yelling inside him, screaming as he charged, holding up his sword, as he knocked on the door.

He had been here twice and met Charlie's gaze and never guessed what her life had been like behind this door, when it had been closed on guests.

Drew, Rob and Henry stood behind him; his rear guard. His mother and father were on their way here too. His father had been arranging rooms at the inn for them all so they had somewhere to take Charlie to.

If she was here...

The door opened.

He swallowed, about to speak, but instead of the door opening to let them in someone ran out of it. A woman. A young ... girl. With red hair. 'Catch her!' He shouted at the others as the door slammed shut, but the girl dodged through them all and kept running. 'Ginny!' He shouted after her as a shot went off inside the house.

Damn.

He spun back around and hammered on the door with the side of his fist. Inside he could hear commotion. 'Let me in!' He yelled, looking back at Rob and Henry. 'Run after her. That was Charlie's sister.'

He turned back to the door and hit it with his fist again and again. 'Damn it, let me in!' Was Charlie in there? Who had fired? Who was hurt?

'Let me in!' He should have brought his pistol.

A man shouted inside, roaring with anger. Hillier.

Finally the door was opened. 'Out of my way.' Harry shoved the servant aside and Drew followed. The noise had come from the dining room, from the room he'd played cards in.

'Send for the guard!' Hillier yelled at the servants as Harry ran in there.

Hillier was standing with the pistol in his hand, buttoning up his flap, and Charlie, she was in there.

The shot had made a hole in the plaster across the room at about knee height, as though the shot had been knocked down or aside. 'Charlie.' She had fired it and then Hillier must have snatched the pistol.

Her gaze turned to Harry just as Hillier gripped a fistful of her cloak and yanked her back, pulling it tight about her neck. Harry lifted his hand. He had no weapons but his hands. But he had Drew with him as a witness and his father was coming, and he did not think Hillier's servants fool enough to seek a prison cell in exchange for their service.

'Let her go,' Harry said, as he saw Hillier turn the butt of the pistol, as though he would hit Charlie with it.

'Let her go,' Drew repeated at his side.

But as Drew said it, Harry could see his fiery wife was freeing herself.

Her hands lifted and pulled the bow tying her cloak loose. Her cloak was left in Hillier's hand as she ran to Harry. 'Good girl,' he said as her bonnet pressed to his shoulder and she gripped his midriff.

Harry's hand lowered. Now he was no longer afraid, the only remaining emotion was anger. 'You have hurt enough people. No more. When the guard arrive they will be told what you have done.'

'And you think they will believe your word against that of a Colonel.'

'They will have enough witnesses; they will not be able refute the truth. My brother, who is a member of parliament, and my cousin, who is the heir to an earldom, saw Ginny run away. And with a duke as my brother, no one would dare to say anyone within my family lied.'

Charlie let him go. 'Where is Ginny?'

'She dodged through us, but Rob and Henry went after her.'

'She will be afraid of them.'

His hand cupped Charlie's cheek. She could not have been here long if she still wore her bonnet. 'She will be fine. We will find her.'

'Harry!'

'No!' Charlie shouted.

Something hard and heavy hit his forehead, making the room spin.

Damn! His hand lifted to his head and swiped at the blood that now ran into his eye. Hillier had used the pistol like a club and then run.

'Are you well?' Drew's hand was on his shoulder.

He was dizzy and confused by the sudden change in the situation, but nothing more. 'Yes. Where has he gone?'

Drew turned and went to the door. Harry followed, wiping the blood from his eye on to his coat.

Someone knocked on the front door. But Hillier was not in the hall. Two of the servants were. 'Where did he go?' Drew asked.

One of the men looked towards a door under the stairs that must lead to a servants' exit.

'Charlie.' Harry looked back. He would not leave her here alone. She was behind him. He clasped her small hand in his now blood-stained one as Drew opened the door and ran ahead of them.

When Harry caught up with Hillier he had no idea what he would do. But as they descended the narrow spiralling stairs he heard the rattle of swords in the hall above. It had been the militia at the door.

They had arrived so quickly, his father must have sent for them.

His feet hurried down the stairs as Drew ran on ahead, while Charlie followed. It was not a big house. As they left it through a servants' door into a garden they saw Hillier passing through a gate at the far end.

He turned to Charlie. 'Where does it lead?'

'To the mews, where his horses and carriage are.'

As Harry wiped the blood from his forehead again, Drew turned back. 'You go on. I will go the other way and out into the street.'

Harry nodded as he found Charlie's hand once more. He pulled her on as Drew turned back, wiping the blood off again on to the sleeve of his coat as they walked.

He pulled open the gate and stepped out into an alley.

'The mews is along there.' Charlie pointed to an open set of gates further along.

Shouting echoed out from the cobbled courtyard of the mews as they reached it, and it was not only Hillier's voice.

There was an arch that led out into the street on the far side and in the centre of the arch stood an auburn-haired man waving his cap in his hand. Hillier was yelling at the man, who blocked his path and his horse reared up.

Damn. Hillier did not have a good control of the animal. He lost his seat as the horse's forelegs kicked out at the man. Good Lord. Hillier's arms flailed desperately, trying to catch a hold of something to stop his descent as he tumbled backwards. There was nothing for him to grasp.

Harry let go of Charlie's hand as Hillier landed on the cobbles with a vicious cracking sound and a heavy thud. His head had hit the stone first.

The courtyard was suddenly full of the militia and he heard his father and Drew as he knelt at Hillier's side. The man's eyes were open, staring as his body convulsed sharply, while his head lay in a widening pool of vivid red blood.

Harry lifted Hillier's head with his already bloody hand and he could feel the broken bone of his smashed skull.

'Ah.' The exclamation was in his mother's voice.

He looked up. 'Turn away, Mama.' Her face was a white mask of horror. He looked back at Charlie. 'Do not look.' He knew such sights could scar a mind for life.

Hillier's body convulsed one last time, then became still as the pulse of the blood running through Harry's fingers stopped and became only an ebbing flow of the final moments of life draining away.

Harry set down Hillier's head on the stone, then unbuttoned his own coat and stripped it off as the Captain of the militia began asking questions of everyone. He covered Hillier's head. Then stood.

'It was that man,' one of the grooms accused, pointing to the man who had been in the middle of the archway. 'He scared the horse deliberately.'

'Rodney.' Charlie was looking at the man too.

So that was the brother.

'I did nothin' wrong. I wanted to stop 'im, that was all. I wanted to speak to 'im. 'E reared 'is 'orse at me!'

Damn this mess. Harry wiped the sticky blood from his hand on to his trousers as nightmares whispered through his head, but he shut them away.

'You are under arrest.' The uniformed men gripped Rodney's arms. He immediately began to struggle.

Harry wiped the blood from his forehead on to the sleeve of his shirt, unsure now what blood was his own and what was Hillier's. He lifted his hand as Rodney's struggle became more violent. 'Stop. Go with them. Do not make this worse for yourself. We will resolve it later.'

'And who are you?'

Charlie gripped his arm, her fingers clasping at his thin shirt. 'My husband.'

'Where is Ginny?'

'Gone. But my brother and my cousin are trying to find her. Go with these men.'

Charlie's brother had already ceased struggling. But as the militia turned him away he looked back at Harry. 'Swear you will find her.'

Harry nodded as Charlie's fingers gripped more firmly about his arm.

'Son.'

Harry looked at his father while Rodney was led out through the arch.

'Your head will need stitching.'

'I have survived with worse,' Harry answered.

His mother was still staring at Hillier's body with wide eyes of disbelief.

'Mama.' Drew put an arm about her. 'Come away. This is not our concern.' Of course he did not know that Harry's mother faced a nightmare she had thought was left behind long ago.

Harry looked at Charlie. 'Go back to the inn with my mother.'

'I cannot. We must find Ginny.'

'Papa and I will find her. You go with my mother. It will be dark soon and I will not have you wandering the streets. I will find her, I promise, and she may already even be at the inn if Henry and Rob caught up with her. Go. It is better that you will be there when one of us finds her.'

'Harry, you should go back too,' his father said. 'To change out of those blood-stained clothes and clean your wound, if nothing else. You will frighten the girl if you found her, looking as you do. Drew and I will go and look. You take your mother and Charlie back to the inn.'

His hand lifted to wipe his eyebrow, but then he saw the amount of blood on him. Yes. He should change. If nothing else. He looked down at Hillier's body. One of the grooms was holding the horse.

'Harry. Hillier's household will see to the body. Leave it to them.' Drew had come to him.

He glanced over to see his father embrace his mother.

'Go and change,' Drew said.

Harry looked at Charlie and his fingers pressed over hers as they still held his arm. 'I will take you to the inn.' His gaze transferred to his mother as he walked Charlie about Hillier's corpse. 'Mama. Come with us.'

She turned away from his father. Harry reached out a hand. Her stillness said that she was confused, trapped somewhere between the past and the present. But so was he and so was Charlie.

They walked back along the seafront. His hand holding his mother's as Charlie gripped his other arm. He was covered in blood and the women looked pale and shocked. They were stared at a dozen times by passers-by.

Ginny was not at the inn and nor were Rob and Henry.

He left Charlie with his mother in the room his parents had taken, then went to another and stripped off his clothes. He washed the blood from his skin, ignoring the screaming in his mind as he saw himself doing the same thing many days over during the war.

The gash in his forehead was not deep. Without stitching there would be a crooked scar, but it had ceased bleeding and he did nothing to it. His thoughts now were for Charlie's young sister, alone in the streets. The sun was setting already. She would be alone in the dark if no one found her soon.

~

It was ten o'clock and the night was cloudy, moonless, and therefore black. Harry was not ready to stop looking. He would not leave the girl on the streets. He had no idea if the others were still looking, but they had not returned to the inn before he'd left it over two hours ago.

He'd decided to go into The Lanes, the area of narrower streets and alleyways. Perhaps she might have felt safer in these enclosed places.

He walked past the 'grand joke' of a palace. What had the old king known of the sinful elements of Brighton? Harry's uncles on his mother's side would probably know. Two of them were dukes and the other an earl and they moved in circles that would have known what the old King did.

Did they know about his mother?

He walked away from the opulence of golden gilded domes and into the narrow streets instead gilded by the glow of gaslight. If she was hiding here. It was folly. She would be more at risk in a narrow street than in a wide one. A wide street had the space to run. Yet she was little more than a child, and with a child's mind these streets might feel safer.

His hands swung at his sides as he walked, but they were held in fists and his right palm itched for his sword hilt to rest on.

He walked past a couple and a man alone and glanced down a narrow unlit alley on his left. He would have walked on, but in a line of yellow-tinted gaslight that fell into the alley he saw the bent legs of a woman sitting on the doorstep of a shop.

He walked into the alley. The woman's legs disappeared as she turned when she heard his footsteps.

It was definitely a woman who was hiding.

212

He did not call out. If it was Ginny, she must be terrified and he did not want her to run again. If it was her. Poor child.

He walked as though he simply walked, as though he was not looking for anyone.

She was only a few paces away from him. He could not see her yet, though, because she had huddled back into the alcove of the shop door.

Then he did see her. A small, slim figure hunched and curled up as she sought to be invisible.

In the dark her hair did not shine out its colour and yet it was auburn with tight curls, like her sister's. Some strands had come loose from a knot and they framed her pale cheek, which was turned away from him. She was still trying to hide.

'Ginny.'

Her head turned, her eyes opening wide, and she scrambled to her feet. But she could not run, he stood in front of her hiding place, blocking any chance of flight.

She resembled Charlie. There was no doubt in his head that he'd found Ginny.

'Do not worry. You have no need to be afraid. I am here to help you. Your sister is at an inn near by. Did you know she has married?'

The girl nodded.

'I am her husband and you have no need to be scared any more. I am going to take you to her.'

She merely looked at him, her eyes saying she was unsure whether or not to believe him.

He had no way to prove himself. He had only his words and his actions. 'You must trust me. I know it shall be difficult to trust another man at this moment. But if you come with me, I will take you to Charlie and there will be supper, if you need it, and a safe place to sleep.' Lord, had Hiller used such words to tempt women back to his home? 'I swear no one will hurt you.' He wished he had thought to bring a maid from the inn with him and yet, in reality, what evidence did that give? Was that how the madams found their girls? The girls who had run away from home …? He could not bear to think of the women he'd lain with before any more.

'Come. Let me take you to safety and I promise that within two days you will be with your mother.'

'Where did y'u meet Charlie?' she asked in a quiet voice that said she was looking for proof.

'Here. On the beach.'

'When?'

'A few weeks ago.'

'And y'u married 'er …'

'I fell in love with your sister.'

'What age was she when she left 'ome?'

'She was fifteen, Ginny, and I know your age too because she has told me, you are twelve.' Just that. Too young to sleep in a doorway. 'Come back with me? I promise to keep you safe.'

He lifted a hand, encouraging her to step out and walk beside him. She hesitated for a moment more, but then she did so.

As they walked, she continually glanced across at him in a way that implied she was still unsure if he was trustworthy.

His father had called him irresponsible for half his life and Drew had mocked him as the family's black sheep – he was not that man now. There were two women he had to protect. He would see Charlie's sister finish her childhood in a safe way, in a safe place. Yet he was meant to go to India in five weeks.

His Uncle Robert who had, he discovered, come with his father but had seen Henry running and joined him, was waiting at the inn and Henry was there too. The others were still looking for Ginny.

She stood to one side of Harry as he introduced her to his uncle and cousin. She did not speak.

Harry took her up to his mother's room, hoping Charlie would be there. She opened the door, saw her sister and rushed past him to embrace Ginny.

'Shall I order her food and a bath?' He asked Charlie, as he saw his mother in the room.

'Yes do. Well done, Harry,' his mother said. 'We will stay with her. Tell your father to leave us alone here.'

He nodded.

When he returned to the taproom, he ordered ale then joined his uncle and Henry. 'My heart is heavier than it ever was when I took the lives of men in war.' It was Gareth he should have said that to. Gareth would have understood.

'At least the girl is safe now,' his uncle said.

'Yes. Yet I feel as though I want to save every woman from such a life. She looked so vulnerable in that dark street. I found her in a shop doorway. If it had been someone else who found her ...'

Henry was staring into a glass of wine. He had used whores too. Harry wondered if Henry now saw the world as he did.

'I am only glad that Hillier is dead,' Uncle Robert said. 'He cannot hurt another woman. I killed a man like that myself. I have never regretted it.'

Henry sat back and glared at Uncle Robert. 'You killed a man ...'

'Once. And, as I said, a man like Hillier who deserved to die. But I did not attack him, he attacked ....' He stopped speaking and looked at Harry.

'Who?' Henry asked.

'No one. It is simply that this situation has thrown my thoughts back through the years.'

His mother. Harry knew it. 'Which man?'

He could tell from the look in his uncle's eyes that he knew Harry had understood. Harry's father must have told his uncle who Hillier was, and his uncle must have known the rest. 'Another man who disapproved of having a woman taken away from him.'

The man his father had taken his mother from ... His mother knew even more of how Charlie was feeling than Harry had imagined.

Henry's gaze turned from Uncle Robert to Harry and back. At least Henry did not understand.

'You have found her.' Harry looked over his shoulder as his father and Drew came into the room.

'Yes. Where's Rob? Have you seen him?'

'He is with John at the barracks.'

'John? Is he here too?'

'He came with us. He did not approve of your mother coming. He came for her sake.' His whole family had rallied again. But the pain in his chest denied any pleasure he might take from that fact.

'John was looking for the girl with Rob, but I told them about her brother being accused, so they went to the barracks to work the magic of a duke and a politician. The Pembroke Pride to the rescue,' Drew laughed.

Once they were all sitting at the table a bottle of whiskey was brought over, with glasses.

~

'Harry!'

Harry stood as he heard the desperation in Charlie's voice. Everyone else about the table and at every other table in the taproom looked across the room to the origin of the shout.

Her hands were clasped together, her clothes creased and the loose strands of hair that had escaped her pins hung in curled little rats' tails about her face. She looked upset, wrung out by shock and grief, and her eyes begged him to hurry to her as he walked across the room. On closer inspection the hazel glistened when it caught the candlelight. She was about to cry, only it did not look like simple tears trapped behind her eyes but an extreme outburst of emotion.

'Is everything all right?' His father asked as Harry reached

216

Charlie. He had followed.

Charlie bit at her lip, silently saying she did not want to say what had distressed her before his father.

'I'll manage it, Papa, sit back down.'

He touched Charlie's arm as his father left them, she had still not said a word. 'Would you like some fresh air? Shall we go outside?'

She nodded slightly.

He turned away, glancing back at the others. They had returned to their conversation.

He was holding her arm gently as they left the inn, opening and holding the doors for her as she seemed to be walking half in a daze.

When he was outside, though, she did not stop walking, but the heels of her boots clicked on the cobbles as she carried on glancing about her with that sense of desperation.

'What is it, Charlie? What has upset you?' Was the past rising up in haunting memories or the scene with Hillier sinking down on her or was it thoughts of her sister … 'How is Ginny?'

The yard was dark, the horses that were here were stabled for the night and the grooms catching some sleep before another coach arrived. But the cloud had cleared and light came from the moon and the stars.

'In here.' She caught hold of his hand and pulled him towards an empty stall.

'What is it?'

'Oh, Harry!' Her sob erupted the moment she had got him to the stall and her arms came up about his neck as the tears that he had seen came hard and fast with hiccups and wails.

'Darling.' His hand stroked over her back as her pain soaked into him like rain into the earth. It hurt to love her. 'I should have come here last night. I know. Forgive me.'

She was sobbing still.

'Was your sister …? Was she …?' God he could not bring

himself to say the word.

Charlie pulled free of his embrace, then held his hand again and pulled him further back into the stall, so they were in dark and out of sight of the yard. He heard the horseshoes on the brick floor in the stall beside the one she had chosen.

The horse whinnied as Charlie began to whisper. 'He did not rape her. I came in time. But he touched her in the carriage and made her touch him and his trousers were undone when I found them and she was on her knees …' Her eyes and expression spoke of memories of the same acts and the same moments.

She began shivering in a violent way. More than she had been shaking the night that Hillier had thrown her out on to the street. He rubbed her arms gently, but her posture said that she would not have accepted an embrace. She swallowed and then her palm pressed against her stomach. Was she going to be sick, as his mother had been?

She straightened, looking as though she clenched her teeth against the nausea. Then she breathed out a harsh breath. 'It is the memories. As you said. We had to force her into speaking, your mother and I. Urging her. Begging and encouraging. Your mother said that it was better that she spoke and that if there might be a child, then there were herbs and medicines that could be used quickly to try to prevent it. It is as though Ginny is a stranger to me. She looks at us both as though we are as cruel as him. I am only trying to help her. Yet I can see she has been told things about me, Harry. Things that are not true. And when I look at myself in her eyes …'

There was a shaky intake of breath and then her hand fisted and struck him hard on the shoulder.

'Ow. What was that for?'

She hit him again. 'You should have gone. We should have gone last night. We could have stopped him fetching her! We could have stopped this!'

Stopped Hillier hurting her sister, or her sister hurting her?

He caught hold of her wrists to end the rain of thumps on his chest. 'I said, I was sorry. I know you are right. I should have trusted your judgement. But you did not trust me and it cut, and my mind was a muddle.'

'Ah.' There were tears again and then her forehead rested against his chest while her arms wrestled in his hold, but as though she did not really want to be free but to fight for the sake of a fight. 'My mind is a muddle too,' she said on a sob, her warm breath seeping through the cloth of his coat.

'I know. It is why I gave you laudanum. But I know that was wrong of me. I am sorry.'

'I keep seeing him. I keep seeing him that first day in the carriage and then in his house and what he made me do for accepting that cake. And I see myself in Ginny's eyes and she hates me. She blames me. I want to help her and I cannot. She does not want to be with me …'

She looked up. Even in the darkness at the back of the stall he could see the shine of tears in her eyes and on her cheeks. 'I gave up my life for her sake …'

He let go of one of her hands and wiped her cheek with the cuff of his oldest coat. His newest coat had been left on Hillier's body. This coat had been worn in battles. 'I wish I could make this right. I wish that I could give you back your life. I cannot. But we have the future. We will make that right. Do not give up on your sister and let us thank God that she was not more seriously assaulted.'

Charlie sniffed back more tears in answer. 'She would not have been assaulted at all if we had left last night.'

'It will do no good to jab at me or yourself with thoughts like that. Hillier would have already left here to fetch her. If we had come last night, they would have still been together in the carriage.'

She gritted her teeth and her glittering eyes caught the small amount of light as they glared at him defiantly.

He shook his head. 'I am not your enemy. I know you are

upset and muddled and looking for someone to blame, but it is not me, darling. You should have just come to me yesterday and not run. If you had talked to me in the first place I would have caught your brother up and come here with him. But I still say, we could not have stopped Hillier from being in the carriage with your sister. Nothing could have been done differently to change that. Though I am sorry for it. But at least you have her here now and we found her before worse things happened.'

She huffed out a breath.

It was not just about her sister. 'I know you are hurting, Charlie. I know. Let me hold you.' She had not come to him to talk yesterday, but she had come to him again today in need of comfort.

Her arms wrapped about his middle. His settled on her shoulders. Then came tears and sobbing again. His fingers ran over her hair.

'Ginny is not even speaking to me. She looks at your mother when she speaks.'

His hand stroked over her hair again as she spoke against his neck. 'She has not seen you for years—'

'She does not even know your mother. She hates me because she has been told by my mother and brother that I did wrong.'

What did he say? How could he provide the comfort that would wipe out the past. His hand stroked over her hair again. 'You make me feel inadequate,' he said quietly. 'I felt inadequate yesterday, and especially when you did not trust me enough to talk to me. I wish I knew how to make you feel better.'

'When you hold me I feel better,' she said against his neck as her arms tightened about his middle.

He held her tighter too. 'I am sure that when your sister comes to know you better, as I do, she will learn to love you again. Forgive her. She must be traumatised today, love her as—'

'I do. I gave myself up to Hillier because Ginny was hungry and crying!'

'I know.'

His hand ran over her hair again. This must feel like such a betrayal. Guilt and a sense of betrayal. He knew those emotions well. 'Darling.'

She sniffed again, then drew away from him, wiping away her tears with the sleeve of her dress. 'I am sorry. I am being selfish.'

'You are not.'

'I have been away too long. Your mother will wonder where I have gone and Ginny might want me.'

His posture stiffened, as hers had, and his lips pursed. He did not think he had helped her. He had tried laudanum, and failed, and comfort and kind words, and failed.

He reached out and held her hand, then lifted her fingers to his lips and felt his ring against them. As he lowered their joined hands he said, 'I have agreed with Papa and John that you, Ginny and my mother will return to John's in the morning. I will stay to help your brother and John will send the second carriage to collect your mother and your brother's wife.'

She nodded. That was all.

His fingers tucked a loose strand of her hair behind her ear. 'Perhaps, during the carriage ride, Ginny will come to know you better.'

'Perhaps.'

I love you. He did not say the words. Now did not feel like the right moment. He did not want his love for her forever tainted by Hillier's death. 'Did you come downstairs for something?'

'Only to speak to you. I just … I had to speak to someone.'

He squeezed her fingers gently. 'I am glad you did. I am glad you felt able to. I am sorry I let you down yesterday.'

'But you did not let me down today, did you? I am sorry I am upset. I am sorry I did not come to you yesterday. I am sorry I stole the jewellery.'

His fingers brushed over her cheek. It was damp with tears again. 'May I kiss you?' He did not want to if her memories were too overwhelming.

There was another small nod.

He leant and pressed his lips against hers and her arms lifted and settled on his shoulders as she embraced him, as she'd first done. He held her too and when the kiss ended he stroked her hair again. 'All will be well. We shall make it so, Charlie ...' There was another last small nod against his shoulder. 'Let me take you back in.'

She breathed out as she pulled away from him.

He led her out of the stall by the hand. 'I was going to let my father sleep in the room hired for us, if you are happy to stay with my mother and Ginny?'

'Yes. I do not want to leave Ginny. Even if she does not really want me there, I—'

'I am sure she is glad that you rescued her, Charlie.'

'Yes.'

He opened the door to the inn. 'And I am sure, even if it does not seem so, your presence is a comfort to her.'

'Perhaps.'

There was no one in the hall. He held her hand still and lifted his free hand and cradled her head, then kissed her again, another press of lips.

Then he opened the taproom door and walked her through it to the stairs.

'I can go up alone,' she said, when they reached the steps.

'Then I will see you in the morning.'

'Yes.'

'Good night.' He kissed the back of her fingers, then let them go.

'Good night,' she answered before she hurried off.

He returned to the table, where his father poured him a fresh drink and slid it over.

'Thank you.'

'Is all well?' Rob asked him.

'All is difficult, as you can imagine,' Harry answered.

When he shared a bed with his father they did not immediately try to sleep but talked quietly. His father told him the whole story of how he came to save Harry's mother. Then Harry told him Charlie's story.

~

After a brief goodbye, Harry and his father had put the women in the carriage and sent them back to John's this morning. Poor Charlie had looked as though she had slept no more than him. Her eyes were red and shadowed and she had been glancing towards her sister constantly, as though she sought to ensure she was safe and happy and yet as though she sought her sister's affection too.

Sadly, he could not make Ginny love Charlie any more than he could take away Charlie's memories, and they had become a greater concern than his own.

He had kissed her before she climbed up into the carriage, said goodbye and whispered an encouragement to speak to his mother, if she had need of someone, and then that had been it. There had been no more opportunity to speak to her privately.

His Uncle Robert, Henry and Drew had accompanied the women on horseback to see them safely back. Immediately after, they had all left the other carriage had been sent to fetch Charlie's mother, sister-in-law and niece and take them to John's.

Harry had remained here to pursue her brother's release, even though he did not like the man. But Cotton had come here to protect his youngest sister, at least, and that had redeemed him a little in Harry's eyes, and it was the one thing Harry could physically do to help Charlie.

His father, Rob, John and he hired horses from the inn and rode out to the barracks. A small rescue party.

The men on guard at the gate saluted as Harry rode up. They had been his men before he had been assigned to another regiment. 'Captain Marlow.'

'You have someone called Cotton in custody,' Harry said. 'We have come to see him.'

'Yes, sir.'

The gate was opened and they all rode in. 'Dismount here,' Harry said in a low voice in the courtyard. 'The men will look after the horses.'

With the horses in the care of others, Harry led the men of his family into the place that had been his home, on and off, for years. They had never entered before. It was the first time that he, the soldier and the man, had come together here.

He caught his father's eye as he walked through the halls towards the cells. His father smiled. He had rarely been the child who had heard the word 'pride' and yet in the last hours his father's gaze and expression had screamed the word at him and even John was deferring to Harry's judgement today.

'Harry!'

He looked back. Then turned around.

'Gareth.' Harry walked back, pushing past the others.

'What brings you back?' Gareth said as they embraced.

'Cotton,' Harry said as he let Gareth go. 'He is Charlie's brother.'

'Charlie …'

Harry smiled. 'My wife's brother. My brother-in-law.'

'You did marry her.'

'Yes.' The man standing before Gareth was a very different man from the one who had lived in these barracks but days before. His heart had been cracked open like a soft egg and his view of the world was a thousand miles wider. He had lived with eyes that saw the world through a microscope. Now he viewed it from horizon to horizon.

'Congratulations. I suppose.'

'Thank you.' Harry turned. 'Gareth, meet my brothers, Rob and John, and my father.' Gareth bowed as they did and then they shook hands before turning to walk towards the cells.

224

'Cotton?' Gareth asked, when they reached the cells.

'Third on the right, sir.'

Even if he had not seen him before, Harry might have guessed it was Charlie's brother. He had the same auburn hair, only his curls were cut close to his head. He was a muscular man and a tall man, though. A man who should have been able to support himself with labour rather than run to his sister to beg her to return to whoring to save his family.

He stood as Harry and the others looked through the bars in the door at him.

Harry glanced at the guard. 'Will you let me in with him?' He had no right to give orders here any more and yet he asked the question in the voice of an order instinctively.

'Yes, sir.' The man stepped forward with a key. 'But just you, Captain Marlow.'

He nodded as the door was unlocked. Then walked through the gap. He was then locked into the cell with Cotton.

The man looked as though he thought Harry might be here to interrogate him. He was a coward. He had not deliberately killed Hillier. The man did not have it in him. He had been doing what he'd said, trying to stop Hillier and that was all and he was afraid of Harry because only days ago Cotton had been urging Charlie to come back here for the wrong reasons.

'Where is Ginny?'

'Safe. With my mother and Charlie, as your mother and your family will be soon.'

"Ave you seen Ginny?"

'Yes. I was the one who found her last night.'

'Was she 'urt?'

Harry did not answer but his demeanour must carry the answer. Yes, but not as Charlie was, not as Charlie had been for years, and why do you not care about her? And why did you turn her sister against her?

'I did no' mean for him t' fall. I was tryin' to protect Ginny. I was tryin' to make 'Illier let 'er go.'

'It is a shame you did not do the same for Charlie years ago,' Harry uttered in a low tone. The man stared at him.

But the past was the past, it could not be changed. The future, though … 'We are doing our best to convince the authorities of that. I saw him lose his seat on the horse and fall.'

Cotton stared at him, then acknowledged. 'Thank 'e. As long as Ginny is safe and my wife and child.'

At least he was thinking of his youngest sister's and his wife's plight not his own.

'We will look after them all and my family have influence. They will do their utmost to see you freed.'

Cotton gave him a glance that said he knew all about the influence of Harry's family and that he disliked and envied people who had wealth and power.

He had imagined he would dislike Charlie's brother, and he did.

But he loved Charlie and he would help her brother because of that. It was all that he seemed able to do.

He bowed his head slightly. Then said, 'My brother has offered your mother and wife a home. I will let you know when they are safe with us.' Harry turned away. The door was opened and the others faced him as he walked out; they had heard the conversation, but there was no judgement of his choice of in-laws in either his father's or John's eyes.

They rode back to the inn with Gareth and they ate in the taproom, discussing their campaign to free Cotton. And while they talked Harry had never felt so connected to his father. His father was the only man here who knew how he felt.

Chapter 15

The maid, who had become Charlie's personal maid for the last five days, secured the buttons at the back of Charlie's evening dress as Ash sat near them watching. Charlie's fingers ran across the fabric over her stomach, smoothing it. Harry had bought her dresses with buttons at the back because, in his world, every woman had a maid to help her dress, but in India she would have no maid and he would not be there each morning to secure her buttons if he was on duty.

So many silly little thoughts like that had crossed her mind since she'd returned here. She could not imagine life in India, yet she had been trying very hard to think of that and not of Ginny, who hid from everyone, preferring solitude and silence, or of her brother, who was still in gaol.

She no longer had to worry over her mother. She had arrived yesterday in a very grand carriage, in clothes that were old, wearing a white linen bonnet with only a sheet wrapped about her few possessions. The duchess would have given her one of the plush rooms as she had insisted that Charlie's mother was a part of their family, but her mother had refused the notion. Her mother was, instead, upstairs in a garret room near the nursery, and now Ginny was there too.

But it was strange to meet her mother after seven years. She had become grey-haired and her face had many lines that had not been there in Charlie's memory and she was colder in nature than Charlie had recalled. She had not even hugged Charlie when she arrived. Charlie's life in the village before she'd made that foolish decision at fourteen to accept a carriage ride for jam, cake and tea, had really been a fairytale that she'd concocted in her head. Her image of Rodney had not been real and nor had her memories of her mother been true.

Harry's mother, Ellen, had held her many times in the last five days. She had stayed with Charlie in this room listening as Charlie had talked and holding her when she'd cried. She had told Harry's mother everything and she had wept over Ginny's silence because it felt as though Ginny was afraid of her. But too much time had gone by and Ginny had been too young when Charlie had left her and too much had happened. They were no longer sisters. Ginny had been waiting for their mother to turn to for comfort.

Ellen had also helped Charlie talk to the others. They had spent an afternoon in Katherine's sitting room with Caro and the three women had helped her begin to sew a shirt for Harry and then they had played cards and it all had seemed a very kind ploy to protect her mind from thinking the thoughts she did not want to hear.

Harry's family were lovely. She was no longer intimidated by their wealth or their blue blood. They had treated her as they would anyone of their own class. While her mother and her sister had kept to themselves and excluded Charlie.

'There ma'am.'

She smiled over her shoulder at the maid. 'Thank you. You may go.' Hark at her ordering the Duchess's servants! She smiled at herself in the mirror as her heart spread an ache through her body – a longing for Harry.

The maid shut the door. Ash came to Charlie's side and nuzzled her fingers.

Charlie's hand ran over the dog's head, then lifted and rested against her stomach again. Her courses were late. But only by days. Yet even so, the thought that there might be a child was moving.

She smiled at herself again. She was going down to dinner alone and she did not even feel scared and that was because Harry's mother was so wonderful. She had taken Charlie downstairs with her grandchildren on one day and they and Harry's youngest brother and sisters had gone out into the garden and spent most of the day playing games. So she had been accepted by the youngest people here too.

That approach had been Harry's mother's preferred method to help Charlie, by working her in to groups. She had taken tea with his older sisters, female cousins and sisters-in-law, and they had all gathered around a piano and sung; she had immediately felt included by it as she'd leant on the grand piano, which was apparently the Duke's. To sing with others was easier than speaking. She had laughed along with them when the harmonies went awry.

Yesterday the men and boys and some of the girls and Harry's sister, Mary, had decided to play cricket. So Harry's mother had sat on a rug beside Charlie, pointing out exactly who was who and explaining all of the married couples. Charlie had then been encouraged to speak to some more of the men, though Harry's mother had not applied pressure on her to speak to anyone.

Charlie had been a stranger to Harry's mother and Harry's mother had spoken to her from the day she'd walked through the door here, as though Charlie was her own daughter. Her own mother had arrived just before dinner yesterday. She had looked awkward and smiled, and spoken to Charlie as though Charlie was a stranger. But when Ginny had come out she had opened her arms and embraced Ginny with relief and love. The sense of exclusion had cut even deeper then and it still did. It had been a sharp knife in Charlie's dreams sawing at her heart all night.

Charlie turned away from the mirror to leave the room.

She had gone to her mother's room last evening, intending to eat with her family. She had expected to be received with gladness. She had convinced herself that her mother's restrained greeting had been due to Harry's family being around them and the opulence of the house. She had thought that privately, in the attic room, it would be different. It had simply been more awkward to be with Ginny and her mother when she was not welcome. Her mother spoke to Ginny and they told her about Rodney's wife and child. His wife had chosen not to come here and her mother said she had only come to see Ginny.

Charlie had not eaten with them, she'd left the room, walked downstairs and spent the entire evening in the company of Harry's mother. She had sat beside her before dinner, during dinner and after. She intended to do the same this evening.

She held her skirt and the bannister as she walked downstairs to the first floor and then on to the ground floor.

It was strange that for years she had craved a happy, simple family life in a humble cottage. Something she had thought she'd once known but which had been only a fairytale. She could never have imagined that she would marry the grandson and brother of a duke and come to a place like this, which ought to be a fairytale.

Voices rose from the drawing room, where Harry's family always gathered before walking into the dining room.

She looked up at the ceiling as she walked down the last wide, shallow flight of stairs. She was becoming used to all the ornate paintings and carvings in the plaster and she had reached a point that she desperately wanted Harry to point at the portraits and tell her how the people painted in them were related to him. She saw resemblances in some of the faces.

In the hall below there was a sudden rise in sound and movement, servants swelled into the hall like the crest breaking on a wave, then the front door opened and they flowed out.

Someone had arrived.

Her feet moved quicker, running down the last half a dozen steps. Harry ... Her heartbeat leapt into a race. Harry!

She hurried across the hall, then looked out of the door. Yes. Yes! Harry climbed out of the carriage.

Charlie gripped her skirt in both hands, lifted it above her knees and ran towards him as she would have run at fourteen, before anything bad had happened to her.

He saw her.

'Harry!'

His arms opened as Charlie continued running towards him, her skirt and petticoats bouncing against her legs in a froth of cotton and muslin. The garments fell as her arms lifted and then they wrapped about his neck.

She was clasped in his embrace and lifted off her feet as their lips pressed together.

Love. Yes, she loved him. She had thought it before. But now she knew it. After days of being without him, she never wished to be without him again. 'I am so happy you are back.'

'I am happy to be back and your brother will be here in a moment. He travelled with John.'

Charlie smiled her gratitude. Oh, he was a clever man.

Harry smiled too. His eyes told her that he cared for her, even though they had never voiced such emotions.

Self-disgust, regret and guilt swept through her with the sharp, abrasive stroke of a besom broom, calling her unworthy of this grand man's love. The thoughts and feelings she had battled beside him in that dark stable were all still there. But it was Mark's guilt she carried, not hers. *Not mine.* Harry's mother had made her learn those words in the last few days; that everything that had happened to her had not been her fault.

She looked back at the house and thought of the warmth and security she had discovered among Harry's family. This was a wonderful fairytale, with its towers of protection and its knight, her cavalry man with his glistening sword, and, yes, there had been a demon, but the demon was now dead.

'My mother is here too,' she told Harry.

'That must make you happy.' He squeezed her shoulder as his arm hung about her, while her hand still gripped about his waist.

'I thought it would, but it does not. It has made me unhappier.' If she was honest with anyone, let her be honest with Harry.

'Why, darling?'

She had loved the sound of that endearment in the stable. She gripped his waist tighter. 'She does not love me.' All that Charlie had longed for, for years, was to be held by her mother and that comfort had not been given to her. Yet it had been given to Ginny. The way they excluded her was cruel.

'I am sure you are wrong. I told you in Brighton, it will take time.'

'Then come and meet her and you will see.'

Charlie had a desire to be proven wrong as she walked Harry upstairs to the attic room. But the desire was a morbid pain in her chest because she knew she was right.

She knocked on the door as Harry stood with her, holding her hand.

'Who is it?' The voice was Ginny's.

'Charlie. I have brought Harry to meet Mama.' She glanced at him. She wanted him to see and she wanted him to tell her that she was wrong. That she was loved. Perhaps his greater experience of a family would see something she had missed, some silent or subtle understanding that she had missed.

The door opened. 'You remember Harry,' Charlie said to Ginny.

Ginny nodded and bobbed a curtsey as she would have to any grand stranger.

Harry gave her his most beautiful smile and bowed his head. But Ginny then turned away from them both without smiling back.

A sigh of misery and mortification escaped Charlie's lips as she pulled Harry into the room. Then she swallowed against the pressure of tears in her throat. 'Mama. I have brought my husband to meet you.' As her mother looked up, Charlie let go of Harry's hand and he bowed.

Her mother stood up to curtsey. 'Captain.' She straightened up. Then blushed and looked at Charlie, as if asking her to take Harry away. She did not say she was pleased to meet him or that she was thankful that he had helped Charlie. She did not care that Charlie was safe – that was how Charlie had interpreted this lack of concern for her freedom.

'Are you comfortable, ma'am? Have you everything you need here?' Harry asked as Charlie's mother sat again.

'Yes. Thank y'u now that Ginny is safe 'ere with me. That is all that I wished for.'

Was that said deliberately to show her disapproval of her eldest daughter? Charlie glanced at Harry. Had he heard the silent dismissal and rejection that she heard? Surely he must see that they did not care for her.

'My brother has said he will find you a cottage of your own.'

'We do not ask for much, only a simple life, Captain, no more than that.'

Every word her mother uttered felt like condemnation of Charlie's choices. Was she denouncing Charlie, as though she had sought the wealth of Harry's family? If she had a chance she would go back and have never climbed into Mark's carriage and have nothing.

Charlie looked at her sister. 'What are you sewing?' She walked over to her.

Ginny looked up. 'It is a cap for Mama.'

'Do na trouble y'ur sister with y'ur doings, Ginny.'

Your sister … Charlie did not even have a name. She was not a member of her own family. She had lost that place. She had no position in their hearts and no place amongst them. When, seven years ago, she had given up her life for their happiness.

233

'Charlie.' Harry beckoned for her quietly to come out of the room as her mother's eyes dropped to the sewing she worked on too.

'Good day,' Charlie said on her breath before she turned to leave. There was no answer.

Harry shut the door in their wake and then he held her as she had longed to be held by her mother.

He was her family. He cared, and he cared as her family never had. 'Do you see?' she whispered.

He pulled away from her a little. 'I do see. I am sorry. Your mother should care more for you. I apologise for her ignorance.'

She struck his shoulder with a gentle slap and laughed quietly. It had been said as a jest. 'You cannot apologise on her behalf.'

He smiled. 'Were you going down to dinner?' He swept the subject aside then.

'Yes …'

'Good, because I am ravenous. We did not stop on the road this afternoon, so we would return earlier.' He had said in the stable that he did not know how to help; instead she guessed he was attempting distraction.

'When you said you would marry me …. When you took me to the inn and said you would look after me … I thought … That is, I feared …' She had to know if he really cared. It would break her to pieces if he did not.

'Feared what, darling? Tell me.' His fingers tucked a loose strand of her hair behind her ear and it tickled her cheek.

'I was afraid that I had trapped you by going to you. That you felt forced, as I once had. That I had forced you into feeling that you had to—'

'Had to help you and marry you …'

'Yes.'

'No.' A bark of coarse laughter left his throat at a pitch that her mother must have been able to hear in the room beside them. 'Believe me, I did not feel forced and I have not been trapped except by—'

It is just that I love you, Harry,' Her hand fell on his chest over his heart, 'and I could not bear it if you came to hate me.' The statement echoed in every bone and sinew in her body. He was everything to her.

A smile parted his lips as another sound of amusement rumbled in his chest beneath her palm. 'Charlie, darling, I love you too. I shall never hate you. You have made me a whole man. I am far more than I could ever be without you.' His embrace became a grip as he picked her up and then spun her about in a circle on the narrow landing. 'I discovered that I love you before I left, but I did not have the heart to say it then or in Brighton. I was afraid you were not in a place to hear it and now you have beaten me to it.'

She laughed, smacking his shoulder to make him put her down. 'I have known that I love you for a long time, but I have been too afraid to say it to you.'

His hands braced either side of her head. 'Never be afraid to say anything to me, promise me that …?'

Yes. Yes. Now Ginny was safe she could promise and everything that he had done for her and her family told her he was trust-worthy, her whole heart believed. 'I promise.'

'Have my family been kind to you?' He took hold of one of her hands and pulled her into motion.

'So very kind. I love your mother too. She has been especially sweet to me. I want her to be my mother.'

'She is your mother; you are my wife.'

Charlie laughed, as now he was here the happiness inside her crept up to the top of a full jug. He was a wonderful distraction She did not have her mother's love, but her sister was safe and Harry was home and she had his family and he loved her. 'I feel as though that is true.'

'It is true.'

When they walked into the drawing room, still holding hands, Charlie did not feel uncomfortable as she had felt on the first day. She was proud, as she had known she would be proud. Proud to be Harry's chosen wife and she was going to be a good wife to him. She would have let go of his hand, but his grip tightened about hers when she tried to let go, so he responded to the embraces of his family one-armed.

When the greetings ceased, Harry let go of her hand and instead rested his arm about her shoulders.

'Would you like some wine?' Harry offered.

'Do you want some?'

He smiled. 'Yes.' They walked over to a servant who was filling glasses.

'Charlie.'

She turned and faced Harry's father. He must have returned with Harry today.

'I have not properly welcomed you to the family. You must think me very crass. Please, think of me as your father, as much as Harry does.' He took one of her hands and held it in both of his, in a gesture that implied genuine affection and concern. More affection and concern than her mother showed her.

It was strange that Harry's family now knew the worst things about her and liked her and welcomed her more, while her own mother…

'Charlie.' She looked across Harry's father's shoulder at the Duke. He had the same colour eyes as Harry, the same eyes as their mother.

He stepped forward as Harry's father moved aside and then The Duke held her hand and lifted it so he could kiss the back of her fingers as his eyes expressed concern and compassion. 'I am very glad that I have been able to assist your family.'

She bobbed an unpractised curtsey. She would have to ask Harry's mother to teach her how to do such things. 'Thank you. Harry said you brought my brother here too. Has he gone upstairs to be with my mother?'

'He asked to see her, but I believe he has now left. He intended returning to his wife.'

He had not even come to speak to her. A bilious sensation clasped at the back of her throat, strangling her. Not one of her family cared for her – or cared what had happened to her.

'Charlie,' Harry said, drawing her attention back to him.

She turned into him, as his arms opened to receive her. 'Do not cry for him. He does not deserve it. I have met him and I do not like him. I'm sorry. I'm sorry that you were cursed with such a man as a brother.'

She pulled away and met his gaze. 'But I rejoice that I have such a wonderful man as a husband.'

His brother and his father had drifted away and no one else paid any attention to them, allowing them a subtle privacy.

Harry pressed his lips down on hers. Love. She could never have imagined this affection and this world and his family … She could still not imagine India.

~

When they lay in bed the emotion in Harry's heart was a hard pull holding Charlie close to him. He had expressed his love and admiration for her with his body and now he lay sated and smiling into the darkness. He had never imagined loving a woman as he loved Charlie.

Charlie rolled on to her side, her head shifting from its place on his upper arm to lie on his chest as her fingers brushed across his stomach.

'I think I am with child,' she whispered into the air. 'My courses are late.'

God. His fingers closed about her shoulder instinctively and gripped tight. A child. He had never in his life imagined himself as a father.

Yet Charlie had been through a lot in the last few days. 'Could it be the result of worry?'

She rolled on to her front, her stomach resting on his hip as her palm pressed on his chest, bracing her upper body. 'No. I want it to be a child.'

He laughed as his fingers combed through her hair. The colour was dulled by the darkness and the moonlight. He wanted her to be with child too. The shock had receded. It was replaced by longing. 'Yes. I like the idea of a child. But I still think a few days' delay in your courses might be worry.'

'How can you know such a thing?'

'Have you not seen how many women I have in my family ...' The conversation had become a teasing exchange, like those they had shared in her little parlour in Brighton.

'They would not speak of such things to you, a man.'

'I did not say they spoke to me. I have ears. I can hear. I have overheard their conversations.'

Charlie rolled on to her back, her hair brushing his arm again and his chest. 'Well, I say I am with child.' He could not see it, and yet he heard the smile in her voice.

He did not answer. Let her believe it. But he would hold his excitement for a week or two.

He rolled sideways and kissed her temple. 'Either way, I love you.'

'And I love you,' she said in return.

Yes. He would like to have a child. Love a child. It was a good thought.

'Do you think I will make a good mother, like yours?'

He kissed her temple again, as he heard the words she had not said: 'or a bad mother like my own'. Except her mother was not a bad mother to Ginny, to Charlie it must feel like a flaw in herself. 'You will make a wonderful mother.'

There was a moment of silence.

'You said I may tell you anything ...' Her breath touched his cheek as her head turned to look at him and her eyes caught the small amount of light in the room and sparkled.

With tears ... His fingers lifted and tucked her hair behind her ear. 'Yes, anything.' His muscle tensed at the thought of what it might be, though. The words she had said in the stable at the inn had remained as ghost-like thoughts.

'I feel guilty, Harry. I always have. I feel as though everything has been my fault and your mother told me that it is not, but my mother … She has always said that it is. That I did wrong when I let him touch me. I blamed you for what happened to Ginny in Brighton because I was upset and I did not want to face how guilty I felt. I knew it was all my fault. If I had never got into that carriage—'

'Charlie. My sweetheart. I know without you telling me that what happened to you was because you felt you had no choice. My mother is right; you have no guilt to bear. What Hillier did is not your sin. He did it.'

The dampness on her cheek caught on his fingers. 'As you have spoken, let me speak too. I want to help you. Perhaps my own honesty can do that. I probably should have said this in Brighton. Guilt is the hardest thing for me to bear in my memories of war and that guilt has shut me off from my family too since I returned. I have not known how anyone might love me when I consider myself a sinful black-hearted man. I have kept my mouth closed and not told them about myself because I did not think that any of them would be able to face me.'

Her hand pressed against his cheek. 'You are not black-hearted.'

'Wait. Let me tell you it all. I bear guilt too. There were so many things about that awful war that were not what I expected. We lacked ammunition, food and medicine and I watched so many men die. Then, when one of my men was hit in the leg and fell next to me, I could stand no more death. In a moment of madness, I picked him up and carried him away from the field. I made that choice and who knew what other men I might have saved if I had continued fighting those that were attacking us. But I picked one man to save and carried him out of range of the guns and the cannons.'

'That was ki—'

'Listen.' He covered her lips with his fingertips. He'd never believed he would tell this to anyone, but now he had begun he had to tell it all. 'I went looking for him a few days later, in the tents that had become hospitals. I always tried to visit my men who were injured, but I wanted to see Martin particularly. I was proud of myself, you see, for saving a life so personally. He was in agony. His leg had been sawn off and the flesh had turned rotten with infection. He was writhing in pain and screaming at me and the wound smelled so badly and looked so awful and there was nothing, no opium or laudanum, to ease his pain and help him remain calm in the hours he had left of life. It took five more days for the infection to claim him. I did not save him from anything. All I did was make his death more difficult. If I had left him on the field to bleed to death or perhaps shot him myself to end his misery it would have been kinder. And who else died because I chose to save Martin when I did not save him at all ...' He swallowed as Charlie wiped his cheek. There was moisture on his skin.

'What else were you to have done? It is not your fault that he died anyway.'

'I do not know what else I might have done. That is the thought that tortures my dreams. But do you see? Your situation is the same. What else were you to have done then? We made choices on the information and the emotions we had then. We thought there would be no harm. It is not your fault, as you tell me it was not mine. You accepted what you thought was a kind offer, nothing more. You had no choice over what came next. There is no fault. Perhaps we should agree to be sad about the consequences but accept that there is nothing we may do to change them.'

Her body moved and then her lips touched his cheek where she had smeared his tears with the wipe of her thumb, and then she pressed her lips against his, before whispering over them. 'I accept it was not my fault.'

'I accept it was not my fault that Martin died, either.'

Chapter 16

Harry tapped on the door of John's library. He'd come looking for his brother for a reason. He'd spent his morning busy but contemplatively.

After breakfast he had spoken with Charlie and his mother, who he'd wanted to talk to about acquiring a ball gown. John and Katherine's ball was approaching and he wished Charlie to feel as confident as possible.

She had said she would not attend, trying to avoid the night. He had refuted that and told her, 'of course she must go to the ball'. If he had been doing what they had planned and taking her to India, it might be her only chance to attend such an event. But he had been thinking all morning about changing his plans.

There was Charlie to protect and her sister and mother. That was where she was now, with them. They could stay here in England, under John's protection. They would be safe and yet they would always feel like Harry's responsibility.

And one day he hoped he and Charlie would have a child for him to care for too.

He knocked again when John had not answered. Then he opened the door.

John was alone.

'Hello,' Harry said as he walked in.

John stood up, smiling at him. 'Hello to you too. Why are you here? You do not usually seek out my company.'

Harry shrugged. 'I have changed.'

His brother walked out from behind his desk. 'It is surprising what a woman can do …'

Harry smirked, but that was true and the sentiment that had brought him here.

'Would you like a glass of whiskey.' John pulled out his pocket watch and glanced at it. 'I do not think it too early.' He put the watch away again. 'And I think we deserve it after the last few days.'

Harry smiled fully. He had always liked John, despite his brother's annoying self-righteous behaviour, but now – now he appreciated his brother far more. He also had a favour to ask.

He walked across the room as John went to the decanter and upturned two of the glasses on a silver tray, then lifted the glass stopper out of the decanter and poured the whiskey.

A need for the liquor eased through Harry's blood. His mind had been spooked like a horse after a thunderstorm these last days – yet his decision was made. 'I need to ask you for something, John. For money again, I'm afraid.'

'Why? For Charlie or her mother? I have a cottage for them. One of my tenant farmers has no family – he has agreed to give them a small cottage without rent if they will wash, clean and cook for him. I did not think they would welcome pure charity. Charlie's mother approved the proposal. They are moving out tomorrow.'

Such a quick resolution. He was unsure if Charlie would be happy with it. Yet she still thought they were going to India and so she had no reason to care where her mother lived.

'Thank you for helping them,' Harry said, as he accepted a glass.

'You are welcome.'

'But that is not the reason I would like your help now, or rather why I would appreciate your money.' He looked his brother in the eyes. 'I would like you to buy me out of the army.'

'What?' There was a very true expression of shock on John's face, which for a man who held his emotions back constantly was quite something. 'Why?'

Because … There was no one else he would feel able to say this to. 'I cannot get the thought of Mama out of my head. Alone in Brussels. No one protected her, as they should have done, when your father died. What if I die in India? On the other side of the world. How would Charlie fare?'

'Mama has told me that Charlie should have all of our addresses and a purse of her own for emergencies.'

Harry smiled. His mother had taken Charlie under her wing. 'But India is a very long way away and if anything happened to me she would have to secure herself a passage home and navigate that entire journey safely. I do not even know anyone in my new regiment. There is not one single person I could trust to help her. No. I have made up my mind. I want to leave the army.' His brother had paid for him to join and now he hoped that he would agree to get him out.

John gave him a slight smile. 'If you are sure.'

'I am sure.'

John lifted his glass and tapped it against Harry's. 'This is a celebratory drink, then. To the future.'

'To the future.' Harry confirmed. Then he tapped John's glass in return and lifted his glass in salute. 'To family.'

'To family.' John smiled before he drank.

Harry drank too, thinking of Charlie and the child she hoped was in her womb.

'So how must this be achieved?' John asked.

'I will need to go to London, I think, to get the papers that release me from my posting and then ensure my new regiment are aware …' It was all very suddenly final. He was going to do

243

it. Leave the army. He had always thought he would die as a soldier. He breathed out, then swallowed the rest of the whiskey in one gulp and put the glass down. 'Will you forgive me if I leave you? I want to speak to Papa.'

'No. As you wish. I will go to London with you, then. Tomorrow?'

'Yes.'

They had only just returned and yet if this was to be done, he wanted it done quickly.

'I shall see you this evening at dinner.'

John nodded.

Harry turned away and his strides were quicker, and his posture increasingly relaxed as he walked from the room. The weight he had carried on his shoulders since the day he'd faced Charlie in the barracks, with her eye struck, had lifted, and even the weight of guilt and memory that he'd carried since his days in the Crimean War had lifted slightly since last night. It felt as though it might lift entirely when he'd paid his way out of the army.

He jogged up the wide, shallow steps, wondering where he would find his father.

The first place he went to was his parents' room.

His mother had taken the children outside to play with the other women and so he hoped to find his father alone there.

Harry knocked on the door of their sitting room, as he had just knocked on the door of John's library.

'Come in!' His father shouted.

'Papa.' Harry opened the door. 'What are you doing?'

His father looked up and smiled. 'Going through some of the accounts and information from the farms at home.' There were papers spread everywhere.

Harry shut the door as his father's gaze turned back to the numerous papers.

'Have you need of more help to manage the estate?'

'Have I …' His father looked back up and straightened. 'Why?'

'I find myself in need of employment.'

'What of the army?'

'John has agreed to pay for me to come out.'

'No. Are you sure that is what you wish to do?'

'Yes.'

His father walked across the room and then Harry was embraced. 'When you returned from the Crimea, when we heard you were coming back, your mother and I rejoiced. But then you came back with darkness and shadows in your eyes. I will not lie and deny that I am gladdened by your decision. Though I know you gave your all, Harry.'

'I wish to give my all to Charlie now.'

His father let him go. 'Your mother will approve it. But there would not be much of an income.'

'I will have my allowance from John and I am serious, is there a position for me with you? I will need work. I could not be idle. I would become bored.'

His father's lips pursed. 'Perhaps. Let me think on it. My steward is getting older. He might accept assistance and when he retires you could take the role and I think if you are to stay here in England and live anywhere, your mother will want you near us. She will want to be able to ensure Charlie's happiness. She foolishly thinks herself partly responsible for what happened to Charlie because she had done nothing to stop Hillier from trapping others.'

'How could she have changed anything?'

'I know. You do not need to say that to me. But such things have twisted her mind. She hides it well, but the scars are deep.'

Harry looked at his father; he'd gone back to work.

'How do you live with it?'

His father looked up. 'What?'

'Knowing what happened; how have you lived with it?'

'I try to not think of it. It is in the past and that is where your mother and I want it; for it to be forgotten.'

'But do you ever forget?'

'No, and nor does she. We just live regardless and seek every minute of happiness together. Today and every day after today is what is important. Think of the future and not the past.'

Harry smiled. Yes. He had seen that attitude in them and they were happy. He would do the same.

'I am going to London tomorrow with John to pay my way out. Will you look after Charlie while I am gone?'

'Of course. Does she know of your decision?'

'Not yet. I'll talk to her now.'

Charlie was with her mother and after taking leave of his father he went in search of her. He was charged up and in a mood to advance his decision, now it was made, to leave the army.

He jogged up the stairs to the attic room. The hallway there was narrower than those downstairs, the ceiling lower and the plaster was not decorated with ornate carvings but painted with a square earthy-coloured pattern.

He could hear Charlie's voice as he progressed. It was a raised pitch, almost a shout. He continued along the hall, his footsteps silent on the narrow length of carpet that ran down the centre of the hall.

'Why, Mama? It is not fair of you!'

His pace slowed as he neared the room.

'I will not talk about it. I do not want to speak of it.'

'But you did not defend me! You should have helped me!'

Ah. She was talking it out with her mother, then. He stopped outside the door. He would not interrupt. It was right that they had this conversation. But nor did he feel like walking away. His shoulder pressed against the wood and he leant closer to the closed door. He could almost hear her mother's silent discomfort as much as Charlie's sense of betrayal.

'You were always a naughty, difficult child. You were never where you ought t' 'ave been.'

'Are you saying it was my fault? It feels as though you think

246

it was my fault. That was what it felt like then and that was why I went to him …'

'The fault lies where the sin is.'

Oh good God. The bloody ignorant woman. What on earth was she saying? He straightened and his hand fisted to knock and interrupt this before it could do Charlie more harm.

'Yes it does, Mama. Yes, it does.' Charlie spoke in a strong, defiant voice, without any hint of the guilt he knew she had been feeling over the last few days. 'And I forgive you. I forgive you for not minding me well and not teaching me of the risk, and I forgive you because I know it was hard when my father died and there was Ginny still a baby. I see why you put her first. I forgive you for not being strong enough to fight against the Colonel and I forgive you for letting me go to him and do what was wrong when you could have helped me. It was not my fault any more than it was yours.'

His hand uncurled and he wished to damn well applaud. *Well said, girl. Well said.*

A sound, more voices, travelled up from the staircase back along the hall. His mother and Ginny. Then this had been some sort of plan. His mother must have taken Ginny away to play with the others so that Charlie could have a chance to speak.

He did not want to be caught here listening. This had been Charlie's moment of freedom from her past. He would not take it away from her.

'I have learned to accept that it was not my fault, Mama. I made a bad choice, but I was not the bad person. The Colonel was wrong to do what he did to me,' he heard Charlie say as he walked away. 'You are not a bad person either. But you must understand that it is the Colonel you have to blame …'

As she had spent the last few days drowning in guilt, he had spent them longing to know what to do to help her escape that. It seemed they had helped each other. By accepting his own lack of control over the past, he had succeeded in helping her do the same.

A smile tugged at his lips as he reached the servants' stairs at the far end of the hall, while he heard his mother and Ginny round the far corner. His smile came from a sense of pride for his wife.

When Charlie came downstairs, she went straight into the garden to play with the children, her expression stiff. It was as though she went looking for a reason to laugh and smile again.

He went outside too as tea was served and excused himself when the children begged him to play. Instead he watched Charlie play the game of blind man's buff, as she cast aside the past and stumbled about in her future. The children squealed 'Auntie Baba!' at her when it was her turn to wear the blindfold and she laughed and ran about with her arms outstretched, as everyone avoided her. She was happy. He could see it. They made each other happy. Whether it was in India or England, they would be happy. But here she would have the family that she had lacked.

He rose, smiling. Perhaps he would play. He had let himself be captured, entirely.

Mary smiled at him as she noticed him walking down the steps.

'Here!' Helen called, distracting Charlie.

Everyone playing now realised what he intended doing.

'This way! This way!' The children all called, drawing Charlie in the opposite direction, so Harry could creep up close behind her.

Then he said near her ear, 'This way.' Her body jolted with surprise before she spun around.

He wrapped his arms about her waist and lifted her off her feet.

'Ahhh! Harry!' She smacked his arm when he set her down, before pulling her blindfold off.

'Caught you.' His hands held her head and then he kissed her. He had made the right decision.

She broke the kiss as the adults applauded them, while the

children exclaimed in various ways from, 'let her go' to 'what are you doing, Uncle Baba?'

'But in the game I have caught you,' Charlie answered. 'So you now have to wear the blindfold.'

Yes. His life from this point forward was blind of direction too. He had nowhere to go and nothing to do, yet he had someone to live it with.

He turned his back. 'Tie it on for me.'

It was when they dressed for dinner that he finally had the chance to tell her his plans, but before he could begin speaking, as soon as he shut the door behind them, she spoke.

'I am not with child. My courses have begun today.'

'Oh, darling.' She had been so pleased with the notion. He opened his arms and she came into them. There were tears.

'There will be children for us one day, God willing.' His hand stroked over her hair and her back.

She nodded against his shoulder.

'I have something to tell you too, sweetheart. I hope you will think it good news.'

She pulled away, although he kept her in the circle of his arms.

Her hand lifted and wiped the tears from her cheeks. 'What is it?'

'We are not going to India.'

'Why?' She sounded disappointed, but after the conversation with her mother perhaps she was looking forward to an escape route.

'I hope you will not be angry with me. John has agreed to pay for me to leave the army.'

'No. Why Harry? Not because of—'

'No.' He pressed a finger on to her lips. 'Listen.'

He took a breath. How to explain the feelings of fear in him, fear for her, for any children they might have – without speaking of his mother's story? His hand cupped her cheek. 'Charlie, I cannot take you there. You have been through enough. I cannot let you be at risk, as you would be, of death from disease or assault if I died in some stupid skirmish. It is not the life I want for us and the children I hope we have. The life I want with you is here. I have asked my father if we can live near them. Would you mind that? Did you fall in love with a soldier and would hate an ordinary man?'

Her arms slipped about his middle, holding him firmly. 'I love the man beneath this coat, not his scarlet coat. I was looking forward to going to India because it was a place for the two of us to make a home—'

'Does my decision disappoint you, then? We will make a home here for the two of us.' He kissed the crown of her head. 'But my mother has fallen in love with you, you know. My father said she will be more than happy to have us live close and so we shall be the two of us yet with our family near.'

Charlie looked up and smiled at him. 'I love her too,' she said on a whisper, still smiling. 'I would rather live near her than my own mother. I think my mother will never be able to forgive me. Your mother is kinder to me because of my past.'

'That is my family, Charlie – Katherine, Caro and Drew will say the same. We are a family who falls for those who have been wounded by life.' And now he understood why his parents were like that, but it was not just his parents, it was his uncles and aunts too…

She turned away, breaking from his hold. 'Well, I do not feel wounded any more.' She glanced back over her shoulder, 'and even though I am not with child, I am very happy.'

It was his wish come true. He'd made her happy and when he looked inside himself, searching his soft, fleshy, heart, there was only happiness too.

'I will have to go to London tomorrow, with John,' he said, as she began to undress. 'To resolve things and end my contract with the army. I shall have to leave you alone again. I'm sorry.'

She looked over her shoulder and smiled at him. 'Then, when you come back we may remain together forever if we wish.'

'We may. There shall be nobody ordering us, or trying to tear us apart.'

'Then you go with my blessing. But hurry back.'

'And when I return we shall put more effort into making a child.'

She laughed at that.

'Do not tell anyone else of my intention to leave the army,' he told Charlie as they walked downstairs. 'Let us keep it as a surprise and remember, while I am away, you have promised to let Mama help you find the most beautiful gown you have ever dreamed of for the ball.'

Her eyes sparkled with tears. 'I have never even imagined a ball gown.' Her voice was high. 'Poor little girls imagine something nice and sweet to eat or a kind working husband who will provide for them, not ball gowns.'

'Then you must try on every single style before you decide which is the prettiest. You need not imagine, you will have.'

Chapter 17

Charlie looked at Harry's reflection in the long mirror in their room. He was watching her with admiration in his eyes and his expression. It was more than that, though, it was pride. There was a glow in his eyes that said he was proud of the way she looked in her ball gown. She had known when they married she would be proud of him; she had never considered that he might ever feel pride in her.

The ghostly whispers of her past breathed as she looked back at her own reflection, but Harry never seemed to hear them and so she closed her ears to them.

She turned and smiled at him.

His hands slipped into his pockets as he smiled back.

'You look stunning, Charlie. Truly. You will outshine everyone who is attending.'

He had only returned today, three hours ago, and he'd come up the servants' stairs, so no one else had seen him. None of his family knew that he was now a simple Mr Marlow and not a captain any more.

And she was Mrs Marlow.

'While you look terribly handsome in a black evening coat, I had not realised the full beauty of the man I married until I saw you in civilian clothes.'

His smile tilted at one side and his hands then slid out of the pockets of his grey trousers. He had a very fine dark-red silk waistcoat on too, and his black cravat was tied about the collar of his white shirt.

'You are such a dashing specimen of a man. But then that was what drew me to stare at you as much as Ash when I saw you on the beach.'

'It is a good job you wrote that first letter to me. I might never have looked back at you otherwise.'

'But that was why I wrote it, because you never did look for more than a second.'

'I thought you were someone seeking a husband, and I was not inclined to be that.'

'I know, you told me. But now you are ...' She smiled.

He walked across the room to her. 'But now I am, and very glad to be, because I met this beautiful woman who changed my mind.' His hand lifted and his fingers touched one of the curls that had been trained to fall on to her bare shoulder. 'When I first met you in an inn, I imagined your hair styled for a ball and I knew then you would make every other woman in the room look dull.'

'I have had dance lessons while you have been away, very hurried lessons, but I think I might stumble through a few dances with you, but please tell everyone else I am yours. I do not wish to make a fool of myself with any other man.'

'You will not make a fool of yourself at all, but no one else will have chance to dance with you because I shall not let you leave my side. No more separations, remember.'

She turned and pulled on her long, white gloves and glanced at herself in the mirror again. Her dress was a deep-purple silk and it looked very grand with its white lace. The contrasting colour made her hair more remarkable too. She looked like someone who lived in the world of Harry's family.

Yet she did live among them and she was not frightened of

this evening, even though his wider family had arrived, more aunts and uncles and copious cousins. She had been introduced to them all, in small numbers, by Katherine or Harry's mother or father. She was liked here. No. She was loved here. And so everyone who came had judged her through the eyes of Harry's parents or Katherine, or Rob and Caro, Mary and Drew, or Henry and Susan.

Phillip, Rupert and Meredith, who had been at their wedding had come for the ball too, and even they had been nice under the light of joy that Harry's mother had expressed on having Charlie as an addition to her family. 'This is my new daughter,' she had said, time and time again.

When Charlie turned around, fully dressed and ready to walk downstairs, Harry leant and kissed her lips.

She pushed him away. 'Harry, we must go downstairs. Mama and Papa are expecting us to be in the receiving line.'

He laughed at her. 'Mama and Papa, is it?'

She frowned. They had become that days ago. 'You do not mind?'

'Of course I do not. The need to be in the receiving line I am not so keen upon, however …'

The ball had become a celebration of their marriage in the last week, and every guest had been written to, to inform them of it. So, of course they must welcome the guests too. 'The ball is in our honour now.'

'So you told me. Come along, then, and I shall enjoy every minute of it because I shall be able to show you off and make everyone else jealous. That is unless you wish to forget the ball and return to bed,' he said the last with a broad, jesting smile. They had already spent an hour in bed since his return.

'No.' She smiled too and lifted her hand like his grandiose relations did. 'Lead me to the ball, sir.'

He held her fingers and then walked beside her as they left the room.

'Oh, you both look splendid!' his mother exclaimed as she saw them walking down the stairs into the hall.

It sounded as though the rest of those staying in the house were already in the ballroom – there was a loud ring of voices coming from the open doors.

'Charlie, you look gorgeous, and Harry, such a transformation.' Katherine voiced with more excitement than Charlie had heard her express before.

Katherine hugged Harry as his mother embraced Charlie. Then they swapped. Then John and Harry's father took a turn in kissing her hand. Harry's father held Harry last of all, holding him with a level of emotion Charlie had never imagined a man might show for another man.

She curtsied time and again, greeting dozens of noble and genteel people. Then Harry lifted his arm, offering it to her as weeks ago he had offered his arm as they had paraded along the front in Brighton, only this time he walked her into a ballroom; a huge room lit by giant gilded, teardrop chandeliers and decorated with marble columns, ornate plaster patterns and paintings.

If she had known that places like this existed when she had lain on top of the hayrick as a child, in the sunshine, chewing on her favourite liquorice root – she would have dreamed of this.

~

Harry's hand held one of Charlie's gently, while his other hand pressed against the middle of her back, firmly, steering her more directly than he would have steered one of his sisters or cousins.

Charlie was not light on her feet, her steps were steady and precise and yet she was confident enough that he did not see her look at her feet once as they waltzed. Instead she looked up at the chandelier that was above them, as though she watched the light sparkling in the abundant drops of cut glass or looked beyond that at the Greek God, Zeus, holding out a hand to those in the room below.

She was truly a stunning woman. Birth. To whom a person was born. Was not something that made the person. Life and love were what made a person.

Charlie had never been loved enough before.

She was loved now.

He had a feeling he had been given someone special to love because fate had known that he and his family were the people for the task. All of his family. It made him feel forgiven for his errors in the past. It made him proud of the parents he had once rebelled against.

She was so lost in her admiration of the room, Charlie had not even realised that the room about them was full of whispers. But they were not cruel whispers. He knew what was being said, the comments would be over his lack of a uniform. Those who had been in the room already when he'd come down were only now seeing that he had resigned his post.

But he was to become a farming man. His father's steward. His father had confirmed it today. He would learn from the man his father had and take over and his father intended to do less now he was getting older. There was a house for them too, which would be rented for their use in the village near his father's manor house.

His Uncle Richard was close to there too and so there would be many of his family near.

It was what he wanted for Charlie.

When the dance came to a close, his brothers Rob, Daniel and David were the first to come over and then his sisters, Mary, Helen, Jennifer and Jemima. All of them exclaimed over his lack of a scarlet coat. 'What?' 'Why?' 'How?' The crowd about him broadened as his cousins arrived to challenge him too. Eleanor screamed with excitement as Margaret and Heather embraced him in turns.

Then he was approached by his male cousins, who had at one time been the friends with whom he'd behaved badly, only they had given that behaviour up long before him. 'Frederick, Gregory, William.' He shook their hands. Then he turned and shook Henry's hand.

'I never thought I would see this day …' Henry stated.

'I could not take this woman to India.' Harry's hand was still at Charlie's back.

'Champagne for the happy couple!' Harry's father's voice reached above the noise of the crowd about him. His father smiled at Charlie first. His father had feared she might feel overwhelmed by the crowd about them and given them an escape route. But as Harry looked at Charlie, her eyes said quite clearly she did not need it, she did not even look as though she was pretending strength, her posture was not stiff nor her chin high. She was merely enjoying all the fuss.

She accepted the glass his father offered her.

So did Harry. Then he looked at his friends as his father turned away. 'And I could not separate her from her new Mama and Papa.' His father looked back and caught Harry's gaze through the melee of everyone else, then he smiled and laughed before turning away again.

Harry had never been so glad of the family he'd been born into. He was a lucky man and now Charlie was lucky too. When there were children, as he knew there would be, then they would create their own family raised in this happiness and love too.

As the next dance began, he leant forward. 'I love you,' he whispered into Charlie's ear, as her gorgeous auburn hair tickled his cheek.

Epilogue

Charlie had been walking back and forth across the grass for the last half an hour, with Ash pacing behind as Charlie rocked the child cradled in her arms, and still Ellen was not asleep.

The sound of the heavy leather ball hitting the willow bat rang through the trees at the edge of the lake. Then voices cheered and called for whoever had hit the ball to run faster.

People were spread out across the lawn before Pembroke Place, where Charlie had first been adopted, and welcomed among them the year before. There was a marquee, where a buffet luncheon was to be served and rugs laid out for the women to watch with the children as the men played cricket.

There was a resounding, unified sigh and then some applause behind her. She guessed the batsman had been caught out. She did not look back.

She had walked away from where the family were gathered as she wanted Ellen to sleep. Ellen had been too busy listening to every sound and watching every face as all of Harry's extended family came to peer at her. Ellen was only two months, the most recent offspring in the family, and so everyone wished to come across and hold her or smile at her.

Charlie was also the newest mother and struggling to learn

how to do things correctly. Though Mama had been willing to take on the task of getting Ellen to drop off for her nap, Charlie wanted to do it. She wanted to be a good mother.

She walked on, bouncing and rocking Ellen, whispering a quiet lullaby in a hurried voice that lacked any musical tone. She was becoming frustrated. 'Please sleep,' she whispered desperately. She wanted to be a good mother.

'Charlie!'

She turned. Harry was walking towards her. Ash bounded over to him.

'Hello,' she called back to him. 'Was it you who was caught out?'

He gave her a wry smile as he came closer, leaning and patting Ash's back. 'Yes. And do not tease me for it. I shall hear enough of that from my cousins.'

'I would not.'

He was wearing only his white shirt and trousers, with his sleeves rolled up to his elbows and his neck cloth removed so his shirt hung open at his collar in a slight V. His red-and-black braces were the only item in his outfit that had colour. But the white set off his dark-brown hair and blue eyes so beautifully.

'How is our daughter?' His hand touched the shock of red hair on Ellen's head. She had been born with her hair, which Harry had said was unusual, but he had celebrated it as a wonderful thing to have a daughter with hair like Charlie's.

'And she has red hair like Charlie's!' he had said to everyone in the villages near where they lived.

'She is refusing to sleep, though she is tired and fractious. I brought her away from the others in the hope they would not distract her.'

Harry's hands came up in a gesture that said, let me take her. She let him do so.

'So my little fighter, you are distressing your mother again are you? We'll have no more of that.'

Ellen's eyes focused on Harry's face as Harry braced her in one arm while his free hand stroked across her cheek.

He was so much easier with Ellen than Charlie was, but then he'd had numerous brothers and sisters and nieces and nephews … He knew what to do with a baby.

'Come along, let us walk down to the lake.' He lifted out his elbow, in a gesture that said 'hold my arm'.

She did so, her fingers curling about his elbow and holding on as she would always hold on to Harry.

He talked to Ellen as they walked with Ash beside him. 'Has your mother been getting herself in a dither, little one?' He looked at Charlie. 'Has she?'

She nodded, tears gathering in her eyes, but they were not really sad tears, they were such happy tears – she had a daughter and a wonderful, dear husband.

'You must not fret. Motherhood must be learned, just as you learned to dance and ride and write and sew. You will become used to it.'

She nodded.

'Now you must smile properly. It is only once or twice a year my family are all together and I will not have you look maudlin and not enjoy it.'

She made a face at him, with a mock smile.

He laughed. 'Not good enough.'

She gave him a truer smile.

He laughed quietly. Oh, she loved him. 'Ellen is lucky to have you as her father.'

'She may not have thought that a few years ago before I met her mother. It is her mother who has made me a good father.' His eyebrows lifted at her, telling her off as he had been doing for weeks, for fearing her capability with Ellen.

But as she looked at Ellen, she saw her eyes had closed. All Harry had to do was walk with her in his arms and talk and she slept. 'She is asleep.'

He looked down and smiled at their daughter, but he did not stop walking. He looked at Charlie. 'We may walk to the lake, then simply to enjoy the view.'

She held his arm tighter and felt her spirits lift. Being a mother felt easier when Harry was with her; she only had to master the moments when he was not. A natural smile pulled at her lips as she looked at him.

'You know we could move into Mama's and Papa's if you wish, just until you get the knack of it and feel more comfortable?'

'No.' Her answer was emphatic. 'I do not want someone else to be a mother to our daughter. I want to achieve it myself.'

With Ellen braced in one arm, his other arm lifted free of Charlie's hold and instead lay over her shoulders. Then he pulled her close to his side as they walked. 'You are her mother, so no one else will fulfil the role and you love her with all your heart, so much so you are trying to do everything just right, when there is no 'just right' with children. So you are the perfect mother and you must stop berating yourself. All that I am worried over is that you are pressuring yourself and upsetting yourself. Ellen has everything she needs.'

Charlie sighed out and leant more into him, her arm reaching about him and her other hand gripping his shirt on his side. 'I love you.'

'I love you too, but promise me no more fears about how good a mother you will be. You love her, that is all that's needed, the rest will come right if there is that.'

'Thank you for being patient with me.'

'Thank you for being patient with me,' he echoed. 'My family have a great respect for you. For accepting the task of taming their black sheep.'

She laughed, her cheek pressing against his shoulder. He was right. Love counted for so much.

'You know that seeing your mother makes you worse. I do not think you should visit any more during our stay. Not this time.

Wait until Ellen is a little older and you are more confident.'

'Yes.' Because every time she faced her mother she saw how unloved she was and she was scared then of not being able to love Ellen enough.

'Charlie, here, you hold Ellen.' He stopped walking.

She took Ellen out of his arms. 'Everything feels right when I hold her and she is happy or sleeping.'

Harry's fingers tucked Charlie's hair behind her right ear. 'Children are allowed to cry, and they will have temper tantrums, and misbehave. I was a terribly naughty child—'

'I know and so was I.' She looked up from Ellen and into his eyes and smiled.

'Then let us allow our daughter to be herself and annoying and frustrating if she wishes to be and love her regardless, no matter what mistakes she makes.'

She smiled. 'Yes. That is what your parents do, isn't it?'

'Yes. That is what all my family have done. A lesson learned from my grandfather's lack of love, and so, if we draw anything from your mother, let it be the same lesson, that we should love each other and our daughter with everything that we are and that will be our legacy.'

'Yes.' She leant and kissed Ellen's cheek, then turned and looked at Harry pursing her lips for a kiss.

He smiled and then obeyed the silent request before whispering over her lips, 'Ellen says, she loves you too, it is in the way she is breathing.'

Author's note

Ah, well. I sort of don't know what to say. I have lived with the Marlow family for ten years, since writing the first draft of *The Illicit Love of a Courtesan*, so they have a very fixed place in my imagination and my heart. It is really emotional to say goodbye to them in this last book in the Marlow Intrigues series. Perhaps I will not be able to let them go entirely and they may pop up as extras in other stories. But it is time for me to turn time back and return to writing in the Regency period in a new series.

I shan't say anything about my next series, but keep an eye out for it and one of the easiest ways to do so is to follow my author pages on sellers' websites. But to belt and braces it, why not follow me on Facebook and ask for emails when posts go up and follow my blog via email and hopefully between the three you'll find out when the new series is released, she says with a smile.

When you read this story, if you have been following the series and have a good memory of the first two books you'll have spotted all the parallels in this story to both the *Lost Love of a Soldier* and *The Illicit Love of a Courtesan*, there was a deliberate resonance in many scenes and I also went back to using inspirations described by Harriett Wilson, a real Regency courtesan. You'll find all of Harriett's true stories on my blog. She was the inspiration for the whole of the Marlow Intrigues series, really. It would never have come to my mind if I had not read Harriett's memoirs.

So, thank you, Harriett Wilson! And thank you to all the readers who have followed the series, posted reviews and share the stories, to spread the word. I am very grateful for your support.

Printed by RR Donnelley at Glasgow, UK